Dead to The World

B. D. Smith

Black Rose Writing | Texas

The author grants the final approval for this literary material.

First printing

This is a work of fiction. Names, characters, businesses, places, events, and
incidents are either the products of the author's imagination or used in a
fictitious manner. Any resemblance to actual persons, living or dead, or
actual events is purely coincidental.

ISBN: 978-1-68433-811-5
PUBLISHED BY BLACK ROSE WRITING
www.blackrosewriting.com

Printed in the United States of America
Suggested Retail Price (SRP) $18.95

Dead to the World is printed in Candara

*As a planet-friendly publisher, Black Rose Writing does its best to eliminate
unnecessary waste to reduce paper usage and energy costs, while never
compromising the reading experience. As a result, the final word count vs. page count
may not meet common expectations.

DEAD TO THE WORLD

BUCKS COVE

SEBEC LAKE

NARROWS

BOWERBANK

NEWELL COVE

TIM'S COVE

SOUTH
COVE
(PEAKS-KENNY
STATE PARK)

PINE ISLAND

SEBEC VILLAGE

GREELEY'S LANDING
(MERRILL'S MARINA)

1.

It was karaoke night at the Bear's Den. Outside, the parking lot was overflowing with snowmobiles and pickups. A few couples were seated in the restaurant, eating a late dinner under the watchful eye of taxidermy gazing down from the walls. The tavern room, in the back, was full of Thursday night revelers. A few were celebrating the extension of the ice fishing season from the ides of March to the end of the month, but most of the tables and booths were crowded by sledders looking forward to an upcoming weekend of fun. The central Maine networks of snowmobile trails around the town of Dover-Foxcroft was in excellent shape, thanks to a recent heavy snowfall and frequent grooming by the Piscataquis Valley Snowmobile Club.

A minor disagreement between members of two local snowmobile clubs – the Milo Devil's Sledders and the Monson Narrow Gauge Riders, had flared briefly earlier in the evening, but the combatants had been escorted out to the parking lot and the glass fragments and broken chairs had been cleaned up. Mary Jo Arnold, a regular at karaoke night, had been halfway through her weekly rendition of "Stand by Your Man" when the disagreement had broken out. Unfazed, she had simply sung louder to be heard over the commotion.

In the far corner, at a small table for two, Don Robertson sat nursing his beer and watching the entrance. Ximena was already a half hour late, but he wasn't surprised. Ximena was a top selling real estate agent in town, and she was having dinner with a potential client that Don had pointed in her direction some months ago. The interested buyer, a wealthy older man and an investor with Don's financial consulting firm, was looking at a million-dollar property near Willimantic, at the western end of nearby Sebec Lake. Don suspected that the rich client was smitten with Ximena, and she had warned Don that she couldn't rush things right now, as a nice fat commission was in the offing.

Don had grown up in Dover-Foxcroft and he recognized a number of the people in the room. He had moved down to the coast more than a decade ago, and only occasionally returned to Piscataquis County. As a result, while he felt at home in the Bear's Den, he stood out from the other patrons in a number of subtle ways: His teeth had been whitened, for example, and he sported a $70 razor cut haircut and a $200 fleece from Eastern Mountain Sports in Portland, along with a $700 pair of designer glasses from a boutique eyewear store.

A big man wearing the uniform of a Piscataquis County Sheriff's Deputy approached Don's table holding a half-full pitcher of beer in one hand and a beer mug in the other. Smiling, he spoke loud enough to be heard over the din.

"Aren't you Don Robertson? Foxcroft Academy? We were both on the football team back then. I'm Jack Walker. OK if I sit down?"

Don reached over and pulled the other chair at the table out for him.

"Let's see what I can remember Jack – you played tight end and were pretty good, but the team sucked, right?"

"Ayup," Jack responded as he filled Don's glass with beer. "If I remember right, you left Dover right after graduation – went down to the big city and I heard you got rich. What brings you back to shire town after what, it must be fifteen years?"

"Fifteen years exactly, Jack. But I've been back off and on, mostly to visit my folks. They moved into assisted living down in Camden last summer, and I'm thinking about renovating the family camp out on Sebec Lake – probably going to move back permanently."

"Why would you want to do that?" Jack asked, clearly interested. His elbow slipped off the table and Don realized he had had a few. Don was feeling a beer buzz himself, and he remembered Jack now as having lots of friends and being a huge gossip in high school - always well informed about who was doing what. Looking at Jack across the table he realized that the deputy's honest interest in what was happening around him had probably been honed into a valuable skill over the past fifteen years, and that Jack had not just randomly wandered over to his table. The deputy was checking out the new guy in town. It was inevitable, Don knew, that people would be curious about his return. Maybe it was a good idea to give Jack an overview of the mid-life crisis that had brought him back to Dover-Foxcroft, with the expectation that the deputy could serve as a town crier of sorts to fill out his profile.

"Good question Jack. I guess I want to come home and start again. Things down in Portland were great the first ten years or so. Turns out I have a knack for investing – got interested in high school actually – from the stock market club. I worked for a brokerage firm for a few years and then went out on my own. My client base grew quickly and it didn't take long for me to consider myself successful. I started moving in the right circles, got married to a smart, successful lawyer, and was living the good life. Then about five years ago it all slowly started to slip away, a little at a time. I lost interest in the social climbing, the dinner parties, and the competitive consumption. I even got tired of all the traffic on Route 1, all the tourists, all the strivers looking for the next step up, hoping for the brass ring move to Boston. It just didn't seem to add up to much in the end."

Don noticed that Jack was listening closely and continued his soliloquy.

"And then a few years ago my life really turned weird. My wife Rosemary got drawn into a cult-like self-improvement group. It started with her dentist inviting her to a local informal gathering and introducing her to some other members of the group. Soon she started going to their get-togethers, and under the guidance of her dentist, a guy named Lee Lamen, who became her so-called 'mentor,' she became obsessed with identifying and cleansing 'negatives' or 'obstacles,' whatever those are, from her 'essential soul,' whatever that is. I mean, these people are into some pretty weird shit. She believed she was making good progress toward 'ultimate clarity,' which was their jargon for self-enlightenment, and even signed up for a weeklong 'multi-layered cleansing.'"

Don knew it was a good story, weird and a little scary, and knew he had Jack's full attention.

"When she returned from being purified, she didn't really want to have much to do with me, other than pressing me to join in her quest for self-realization. We had a huge argument and her mentor - this Lee Lamen guy, soon labeled me a 'suppressive person.' Rosemary was warned that she might be identified as potential trouble if she didn't cut contact with me. It didn't take long for her to inform me that 'disconnection' was necessary. I got the message and moved out of our condo, which she owned. I haven't heard much from her since - she's probably figuring out how best to screw me over when we get a divorce."

With a stunned expression, Jack asked: "Just like that? There must have been more to it."

"Not that I could see - I figured she had a thing going with this Lamen guy, but I never called her on it."

"Isn't there anything you can do – an intervention or something?"

"I thought about it Jack, but this Lamen guy made it quite clear that any efforts on my part to contact Rosemary or change her mind could seriously hinder her progress toward ultimate clarity, and they couldn't allow that to happen. He said that I was close to being declared what they call 'fair game,' and that I could be targeted for many different forms of retaliation. At that point I figured it was a good time to cut my losses, get a divorce, and make a new start. Almost all of my interaction with clients and investment planning is done online or on the phone, so as long as I have internet, I can run my business from anywhere."

Jack filled Don's glass again and was about to ask another question when Don looked past him, smiled, and stood up. Turning, Jack saw Ximena Lapointe making her way across the room, waving to people she recognized and shedding her snowmobile suit. Patting Jack on the shoulder in greeting, she threw her arms around Don's neck and leaned in for a kiss. Standing now, Jack slowly retreated to an adjacent table, nodding his head and muttering to himself.

"Ximena Lapointe – now there's a very good reason to come home to shire town."

Jack and Don weren't the only customers to notice Ximena's arrival. She had been an avid runner and cross-country skier since high school, and the brightly patterned leggings and form-fitting running jersey she wore under her snowmobile suit showed off her athletic physique. Ximena noticed a booth opening up and grabbed it while Don went to the bar and ordered burgers and a fresh pitcher of beer. When he returned, he slid in next to her, stroking her thigh with one hand as he poured her a beer with his other.

"Where were you? I was worried you weren't coming. I hope you haven't forgotten what I told you about your dinner companion. He might seem like a harmless geezer with a crush on you – but he's not someone to take lightly."

"Sorry I'm late. It's not the client. Nigel's being the perfect gentleman. It was my babysitter. She was late again, and then my sled got stuck on the way here."

Don's hand slid further up her thigh and he leaned in to nuzzle her neck.

"I was thinking maybe we could head up to the cabin after we finish a pitcher or two here – get away from all the noise."

Ximena laughed and clicked glasses with him, her smile bordering on a leer.

"I have to be home to relieve the babysitter by one or so, but that will give us plenty of time."

An overweight middle-aged man with a scruffy beard entered the tavern from the restaurant, taking a seat at the end of the bar. Glancing around the room he noticed Don and Ximena canoodling in the booth. Pulling out his phone he keyed in a number.

"Hey Wes. It's Gary. You asked me to call when I got here. Don Robertson and Ximena are in a back booth. They're looking pretty horny. I'm guessing they'll be heading out to his cabin soon."

Gary listened to the reply and then answered.

"Sounds good. I'll be here."

Twenty minutes later, as Ximena and Don were finishing up their burgers, Don felt a shift in the room. The Karaoke singer, an older man in a wheelchair, paused in his rendition of "My Way," as the noise level dropped. Don looked up just as Wes Fuller, Ximena's ex, slid into the booth, facing them. Conversation had gone quiet at adjacent tables, and Don noticed many of the men sitting at the bar had turned around and were looking toward their booth with interest that bordered on anticipation.

Fuller was about Don's size, maybe five ten, but probably outweighed him by twenty pounds, most of it muscle. Ignoring Don, Fuller folded his large hands on the table and focused on Ximena.

"How ya been X? Haven't seen you around lately."

Ximena did not look up as she whispered to Don.

"Let's go Don, I'm finished eating."

"Don't leave yet. I just got here." Fuller urged.

Suddenly angry, Ximena looked across the table at Fuller and answered him in a barely controlled voice.

"You're a sick man Wes. You need help. I'm calling the cops to report you as soon as we leave. Or don't you remember the protection from abuse order the court slapped on you? No indirect or direct contact with me is allowed."

"That order runs out pretty soon. Don't be so stubborn."

"No way Wes. I requested an extension last week, and now for sure it will be renewed."

Fuller leaned across the table and reached for Ximena's arm. Don grabbed Fuller's wrist with one hand and cocked his other arm, clearly intending to punch Fuller in the face. Jack Walker, who had stood up from his place at a nearby table, suddenly loomed over their table and placed his hand on Don's shoulder.

"No need to nail him Don, he was just leaving."

Turning his attention to Fuller, he continued.

"Wes, in case you forgot, I happened to be in the courtroom when Ximena's protection from abuse order was issued against you. I'm ready to recount to the court what just happened here, and if Ximena wants to come by and file a complaint I will certainly back her up."

With an enraged expression, looking ready to lash out, Fuller pulled his hand away from Don's grip. The deputy sheriff set his beer glass down on the table and spread his feet a bit, flexing his knees, and smiled at Fuller.

"What's it going to be Fuller? We got a cell just waiting for you down at the jail, and Debbie and her team can fix you up a real nice home cooked breakfast in the morning."

Staring at the deputy, doing his best to hose him with fear, Fuller finally slid sideways out of the booth and started to walk toward the exit, rasping out a final threat in Don's direction.

"You can count on it Robertson –you're gonna end up a big-time loser. I'm gonna fuck you up."

After Fuller had left, Ximena and Don thanked Jack and decided to take him up on his offer to walk out with them. The wind had died down and a light snow had begun to fall. Starting their sleds, Don and Ximena pulled out of the parking lot, waved to Jack, and headed out east of town on ITS main trail 82.

It was a beautiful night for sledding and the trail was well groomed and smooth - winding through dark green walls of hemlock and white pine. They made good time and reached the cabin, located a few miles downstream from Sebec Village on the Sebec River, in less than an hour. Once inside Don fired up the kerosene heater, placed it in the fireplace for venting to the outside, opened the damper, and lit two large candles on either side of the hearth. Ximena dove under the down comforter on the bed before starting to undress.

"Jesus Don, it's fuckin freezing in here. Can't we have a decent fire in the fireplace?"

"No way lover. I have this bad reaction to wood smoke. Even a little bit messes up my sinuses and gives me an instant headache. But this cabin is really snug, and the heater warms up the place in no time. Plus, I can help."

Don stripped off his snowmobile suit, boots, and the rest of his clothes before joining Ximena in bed. She greeted him with open arms, and entwined, they giggled and gasped as their cold hands explored and the candles flickered in the dark cabin.

Ximena and Don had been a couple for most of their last two years of high school, but they broke up when he moved down to the coast after graduation. When they ran into each other at the Whoopie Pie festival the previous summer, after fifteen years, there was an immediate and intense rekindling of their attraction. They had lunch at the Mill, and while Ximena called a babysitter for her son and watched the out-of-town throng stream across the Piscataquis River Bridge on their way to the festival, Don got them a room in the boutique hotel above the restaurant. They emerged briefly for dinner at Allie Oops before returning to their room to get caught up on their lives and see how much they had changed over the past fifteen years. Ximena knew immediately that they could have a future together, and by the morning, Don was also convinced. He told her all about his failed marriage and his potential move back to Dover-Foxcroft, and pressing up against him in bed, Ximena enthusiastically endorsed his plans.

Wes Fuller, who Ximena had briefly dated the previous winter, and who refused to accept her rejection, had continued to harass her on and off over the past year, but the confrontation at the Bear's Den had been a disturbing escalation of his hostility toward her and her new man. Don downplayed Fuller's behavior, remembering him as being pretty much a loser in high school, but Ximena was definitely getting creeped out by his unhealthy fixation on her. She knew he was involved in the drug scene in the county and had been arrested several times for assault. She had thought that the protection from abuse order she had obtained would put an end to Fuller's harassment, but clearly it hadn't worked.

The snow was coming down more heavily, muffling sound outside the snug cabin on the Sebec River. Ximena and Don drifted off to sleep, warm now and entwined beneath the thick down comforter. Just after midnight Ximena's Fitbit alarm woke her out of a deep slumber. She slipped out of bed and dressed slowly, trying to shake off her grogginess. Don was lying diagonally on the bed, tangled in the comforter, and snoring loudly – dead to the world. Looking out the window, Ximena was surprised by the heavy snow accumulation and worried about the trip back to her place. She took several deep breaths as she stepped outside and immediately felt better. It was hard sledding through the deepening snow on the trails back to her place, and the babysitter was pissed when Ximena finally showed up a half hour late. An extra five dollars mollified her somewhat. Checking on her son and pulling the covers he had kicked off back up to his chin, Ximena then headed off to bed, already thinking about tomorrow. Other than a scheduled meeting with a couple that were planning on putting their Sebec summer cabin on the market in the spring, her day was clear, and she had promised Don to be back at the cabin first thing in the morning.

Bright and early the next day Ximena stopped off at the Center Theatre Coffee House and picked up two lattes and several Elaine's donuts for her Sunday morning snuggle with Don, and headed out to his Sebec River cabin. The snowstorm had cleared off and the temperature had dropped overnight, with a strong wind out of the west. The snowmobile trails had seen some use that morning and the snow was well packed. Ximena made good time. Pulling up next to Don's snowmobile, Ximena expected him to be peaking out the cabin window. Don was a huge fan of coffee and Elaine's donuts. But the cabin was silent. Pushing aside the foot or so of snow that had drifted up against the door, Ximena juggled the coffees and bag of donuts and opened the cabin door. Inside it was pitch dark and ice cold.

2.

Anne Quinn's phone rang as she was getting out of her truck in the parking lot of the Piscataquis County Sheriff's Office in downtown Dover-Foxcroft. She wasn't surprised when Ximena's name showed on the screen – they had planned to go cross-country skiing that afternoon so Ximena could show her the basics of free skate techniques.

"Hi Ximena. Are we still on for this afternoon?"

"Anne. He's dead. I'm at the cabin. What should I do?"

"Who's dead? What cabin?"

"My boyfriend, Don Robertson. His cabin is out by Sebec Village."

"Are you sure he's dead?"

"Oh yeah, he's dead. Like frozen dead."

"OK Ximena. Help's on the way. Don't touch anything. Can I reach the cabin in my truck?"

"No way Anne. The snow's too deep."

"OK. Here's what we'll do. Go back out to the Sebec Village Reading Room and wait for me. I'll meet you there and ride with you back to the cabin on your sled. I'll be there in twenty minutes."

Anne continued walking into the courthouse complex that housed the sheriff's office, looking for Jim Torben, the sheriff, or Jack Walker, the deputy she often worked with.

Seeing Jack at his desk she told him about Don Robertson being found dead out at Sebec Village and asked him to hitch up the trailer with the snowmobiles and a sled for the body and follow her out to the Reading Room as soon as he could. Jack looked stunned and mentioned as he got up from his desk that he had talked to Robertson just the night before.

Ximena was waiting when Anne pulled up at the Reading Room and she gratefully climbed into her truck to warm up. She was shivering from the cold and the shock of finding her lover dead, and she was crying. Ximena immediately started talking, and Anne didn't interrupt.

"Don and I went out to the cabin last night after karaoke at the Bear's Den. I had planned on staying the night with him but then my babysitter informed me that she had to be home by one. I left the cabin last night about midnight and then came back out here this morning."

Ximena's narration was broken by a deep sob, and the sound of her ragged breathing filled the cab of the truck for several minutes before she continued.

"Don was still in bed when I went into the cabin this morning and at first he seemed fine, all wrapped in the comforter with just his head out, pretty much the way I left him last night. But he was ice cold when I touched him, and he wasn't breathing."

Anne leaned over and hugged Ximena, reassuring her that she would be OK. Everything would be OK. It looked like more than a foot of fresh snow had fallen overnight and it began to snow hard again as they rode Ximena's sled back to the cabin. When they arrived, Anne made a quick search of the surrounding area. With the exception of Ximena's footprints from that morning going into and out of the cabin's front door, the area was blanketed with a smooth unbroken expanse of snow.

The cabin door stood ajar. Anne stopped just inside and scanned the room. There was no sign of a struggle and nothing out of the ordinary jumped out at her. A kerosene heater was sitting in the fireplace, flanked by two large candles which had burned out. She touched the heater and it was cold. She shook it, confirming that it had run out of fuel. Approaching the bed, Anne was surprised by Don's appearance. Only his head was exposed, cradled in the folds of the down comforter. She had expected his face to be drained of color, but instead his lips were cherry red and his cheeks were a healthy pink. Reaching to check for a pulse in his neck, Anne quickly pulled her hand back. He was ice cold to the touch.

Deciding to err on the side of caution, Anne retreated from the pink-faced corpse. Closing the cabin door on the way out, she called Doug Bateman, catching him at home. Bateman was a detective with the Maine State Police, out of the Major Crimes Unit-North in Bangor, but he lived just up the road from Sebec Village in the town of Bowerbank, on the north shore of Sebec Lake. He was also Anne's lover. He picked up on the second ring.

"Hi sweet Anne. How about meeting up for breakfast at Spencer's?"

"Doug- I'm over at a cabin on the river by Sebec Village with Ximena Lapointe. She found her boyfriend Don Robertson dead here this morning."

"I'm on my way – what've we got?"

"I'd guess an accidental death – carbon monoxide maybe. Looks like he died in his sleep. You won't be able to reach the cabin in your jeep. Jack Walker should be on his way out to Sebec Village with snowmobiles and a towing sled for the body. You can meet him there and ride back to the cabin – just follow our tracks on the road going east out of Sebec Village between the dam and the Reading Room."

Jack and Doug reached the cabin about half an hour later. Doug took in the undisturbed snow cover, the cold kerosene heater, and Don Robertson's surprisingly healthy-looking dead body, and agreed with Anne's assessment. He checked the chimney, noted that the damper was open about halfway and that the chimney looked clear. Following protocol, Doug called down to the Chief Medical Examiner's Office in Augusta for guidance. Mike Bowman must have had Doug included in his call recognition list and answered with his standard greeting.

"Douglas Bateman – when are you bringing me some of those donuts from Elaine's? It's been a while you know."

"Next time I come down. I promise. But right now I'm hoping you can help us with a body discovered up here in Sebec this morning. Looks to me like an accidental death. The victim is a man in his thirties – dead in bed. It's an isolated cabin, deep snow, no evidence of foul play, and a kerosene heater out of fuel. Looks like it could be carbon monoxide poisoning. The puzzling thing is that the heater was in the fireplace and the damper was half open, so it looks like there was adequate ventilation in the cabin."

"Yeah, we get those occasionally," Bowman replied. "If the outside temperature is very low a cold air plug can form in the chimney. It can block the kerosene heater's carbon monoxide fumes from escaping up the chimney, even if the flue is otherwise unobstructed. The CO gets trapped in the house. A clear, odorless gas, it's a silent killer. It interferes with your body's oxygen delivery system. You are literally starved of oxygen at the cellular level."

Pausing for a moment to think, Bowman continued. "This would be the third case of CO poisoning this winter, I think, which is more than average. But it's been unusually cold this year, even for Maine, beginning way back in November."

Even though Doug had been investigating suspicious deaths and homicides for more than a decade, this was the first case like this he had encountered.

"Is there anything I can look for that might confirm he died of carbon monoxide poisoning?"

"Have you had a close look at the body? Describe it."

"Looks like he died in his sleep, wrapped up in a comforter, just his head showing. The weird thing is his face is a nice rosy pink."

"Bingo – a classic sign of carbon monoxide poisoning - The carboxymyoglobin content of the blood colors it pink, creating a false image of good circulation rather than being starved of oxygen. Carbon monoxide kills because it's hundreds of times stronger than oxygen in binding to hemoglobin – that's the protein in your red blood cells that carries oxygen from your lungs to the rest of your body. As you breathe in carbon monoxide it restricts the oxygen-carrying capacity of your blood and reduces the delivery of oxygen to tissues. I'd say this is likely an accidental death. Bag up the body and send it down. We can run a CO-oximeter analysis of a blood sample and have a quick answer for you – it only takes a few minutes."

After they placed Robertson's body in a body bag and carried it out to the towing sled, they retraced their path back to the Sebec

Village Reading Room. There they transferred the deceased to Jack Walker's SUV for the long trip down to Augusta and the Chief Medical Examiner's Office. As expected, when the lab result came back the next day it showed that Don Robertson had a carboxyhemoglobin level of 61% - clear evidence that carbon monoxide poisoning had killed him. His death was officially classified as accidental, and the investigation closed.

. . .

Several months later, however, Don Robertson's cause of death would be revisited. Spring had finally arrived in central Maine. The black fly season was well along and Dover-Foxcroft was starting to gear up to host the Whoopie Pie festival in several weeks. Anne noticed the blue tubing strung between sugar maples as she drove along Route 6 and wondered what kind of a yield Bob's Sugarhouse in town got this year. She had read that climate change was hitting the maple sugar industry hard – narrowing the temporal window of sap flow, and pushing it back earlier in the spring.

Jack Walker had called early that morning and asked her to meet him out at Don Robertson's cabin. There was someone she needed to talk to. Anne had initially resisted, saying she had a lot of work to catch up on, but without giving any further explanation, Jack insisted it was important. Pulling up to the cabin, she parked next to Jack's SUV and an older pickup that had several ladders, rakes, and pole saws sticking out of the bed of the truck. Yellow crime scene tape still hung from the cabin's door frame, waving in the light breeze.

Jack was sitting on the front porch next to an older man sporting an impressively bushy white beard. They were clearly enjoying the mid-morning sunshine. Jack introduced the older man.

"Anne, this is Gavin Anderson. He opens and closes camps for summer people on the lake, including Don's cabin here. Don's widow is putting the cabin up for sale and asked Gavin to get it ready for the realtor. He came out this morning to check out what might be needed to be done – any downed trees or burst pipes, or just general cleanup. He discovered a few things he thought we would be interested in."

Anne shifted her attention to Gavin, and he picked up the story.

"A couple of things caught my eye. When I went to the storage shed the ladder wasn't where I usually keep it – hung on the outside wall."

Gavin led them over to a small shed behind the cabin and pointed to an area of beaten down grass along the base of the shed.

"I found it right here, lying on the ground."

"Couldn't it just have fallen off where it had been hung?" Anne asked.

"No, not really. I hang it on the other wall, not here,"

Gavin walked around the corner of the shed to point at the hooks where the ladder was usually stored.

"OK," Anne responded, giving Jack Walker a puzzled glance. "Someone took it off the hooks where you store it and used it for something. So what?"

Gavin smiled, catching Anne's bemused reaction, and pointed back toward the cabin, where a bright red fiberglass extension ladder leaned up against the chimney.

"Right," he replied. "They used it for something."

Smiling broadly now, he continued.

"When I got here this morning the first thing I did was pick up the ladder from where it was on the ground here by the shed and set it up so I could seal off the chimney opening. Chimney swifts can be a real problem around here if you don't put a board or something to block them from getting down the flue and nesting, and that's one of the things I do every spring here at Don's. I figured a chimney full of chattering birds wouldn't help to sell the place. When I climbed the ladder with the slab of slate I use to block the chimney I saw something weird, and called Jack. He's been up there too. Why don't you take a look?"

Anne climbed the ladder, looked at the top of the chimney, and called down. "What am I looking for?"

"Look closer," Jack replied.

Turning back to the chimney, Anne looked again and noticed several fragments of dark gray fabric – likely canvas, caught on the sharp edges of the metal flue encased in the surrounding cement and stone of the chimney. Climbing back down the ladder, Anne looked over at Gavin, who said out loud what she was already thinking.

"Someone used the ladder to climb up and cover the top of the chimney with a tarpaulin. When they removed it, they didn't notice that some of it got caught in the metal sheathing of the flue. I've been doing work at this camp for more than a decade and I've never used a tarp to cover the chimney, and those torn fragments were not there when I took the cover stone off last fall."

Anne looked at Gavin with new appreciation.

"Mr. Anderson, thanks for calling Jack and alerting us to what you've found."

Gavin smiled again.

"I've been watching those crime shows – you know, the CSI shows – you think I might be on to something here?"

"Maybe so Gavin. Let me make a call and see if we can follow up on this."

Anne called Doug over at the Maine State Police barracks in Bangor and described what they had found at the cabin. He agreed it was worth looking into. The State Police Evidence Response Team down in Augusta was alerted and several crime scene technicians arrived at the cabin by mid-afternoon. They photographed the chimney and the fabric fragments before bagging them. They also dusted the extension ladder for prints – not really expecting to recover any, given the length of time that had passed and its exposure to the elements.

Knowing that the recovery of fabric pieces from the chimney would not be enough on its own to justify opening a suspicious death investigation, Doug and Anne assembled an informal group of several dozen volunteers the next morning and began a search in hopes of finding the chimney tarp discarded somewhere nearby.

Conditions were not the best – it was black fly season and understory vegetation was thick in some places.

Working outward from the cabin and focusing on road margins and trails, the search turned up nothing of interest through the morning. In the afternoon they widened the search to include both sides of the Sebec River and the surrounding forest.

By mid-afternoon one of the volunteers – George Moser, an avid fly fisherman who knew this section of the river quite well, had worked his way downstream several hundred yards from the cabin when he saw something. He hadn't really been looking for the tarp so much as searching for promising fishing spots when he noticed what looked like a bright red snake caught on a rock mid-stream. Looking closer, George realized it was a bungee cord attached to a large piece of gray canvas. Using a long branch he picked up from the forest floor, George snagged the canvas and pulled it to shore.

Roughly rectangular and ragged around the edges, the canvas measured about three feet on a side and was covered in paint spatters. Along with the red bungee cord, a thin cable maybe twenty feet in length was attached to the canvas. Leaving the tarpaulin on the ground, George went to report what he had found. It was bagged and driven down to the crime lab the same afternoon. Analysis soon confirmed that the fabric fragments recovered from the chimney at the cabin were a match with the tarp recovered from the river. A solid case for the death of Don Robertson being a homicide could now be made. It had been an ingenious and well-thought-out killing, and if Gavin Anderson had not been such a fan of television crime scene shows it would quite likely have gone undetected.

It had been a simple plan. At some point prior to Don and Ximena arriving at the cabin the killer had used the nearby extension ladder to reach the top of the chimney and seal off the flue with the tarp, using the bungee cord to hold it in place. The length of cable was left dangling down the side of the chimney. There was little chance, given the dark night, that either Don or Ximena would notice the tarp when they arrived at the cabin. Returning in the last hours before dawn, the killer could simply pull the tarp off of the chimney, using the attached cable, and then disappear back into the darkness. Not wanting to risk being seen with the murder weapon, the killer had later dropped it in a snowbank on the ice-covered Sebec River, confident that spring floodwaters would carry it downstream.

3.

Soon after he was elected Sheriff of Piscataquis County, Jim Torben got rid of the large ornate desk his predecessor Don Hudson had been so proud of. Hudson, a transplant from Massachusetts, had been arrested on federal drug charges and removed from office a while back. In stark contrast to Hudson, Torben was not "from away." He had been born and raised in Dover-Foxcroft and had joined the sheriff's department soon after graduating from Foxcroft Academy. Steadily working his way up through the ranks in the sheriff's department, Torben had gained the respect of the people he worked with on a daily basis, as well as many of the communities dispersed across Piscataquis County - one of the largest and least populated counties east of the Mississippi. In place of Don Hudson's desk Torben had picked up a large and well-used oak library table at the Chesley Auction House over in East Corinth, twenty minutes away down Route 15.

The morning after the discovery of the piece of canvas that had been used in the murder of Don Robertson, four people sat around the sheriff's oak table and contemplated how to approach what they all recognized would be a difficult if not impossible case to crack. Doug Bateman sat next to the sheriff, with Anne Quinn and Jack Walker facing them across the table. While Anne, Doug, and Jim had previously worked together on a number of high-profile cases, Jack was new to the group. He hadn't worked any major crimes before, but Anne had been partnered with him on and off for the last six months or so and thought he might be ready for the challenge. Torben had agreed with her suggestion, and assigned Jack to the case.

Stan Shelter, who was Doug Bateman's boss at the Major Crimes Unit North over in Bangor, was also in the meeting, on the speakerphone. He would probably have nothing to offer to their discussion, and it wasn't clear that he was even listening. That was fine with Bateman – the last thing he wanted was interference from Shelter – a consummate bureaucrat with little experience in major crimes and a penchant for long-distance micromanagement of the MCU's widely dispersed detectives. MCU-North's jurisdiction encompassed almost half of the entire state of Maine - the five predominantly rural northern and easterly counties, covering 20,000 square miles and encompassing over 300,000 people.

Setting down his coffee cup, Jim Torben turned to Doug.

"Doug, now that the Robertson death is considered a homicide, the investigation is in the hands of MCU. Stan Shelter and I talked this morning and he's assigned you as the lead detective in the case. He also requested our assistance in the investigation, and I agreed."

Looking around the table, Doug frowned.

"Well, it looks like we're starting from absolute zero, and we're already several months behind. We know how Robertson was killed, and when. We also know that the murder was premeditated and carefully planned, and that the killer knew that Don and Ximena would be spending the night in the cabin. But that's it. We don't have any suspects or any motives, no convenient CCTV footage or much chance of locating any witnesses. Not too many people were likely out and about in the woods in the middle of the night, except of course for the killer."

Looking across the table at Anne and Jack, Doug continued.

"The case is also complicated in that Robertson was back and forth between here and Portland, so we need to look for leads in both places. The most logical way to divide up the work is to have my partner Tom Richard and I look into his life on the coast, and for Anne and Jack to pursue the case here."

Doug paused in anticipation of Stan Shelter interrupting over the speakerphone. He thought there was a good chance his boss would veto the involvement of his partner Tom Richard, who was once again the subject of an internal review involving a claim that he used unnecessary force in subduing a suspect in a rape case. Doug waited for any response from the speakerphone and realizing with relief that Shelter did not appear to be paying attention, he hurried on.

"Anne, Jack, are you two OK handling things here in Dover?"

Both nodded, and Jack raised his hand to speak as he glanced down, opening his iPad.

"I might have some leads on possible motives and persons of interest, both here and down on the coast."

Glancing around the table, Jack smiled at the looks of surprise that the rookie was speaking up, and continued.

"I ran into Don Robertson at the Bear's Den the night before he was found dead. We were both on the football team back in high school and he remembered me. We ended up sharing a pitcher of beer and getting caught up. He'd had a few beers already and did most of the talking – filling me in on why he was planning on moving back to Dover, and all his personal problems down in Portland."

Holding up his iPad, Jack continued.

"I often take contemporaneous notes on conversations I have with people when I think it might come in handy later. Given what happened that night at the Bear's Den, I made sure to take notes on my conversation with Robertson. Don told me he and his wife Rosemary were heading for a divorce and that she was deep into a cultish self-help group down in Portland. It sounded pretty hostile, with him being warned by cult members to stay away from his wife. So on the Portland side of the investigation, his wife and her involvement with this cult might be a good starting point."

Jack checked his iPad again.

"Don mentioned his wife's dentist, a guy named Lee Lamen, as being her mentor in the group, and intimated that Lamen had threatened him."

Pausing, Jack looked across the table at Doug and the sheriff. Nodding his head, Doug responded.

"That's good work Jack. Don's wife and Lee Lamen are solid places to start. What do you have on the Dover side of things? What happened that night at the Bear's Den?"

"Ximena Lapointe showed up and joined us. She made quite an entrance. She and Don embraced and kissed, almost showing off for the karaoke crowd. I remembered they'd been an item in high school. Don's interest in returning to town made much more sense with Ximena in the picture. Doug, you remember Ximena from high school, don't you?"

With a mock serious expression, Anne spoke up before Doug could respond.

"Yes Doug, do tell us about Ximena Lapointe."

Frowning now and looking to both Jack and the sheriff for support, Doug absently pulled at his right ear as he replied.

"Well, to be honest, Anne, I didn't know Ximena in high school. She wasn't part of my crowd at Foxcroft Academy. I know who she is, of course, and I've run into her a few times over the years, but nothing beyond that. I can confirm Jack's assessment though – she's a looker."

Anne settled back in her chair, surprised at Doug's response – not what he said, but his body language. Although she had never mentioned it to him, she knew Doug had a distinctive "tell." Whenever he was being evasive – not exactly lying but being careful with his words and perhaps not being fully forthcoming, he would tug at his right ear. "Interesting," she thought, filing Doug's evasion away for future discussion when they were alone.

Doug looked to Jack, who resumed his account of the karaoke night drama at the Bear's Den.

"Maybe a half hour later, Wes Fuller walked in and initiated an argument with Ximena and Don. It turns out Fuller and Ximena had dated a year or so back, but when he started trying to control her Ximena abruptly dumped him. Fuller didn't take the rejection well and began stalking her. Eventually she was forced to get him served with a restraining order. He clearly didn't like seeing Ximena and Don Robertson together at karaoke night and was getting aggressive. I stepped in and suggested he leave, which he did, but not before he threatened Don."

Looking down at his iPad, Jack found the passage he was looking for.

"Let's see – here it is - 'you can count on it Robertson, I'm gonna fuck you up.'"

Doug, Jim, and Jack all agreed that this sounded like typical bluster from Fuller. He had been a big talker but short on follow-through ever since high school.

The first steps they needed to take in the investigation seemed clear enough, based on Jack's observations, and it only took another twenty minutes or so to lay them out. Doug would head back to Bangor and he and his partner Tom Richard would start pulling together background information on Don Robertson, his wife, and the group she had joined, in advance of setting up some initial interviews with her and her mentor Lee Lamen. Anne and Jack would interview Wes Fuller, but first they needed to talk to Ximena Lapointe and see what she could tell them about Fuller, and which of his friends she thought might have worthwhile information.

Anne spent the rest of the morning learning more about Fuller - their prime suspect on the Dover side of the investigation. Other than the protection from abuse order that Ximena had obtained, Wes Fuller only had a few other run-ins with law enforcement – mostly bar fights, suspected drug dealing, and numerous complaints regarding his boating habits on Sebec Lake. Given his obnoxious profile, Anne was not surprised to learn that Fuller was the owner of the bright red "go-fast" boat designed for offshore open ocean racing that far too often could be heard out for high speed runs on Sebec. It was loud, and irritated onlookers could hear it coming from a mile or more away.

Fuller's boat was in fact at the top of the list of watercraft that Anne had decided would be permanently banned from the lake when she ascended to her imaginary throne and became "Queen of Sebec." Anne lived in a cottage on the south shore and summer evenings would frequently find her and Doug on her dock sharing a bottle of wine and watching the sunset. Over the past few summers they had developed and refined a comprehensive set of regulations for watercraft that would be imposed once Anne became queen. Canoes, kayaks, and paddleboards on the lake, for example – any human-powered craft, would be entitled to a $100 annual payment. Sailboats – any wind-powered vessel, would be allowed free of charge. Powerboats, on the other hand, would in general be charged on a sliding scale based on their horsepower rating. Any boat powered by an engine of less than ten horsepower would be charged an annual fee of $25. Ten to fifty horsepower would face a fee of $50, and fifty to one hundred horsepower a fee of $200. No boats with a horsepower rating above one hundred would be permitted. And of course, jet skis – personal watercraft, would be banned and subject to hefty fines.

Anne and Doug agreed, however, that there should be two notable exceptions to this fee structure. Pontoon or "patio" boats, regardless of their horsepower rating, would not face any fees. This exemption was based on the general quietness and the slow, stately progression of patio boats – they usually slipped past in a leisurely and dignified manner, like royal barges on the Thames. The second exemption was for vintage boats – those manufactured before 1960, and in particular any wooden boats or "woodies." There were not very many such boats on the lake, and since Doug owned one of the few woodies on the lake, a 1952 Chris Craft, an exemption for them seemed only appropriate.

Anne was surprised to learn that Wes Fuller ran a small company that plowed snow in the winter and cleared brush and downed trees in the summer months. It was not in the same category as Blue Water Tree Service or some of the other more established local firms. It certainly didn't appear to be a source of income sufficient to support his ownership of a go-fast boat, or the large compound he owned on the south shore not too far from the Sebec Village. It was suspected that drug money laundered through his business was a substantial portion of his income, but so far proof had been hard to come by.

Anne knew that Ximena mostly conducted her real estate business from her home on Davis Street on the Foxcroft side of the Piscataquis River, and she and Jack Walker decided to drop in on her unannounced that afternoon. As they pulled up to her house Jack admired the new high-end Ford pickup parked in her driveway. His own truck had over 180,000 miles on it and was showing some serious rust.

Ximena was puzzled but welcoming, and ushered them into her home office.

"Sorry for the mess, guys. I've been swamped with new listings coming on the market for the spring sales season. What's up?"

Anne and Jack had agreed that Jack would begin the questioning, given his long acquaintance with Ximena.

"Sorry for the interruption, Ximena. We're hoping you can provide us with some additional information both about Don Robertson's death and about Wes Fuller. I heard him threaten Robertson at the Bear's Den on karaoke night. Was there a long-standing beef? Had he made similar threats earlier?"

Looking from Jack to Anne, and back to Jack, Ximena furrowed her brow.

"What's this all about? Why do you want to know about Fuller and his dislike for Don? Don's dead, what difference does it make now?"

Jack looked over to Anne and she picked up the questioning.

"Ximena, Don's death has been reclassified as suspicious. We don't think it was an accident. I can't go into the details right now, but it looks like he was murdered. Since Wes Fuller threatened Don in public a few hours before he died, he's on our list of people of interest. We're hoping you can tell us more about Fuller, and about that Thursday night - both at the Bear's Den and later at the cabin."

Stunned into silence, Ximena stared past them, out the window. Finally, she replied.

"But Don died of carbon monoxide poisoning. He wasn't murdered."

Anne shook her head.

"No, it was a deliberate killing. Someone covered the chimney to trap the carbon monoxide fumes in the cabin. And we need your help to catch his killer."

Visibly shaken, Ximena sat forward in her chair and replied.

"How can I help? What do you want to know?"

Jack opened his iPad and started through his list of questions.

"Let's start with that night. Don told me that you were late getting to the Bear's Den. What delayed you?"

"Well, I had a dinner meeting with a big potential buyer for a property on the lake. That wrapped up on time, but my babysitter, Suzie Arter, was late, again, and then I managed to run my sled into a ditch on the way to the Bear's Den."

"Who's the buyer? Anything unusual there?"

"His name is Nigel Underwood. He's a Brit who lives down on the coast somewhere. He's an older man – maybe mid-sixties, sharp dresser and a bit smarmy. Nigel seemed normal enough, but it was a bit unusual the way he dropped off the face of the earth after our dinner meeting that night. He said he would be in touch with me the following week to make an offer, but then never followed through. I tried to contact him, but all my calls, texts, and emails went unanswered. If you wanna know the truth, it pissed me off."

Jack asked for the contact information for Underwood, added it to his iPad, and went to the next question on his list.

"Let's talk about your babysitter, Suzie Arter. I think I remember you telling us earlier that you had to be home by 1AM that night. She had stayed overnight for you a number of times previously, hadn't she? Why didn't she stay over that night?"

"I think she had a big test the next day – her SAT test if I remember right."

"We'll check on that with Suzie. OK, next question. Do you remember anything unusual about that night after you left the cabin – you said it was about midnight?"

"Yes – right about midnight. I had set my Fitbit to wake me. I don't remember if the heater was still on when I got up, but it was still warm in the cabin. I remember that. I woke up with a headache and figured I had too much beer at the Bear's Den. But it cleared up soon after I stepped outside. The snow was coming down really hard then, and it took me longer than I expected to get home."

"You didn't see anyone around the cabin or on the way home? You didn't hear anything?"

"Nope. The snow muffled sound pretty well, and visibility was down to almost nothing. It was hard to even see the trail. I was afraid I was going to go in the ditch again and would have to call someone to come and get me."

"OK, let's talk about Wes Fuller. How long had he known about you and Don? Had he made previous threats?"

"That was a real surprise to me. I don't think Wes and Don had ever run into each other since high school. Don never mentioned Wes having bothered him before, and I had not had many real problems with Wes since I got the restraining order. Him showing up and harassing us at the Bear's Den that night was right out of the blue."

"Anything else you think we should know about Wes Fuller before we talk to him?"

Ximena went still for a moment. Taking a deep breath, she replied.

"Looking back on it, I can't believe I ever got involved with the creep. He seemed nice enough at first, and being the subject of gossip myself, I chose to ignore all the badmouthing I had heard about him. Plus, he always had excellent weed. Everyone in town thinks he's just a blustery fraud – always making threats and posturing but never really following through. That's how he comes across. But it's a mask. As soon as I saw what's behind the mask, I got away from him as fast as I could. He scares me. Wes is involved in drugs – no question, and a bunch of other ugly stuff. And he's really smart. Or sly, I guess would be more accurate. I wouldn't be surprised if he was behind the murder of Don Robertson."

Anne thanked Ximena for talking with them, asked her to keep their conversation private for the time being, and indicated that they would have some more questions for her as the investigation progressed. As they walked back to their car, Anne and Jack both admired Ximena's new pickup. Having just bought a new truck herself, Anne wondered how Ximena could afford such an expensive vehicle on her real estate agent earnings.

4.

The next morning Jack and Anne drove out toward Sebec Village, turning left onto Sunset Ridge Road just before they reached the curve down into the town – if you could still call it that. In the 1800s Sebec Village had been a bustling town with lumber and woolen mills, carriage and cedar tub factories, and a variety of retail establishments. Today all that remained was a small hydro-electric generating plant, a few historic structures, including the Sebec Reading Room, and a few long-vacant stores, all clustered around the dam.

Neither Anne nor Jack had been to Wes Fuller's place before, and both were stunned to silence when it came into view a few minutes later. Shoreline zoning regulations ensured that a hundred-foot wide strip of vegetation, including mature birch and maple trees, remained intact along the lakeshore, but the remainder of his two-acre property had been entirely cleared of vegetation. Where mixed hardwood forest had once flourished, a vast expanse of gravel now covered the ground. A relatively new doublewide mobile home occupied the center of the lot, with a three-bay garage set back eighty feet or so from it toward the wooded lakeshore. A half dozen trucks and trailers of various sizes and states of repair, along with a well-used tree chipper, were scattered, seemingly at random, around the property. Several of them were covered with ratty and frayed canvas tarpaulins.

The sound of an edge grinder drifted over from the garage as Anne and Jack stepped up onto the porch of the doublewide and knocked on the door. After a few minutes, and more knocking, they could hear movement inside and the door was opened by Gary Crites. Gary looked like he had slept in his clothes and his belly peeked out from under his sweatshirt. Gary's expression went from belligerent to guarded as he recognized who his visitors were.

"What?"

"Good morning Gary," Jack replied. "We're looking for Wes Fuller. Can we come in?"

"No way Jack. No can do."

"Well, can Wes come out and talk with us?"

"Wes ain't here. Don't know where he is."

"Who's out in the garage Gary?"

"Not sure. I just got up."

Exchanging a glance, Anne and Jack turned away from Gary, stepped down off the porch, and started toward the garage. They heard Gary making a phone call behind them, and when they were about half-way to the garage, Wes Fuller burst out a side door, bellowing angrily.

"You're trespassing on my property. You need to leave. Now."

Noticing the hammer Wes was holding in his right hand, Anne extracted her 21" telescoping Monadnock baton from her coat pocket, extended it with an audible snap, and casually began tapping it against her leg. Next to her, Jack rested his hand on the butt of his holstered Glock as Anne responded to Fuller's demand.

"You plan on doing something with that hammer, Wes?"

Fuller stopped his advance toward them, held the hammer out in front of him, and dropped it.

"Sorry about that – I didn't realize I still had it in my hand," he sneered.

Collapsing her baton and slipping it back into her coat pocket, Anne gestured toward the garage.

"What are you cooking up in there Wes – a fresh batch of crank?"

"No, nothing like that. None of your business."

Starting toward Wes, Jack pointed again at the garage.

"Mind if we take a look-see?"

Wes stepped in front of the much larger man.

"Yes, I mind. Don't you need a warrant or something?"

Jack turned his head and glanced at Anne, who answered Fuller's objection.

"Without your permission, Wes, yes - we would need a search warrant. Jack can wait here with you while I go and request one. It might take a while. Or you can just let us take a quick look. That is, assuming it's all kosher in there."

"OK, fine. You can check it out. But you have to promise not to blab about this around town."

Leading Anne and Jack to the garage, Wes opened the side door and with a deep bow, ushered them inside. Fuller's trailered go-fast boat that Anne detested took up the first bay of the garage. Beyond it, the floor of the other two bays was covered with what appeared to be the disassembled parts of a patio boat. Its two large aluminum pontoons were sitting on sawhorses, and a variety of tools – wrenches, cutting torches, edge grinders, and drills, were scattered around on the floor.

Anne looked around with a quizzical expression, while Jack immediately let out an audible snort as he turned to Wes, who was still standing in the doorway.

"Is this is what you're keeping secret Wes? Looks to me like you've stripped down your patio boat and are getting started on customizing it for the big race."

Jack glanced at several of the parts on the floor and then ran his hand along one of the highly polished pontoons.

"Looks like a Bennington twenty-two-footer. The twenty-two feet and under class is shaping up to be tough this year, Wes – think you can compete? Not changing anything below the waterline, are you?"

"Fuck you Jack. It's all within the rules. I just don't want anyone to get wind of what I have planned."

Still confused, Anne asked "What big race?"

"It's the third annual Sebec Pontoon Boat Challenge, Anne," Jack replied. "It's coming up in July. I'm not surprised it doesn't loom large for you – it was really small the first two years – maybe a dozen or so local competitors. But it's really taken off this year.

Rumor is it could have maybe a hundred boats coming from all over New England."

Turning her attention to Fuller, Anne switched topics back to the reason for their visit.

"Wes, we don't care what you're planning for your patio boat. Let's go up to the house and have a conversation. Or we can go downtown and talk there. Either way's OK with us. We have a few questions about Don Robertson and your confrontation with him at the Bear's Den a few months ago."

It was Wes Fuller's turn to look confused.

"Sure. Come on up to the house. I got nothing to hide. Don Robertson? What about him? He offed himself, right?"

Jack and Anne didn't offer any reply to Wes until they were seated around a Formica table in the kitchen of his doublewide. Anne rested her hands on the table, only to fold them in her lap when she felt its sticky surface.

"Wes, it turns out Don Robertson's death was not accidental. He was murdered." Anne said in a neutral voice. She paused to let that sink in, and then continued.

"Back a few months ago a number of witnesses, including Jack here, heard you threaten Don Robertson at the Bear's Den. Why the threat? Couldn't you accept that Ximena dumped you - that she got a new man?"

Still looking confused, Wes sat silent, then uttered a short, sharp laugh and replied.

"You think Don was murdered? And that I killed him out of jealousy over Ximena? Now that's a good one."

Fixing Anne with a serious stare, Wes continued. "You got the wrong guy. I could care less who Ximena is fucking. I admit to jerking her around whenever I run into her, but that's just cause she's such a bitch. And I'm certainly not grieving over little Donny Robertson. He was a slimy piece of work. But I didn't kill him."

Anne tried to ignore the pile of dirty dishes in the sink and the smell of rancid grease that floated over from a cast iron skillet on the stove.

"How well did you know Robertson?"

"I knew him from high school. He was a prick even back then. Thought he was some sort of investment genius. I hadn't seen him in maybe ten years, though, until the Bear's Den."

"So why do you say he was a slimy piece of work if you hadn't seen him in the last ten years?"

Fuller pursed his lips, trying to decide how much to say. Reaching a decision, he seemed to relax, leaning back in his chair and answering Anne.

"Robertson thought he was a big shot. He went down on the coast and made a lot of money. Then he decided to move back here and lord it over all of us. I heard from someone downtown that part of his grand return to Dover, in addition to Ximena, was going to involve winning the unlimited class, the main event, at the Sebec Pontoon Challenge this summer. But being a sneaky prick, he was planning on doing it with a fancy pontoon boat out of Indiana he was getting on loan – one of those rich man Manitou boats."

Anne turned to Jack for translation.

"It's a long story Anne. I can fill you in when we're done here. The short answer is that the Sebec Challenge was initially set up to be mostly for regular people, not rich folks. It's the antithesis of Lake Winnipesaukee and its Gentleman's Racers. But an unlimited class has been added this year. It's meant to attract the high-end crowd and their wallets."

Anne turned back to Fuller.

"Let's get back to karaoke night at the Bear's Den. Can you fill in the timeline for us? Where were you earlier in the evening? Did you know Ximena and Robertson would be there? What did you do after you left the bar that night?"

"I was at home, packing for a trip down to Portland. Gary called from the Bear's Den to let me know Ximena and Don were there, and I figured I would stop by on my way out of town, just to jerk them around a little. Gary can confirm the phone call. Ask him."

"We will," replied Anne. "And we will check on the phone records – was it a mobile phone or a land line?"

"A land line."

Wes pointed to a vintage Trimline corded wall phone next to the refrigerator.

"You were on your way to Portland?"

"Yeah. I had to see a man about a used Vermeer chipper he had listed on craigslist."

"So you drove down that night?"

"Ayup. Got to my friend Sylvia's place about midnight. Checked out the chipper first thing in the morning – it was a piece of shit. I hung out with Sylvia for the rest of Friday, and then drove back up that night. You can check with Sylvia."

When they had finished up their questioning of Wes, Jack drifted off to look at the machinery scattered around the property, and Anne tracked down Gary, who had gone out to the garage. He confirmed his phone call from the Bear's Den on karaoke night, but had little more to offer, and Anne walked back to the car to wait for Jack. As he returned from his casual wandering among the scattered equipment, Anne noticed that he had picked up several fragments of canvas, along with a red bungee cord, all of which looked to be a good potential match with the tarp and attached cord that had been used to cover the cabin chimney where Don Robertson had died.

As they got into their SUV, Fuller suddenly burst out of the door of the doublewide, and Anne thought he was going to complain about Jack's collecting activities. But Fuller had a different message.

"It's pretty funny you're putting me in the picture for that prick's killing. Ximena is the one you should be talking to. Maybe you should ask her where she got the cash for that fancy new truck."

Driving back into Dover, Anne and Jack discussed their next steps and divided up the loose ends to be pursued. Once back in the office, Jack arranged for the tarp and bungee cord he had collected to be sent down to the crime lab in Augusta for analysis, and then headed over to the Prouty Ford dealership in town to check if Ximena had purchased her new pickup from them. Meanwhile, Anne followed up on Wes Fuller's alibi for karaoke night. Her check of phone records showed an incoming call from Gary to Fuller's Trimline on karaoke night, and Fuller's friend Sylvia confirmed his arrival in Portland about midnight that same night. So far at least, part of Wes Fuller's alibi seemed solid. There was no way he could have removed the tarp from the cabin's chimney in the early morning hours of Friday. But he had no alibi for earlier in the evening and could have put the tarp in place.

Jack came up empty on the pickup purchase. The sales manager at the Prouty dealership had no record of selling a truck to Ximena Lapointe, saying that they were losing far too many sales to dealerships in Bangor and beyond. People were looking to save a few hundred dollars rather than supporting local businesses. It took Jack most of the rest of the morning to find the source of Ximena's shiny new truck. She had purchased it from the Quirk Ford dealership down in Belfast and had paid cash – a little more than $43,000, which was a sizable sum for a real estate salesperson to have laying around.

Her cash purchase of such an expensive truck certainly warranted another interview with Ximena, and Anne remembered that they hadn't yet talked with her babysitter, Suzie Arter, to see if she could confirm Ximena's account of karaoke night. Anne called the Foxcroft Academy, and a check of their records showed both that an SAT exam had been given on that Friday in March, and that Susan Arter had taken the test. They would still need to interview Suzie to see if her story matched Ximena's account of karaoke night, but Anne expected that it would.

It was almost noon, and Jack suggested that he could tell her all about the Sebec Pontoon Boat Challenge over lunch at the café located in the renovated woolen mill. It was a beautiful spring day, and they walked down Main Street to the restaurant. Once they had ordered at the counter, grabbed a couple of ginger beers from the cooler, and found a table that overlooked the Piscataquis River, Jack took a sip of his ginger beer and began.

"It started three or four years ago on a sort of dare. A few guys with patio boats on Sebec Lake were boasting one night at Pat's Pizza about how fast their boats were, and they decided to have a race. Maybe a half dozen boats took part that first year, and they had a barbeque afterward at the beach by Greeley's Landing. Word got around, the local paper picked it up, and some local boosters, including the Chamber of Commerce and the Kiwanis Club, got behind sponsoring an annual patio boat race on Sebec Lake."

Jack paused as their lunches arrived, and then continued between bites of his sandwich.

"Summers in Maine don't last that long. There's a short three-month window for small towns to draw in visitors, and starting in early June you can find a weekend festival of some sort somewhere in the state, as different localities try to attract people and their pocketbooks. About ten years ago Dover-Foxcroft hit the jackpot with the town's creation of the Whoopie Pie Festival. Held in late June, the festival draws five thousand or so people every year, doubling the town's population. It was hoped that the Sebec Pontoon Boat Challenge would give the town another big summer weekend."

Jack took a quick bite of his sandwich and continued.

"Things started taking off the second year. With wider promotion the race drew maybe thirty boats from across Maine and several neighboring states. It became obvious, however, that the event needed more structure, more organization, if it was going to continue to grow. So last fall a set of overall rules were developed, and different classes of competition were established."

Jack pulled up a web site on his iPad, scrolled down briefly, and continued.

"Let's see – there are now four different categories or classes that entries fall into. The first two are for boats that are twenty-two feet or less in length, with motors having one hundred and fifty horsepower or less. One of these classes is limited to women pilots – the "Powder Puff" class. The other twenty-two foot and under class is open to anyone. The third class is for boats over twenty-two feet in length, powered by three hundred horsepower or less, and the fourth class is unlimited – any length, any horsepower. This unlimited class is for the high-end competitors, the gentleman racers, who can afford $150,000 pontoon boats that can hit sixty mph or more. I think the current speed record for a pontoon boat is 114mph."

Anne interrupted.

"What sort of rules are there for boat modification, like what we saw with Wes Fuller?"

"Obviously, the unlimited class has no restrictions at all. For the other three classes, any and all modifications above the waterline are allowed. You will see some airfoils and other nonsense, and a few comedians have charcoal grills welded to their decks. But below the waterline the boats have to remain stock. No changes are allowed. Now that things are more formalized each boat will go through a pre-race inspection before they are launched – first to ensure that they won't introduce any invasive plants – Sebec is one of the lakes in the state that does not yet have any exotic introductions. In addition, each boat will be inspected to make sure there are no enhancements below the waterline."

Anne was starting to see the rationale for the pontoon boat class structure and smiled.

"I like this a lot Jack – let the rich kids fight it out in the unlimited class, and bring all their money to town, while at the same time preserving the other three classes for competitors of more modest means. If you want you can compete in your everyday patio boat that you use on the weekends for towing kids on tubes and for sunset cruises, both above and below the twenty-two-foot dividing line. Or, for all those more adventurous competitors with a heated garage, and facing Maine's long winters, you can do what Wes Fuller is doing, and customize your own racing pontoon boat from the ground up. How can we check on Don Robertson's entry in this year's race, if there was one?"

"Well," Jack responded, let's go talk to Bob Lutz, he's involved in the organization and running of this year's race."

They found Lutz sitting at his desk at Dave's World, Dover's local appliance store, surrounded by displays of heat pumps, refrigerators, stoves, flooring, and more. Lutz was just finishing up his brown bag lunch. Jack introduced Anne, and when they asked about the Sebec Pontoon Challenge, Bob reached over and opened his personal laptop. Calling up his list of registered entries for the race, he scrolled down until he found Don Robertson's name.

"Yeah, Don's still on the list, even though he obviously won't be competing, being dead and all. But the other person listed with him is still intending to participate. His name is Nigel Underwood. He's one of the race organizers this year. He and Don entered a Manitou in the unlimited class, and he is still intending to race. He's already paid the $500 non-refundable entry fee. We thought the rich folks with expensive boats wouldn't mind a nice hefty fee up front to experience our beautiful lake."

"I know that name," Jack murmured. "He's the potential buyer that Ximena had dinner with on karaoke night. We need to talk to him."

Anne nodded in agreement and turned back to Lutz with more questions about the race.

"How many people have registered for the race, Bob?"

"Maybe sixty so far, but we expect that to surge from now until race day, particularly given the recent media deal that's been signed."

"What deal's that?" Jack asked.

"ESPN is going to carry the race. They've been getting involved in lots of quirky competitions – apparently there's a growing viewing audience for offbeat events, and they've contracted to cover the race. We're keeping that quiet until the big reveal, but the race could eventually be bigger than the Whoopee Pie Festival."

5.

"ESPN?" Doug exclaimed, setting down his glass of sauvignon blanc and looking with incredulity across the table at Anne. "You have got to be kidding."

They were having dinner at Allie Oops, the sports bar in Dover-Foxcroft. Sitting at a corner table, waiting for their pizza to arrive, Anne was filling him in on the unfolding plans for the Sebec Pontoon Boat Challenge.

"I know," Anne responded. "I'm not sure if I should be pleased or horrified. I'm not ready for Sebec to be discovered, to be showcased on ESPN as a center for patio boat racing. What will exposure like that do to the community?"

Doug was still stunned.

"No way to know right now Anne. Sounds like it could be a nice boost to the local economy, and it would only be for a few days each summer. I haven't seen too many down sides to the Whoopie Pie festival. Maybe it will be the same sort of thing."

Their pizza arrived before Anne could respond, and both Anne and Doug were surprised by who brought it to the table.

"Katie, what are you doing back in Dover?" Anne asked. "I thought you and Lou Binford were exploring urban adventures down on the coast."

Brushing back her long red hair, Katie hugged them both before sitting down at their table.

"I'm back for good, I think. It took me a while to get past my initial crush on Louise, but when I did it got pretty boring, and sort of scary now and then. She works a lot, and when she's not working, she wants to party hard and to impress people. Me, I'm more of a stay-at-home gal – quiet dinners and snuggling up in front of the TV."

"Well, we're glad to have you back Katie," Anne responded. "Was the breakup mutual?"

"Ayup," Katie responded. "Lou was happy to see me go and I was relieved to escape in one piece. She left the state police. I'm not sure if it was voluntary. She started a consulting business – drones for hire. She does real estate flyovers along with some crime scene stuff, natural disasters, and sporting events for media outlets. She's not too successful yet, but she's staying afloat."

Dropping her voice and glancing over her shoulder, Katie continued. "I don't know how well you got to know her when she was up here working on your serial murder case, but Lou has lots of issues, maybe left over from her time in the military."

"Like what?" Anne asked.

"Lou Binford makes shit up all the time – and it's not clear if she actually can tell the difference between her fantasies and reality. At first I challenged her on her stories, thinking she was doing it for fun, but she was dead serious. And Lou's quite volatile - she can fly off the handle pretty easily. With all her marital arts experience, I was never sure what she might do. I got nervous just being around her toward the end."

Katie jumped as her name was yelled out from behind the bar. Getting up and moving away, she called back over her shoulder. "Sorry, gotta get back to work. Talk to you guys soon."

Doug slid a slice of pizza onto Anne's plate and added to Katie's breakup tale.

"The story I heard was that Lou was allowed to resign – she apparently was caught up in some sort of sexual harassment complaints. Sounds like Katie is well rid of her."

A rerun of one of the Patriot's games was playing on the TV above the bar, and Doug glanced at it as Anne unfolded a printout from her coat pocket.

"Look at this Doug. I got it from Bob Lutz. It's the draft schedule for the pontoon boat race. It's a two-day event – Friday and Saturday. Friday is preliminary time trials, with individual boats starting at intervals and covering a course that goes from a start/finish line by Greeley's Landing, east around Pine Island, and then back. Then on Saturday there are one-on-one match races between the top four finishers in each of the four classes of competition. They'll start by Greeley's Landing again, but go west through the narrows, into and out of Buck's Cove, down toward the Peaks Kenny State Park beach in the South Cove, then back through the narrows to the finish line."

Doug responded before sliding a pizza slice onto his plate.

"How is ESPN going to make a show out of patio boats racing around? Sounds pretty boring to me."

"Oh, I think it will be great on TV," Anne countered. "The Friday prelims will probably be boring, but the Saturday match races will be anything but – they have a bunch of corners built into the course that the boats will have to maneuver around, trying to get the inside track, and the channel into Buck's Cove is only wide enough for one boat at a time. And don't forget, there's always the weather – if we get any sort of waves on the big part of lake, west of the narrows, it could get ugly."

"Maybe," Doug replied. "But how are they going to get cameras on the action?"

"Lutz said ESPN is planning on stationary cameras on Pine Island, and most importantly, at the Buck's Cove channel, and then cameras on boats that will follow the competitors, like the motorcycle cameras they use for the Tour de France. Each of the competitor boats will also have cameras, and they plan on wall to wall drone coverage."

"I hope they also get wall-to-wall insurance coverage. If a couple of guys who have been building their boats back in the woods and dreaming of victory all winter end up running neck in neck as they approach the Buck's Cove channel, there could be some epic crashes."

"Great TV," replied Anne, reaching for another slice of pizza.

"So, do you think the patio boat race has anything to do with our murder investigation?" Doug asked with a puzzled expression.

"Maybe." Anne responded. "It turns out Don Robertson and a guy named Nigel Underwood had a high-end entry in the unlimited class of the race. Underwood apparently is still planning on competing. Underwood is also the rich prospective buyer who had dinner with Ximena on karaoke night to discuss a property here on Sebec Lake. But he's dropped off the map since the killing. I think you can include him in the people you and Tom Richard need to talk to down on the coast."

"I will add him to the list," Doug replied. "I wonder what his other business dealings with Robertson were. We haven't gotten very far with our interviews yet. Tom Richard has been cleared to work the case, and we'll be talking to the widow Robertson tomorrow. Lee Lamen, the dentist character who is her spiritual mentor, is at a convention in Atlanta, and we're not clear yet when he'll be back."

"How about Robertson's estate?" Anne asked, "anything there?"

"It went through informal probate, with his wife Rosemary filing with the court as the personal representative or executor. In the absence of a will the entire estate went to her. I hope we can go over what was in the estate with her tomorrow and see if it represented much of a motive for Rosemary to knock off her husband. We also need to see if there was a life insurance policy and ask if there are any disgruntled or suspicious investors. If we're really lucky his computer files and investor records will still be intact, but who knows what his widow has done with them."

Catching Katie's eye behind the bar, Doug held his empty wine glass in the air and held up two fingers, then asked Anne how the interviews with Ximena and Wes Fuller had turned out.

"Well, we still have some aspects of their alibis to nail down – Ximena's story about leaving the cabin at midnight because of the babysitter's test the next day seems to check out, but I need to confirm it with the babysitter, Suzie Arter. And once you talk to Nigel Underwood we can see if the account of their dinner meeting that night holds up - a time-stamped receipt would be nice, or a statement from their waiter. Maybe they were out putting a tarp over the chimney of Don Robertson's cabin."

Anne took a sip of wine and continued.

"It's pretty much the same situation with Wes Fuller. He has a good alibi for after the confrontation with Robertson and Ximena at the Bear's Den – his trip down to Portland checks out, and he doesn't have a clear motive unless it's the fact that Robertson was entering a fancy pontoon boat in the upcoming race. But that doesn't seem like enough of a motive for murder – particularly since their boats would not have been competing against each other – Fuller is in the under twenty-two-foot class and Robertson was in the unlimited category.

"How about his buddy Gary Crites?" Doug countered. "Maybe Fuller placed the tarp before heading to the Bear's Den that night, and then George went over and pulled it off in the early morning hours."

"That could play," Anne agreed. "We collected some tarp samples and a red bungee cord out at Fuller's camp – maybe the lab results will link them to the killing. And Jack and I can have a talk with Gary. He's not exactly Mensa material, and it should be easy to get a read on him. Actually, neither he nor Wes seem too sharp – I doubt they could pull off such a carefully planned scheme."

Allie Oops was filling up and the noise level had increased considerably. Doug went to the bar to pay their tab, and Anne, remembering something, came up beside him.

"I have another loose end Doug – Ximena recently bought a new truck from the Quirk Ford dealership down in Belfast and paid cash. Jack and I are both curious about where she got the money, and Wes Fuller pointed the finger at her for Robertson's death, suggesting that we look into the truck purchase."

Doug glanced up from signing the bill and was about to respond when he saw the look of surprise on Anne's face and turned to see what had spooked her. Announcing their entrance with loud laughter, Louise Binford and two sketchy looking men came in the front door of Allie Oops. Both men made a beeline for the bathroom at the back of the bar, but Lou, noticing Anne and Doug, drifted over and greeted them enthusiastically. She was still a striking individual, a little over six feet tall, with short purple hair, black boots, tights, and jacket, and an aggressive personality.

"Hey guys – how's it goin up here in the boonies? Rogue moose keeping you busy?"

Doug smiled and shook Lou's outstretched hand. Anne managed to avoid Binford's clumsy attempt at a hug, while also watching Katie, reflected in the mirror behind the bar, as she grabbed her coat and slipped out the back door. Anne wondered if Lou was in town because of Katie, but wasn't going to ask, when Doug asked in a more general way.

"What brings you back to Dover, Lou?"

"Never thought I would be back up here in the middle of nowhere, but it looks like I have a shot at getting the contract for drone coverage of the big patio boat race on Sebec. I still have to make a pitch to this Nigel Underwood guy, but it's looking pretty good."

After a few minutes of awkward chit-chat about the race, Anne and Doug managed to escape Lou Binford and the noise and growing intensity of the bar. They walked back to where Doug's Jeep Cherokee was parked in the large lot behind Allie Oops. It was a short twenty-minute drive to Anne's cabin on the south shore of Sebec Lake, and they were planning on spending the night there.

Anne and Doug had been together for more than a year now, but they still each owned their own lakeside cabins, Anne on the south shore and Doug on the north. They spent about an equal number of nights at both camps without paying much attention to which place they stayed. The important thing was they rarely spent a night apart. Anne had left her truck in the parking lot at the courthouse, and Doug would drop her off there in the morning before he headed into work at the state police barracks in Bangor.

As they approached Doug's jeep Anne heard something and turned to see a dark shape maybe twenty feet behind them – some sort of animal dimly visible in the darkness. She grabbed Doug by the arm and they both stopped and turned to watch a large stray dog approach them. It walked slowly, with its head down, and reaching them, leaned against Doug's legs and looked up at him. It didn't have a collar or tags and had been living on the street for a while, judging from the absence of a collar, one tattered ear, ribs showing, and matted fur. It looked like a German Shepard but with a tawny-colored coat. Doug reached down and scratched the dog behind the ears, murmuring "what a sweet dog," and Anne could tell it was love at first sight. Crouching down, Anne put an arm around the dog's neck and looked up at Doug with a smile.

"We need to take this dog home. Let's go to your place tonight – we can stop at Will's and buy some food, and maybe some dog shampoo, and then tomorrow we'll take it to vet to get him checked out – see if it has a chip, get it dewormed and vaccinated, and take it from there."

Doug nodded, reached down, and cradling the dog, placed it on the back seat of the jeep. Stretching out, the dog slapped its tail a few times on the seat and closed his eyes.

"I'll be surprised if he doesn't have a chip," Doug remarked as they pulled into the parking lot at Will's Stop 'n Save Market. "He's neutered, maybe a year or two old, and unless I'm mistaken, he looks to be part or all Chinook. They're still pretty rare – sled dogs that were first bred in New Hampshire in the early twentieth century. He's maybe fifty pounds now but will probably reach seventy-five or eighty pounds when fully grown. Melinda Blood – the professor you met at the University of Maine last year – her Chinook, Jack, died just last year. They're wonderful dogs."

Will's had everything they were looking for, and Anne smiled as they passed the post office on the way out of town with a big bag of dog food, dog shampoo, several squeaky toys, and a new collar in the back of the jeep – she knew that chip or not, this dog had a new home. After a full bowl of food and a bath he didn't particularly enjoy, the dog sniffed around the living room before picking up a squeaky toy and curling up in front of the fire. He was soon snoring contentedly.

Later that night Anne woke up, surprised that Doug was hogging the bed, which he rarely did, only to realize that it wasn't Doug pressing up against her. There was a large freshly bathed dog stretched out between them, chasing something, no doubt a red squirrel, in his dreams.

6.

Doug Bateman and his partner Tom Richard paused at the corner of Pearl and Middle Street in Portland and waited for several cars to pass before crossing. Tom had driven down from Bangor, and Doug from Dover-Foxcroft. They were on their way to interview Rosemary Tremblay, Don Robertson's widow, whose office was a half block farther up on Middle Street. She was lawyer in one of Portland's largest law firms and had somewhat reluctantly agreed to give them a half hour of her valuable time. Doug checked his watch to make sure they were on time, causing Tom to snicker next to him.

"Jesus Doug, we're not on our way to the principal's office. She might say she's very busy and only has a half hour for us, but once we sit down, we can take all the time we want. Plus, judging from her last name her family has roots in Quebec, and I can snow her with my Québécois patter. She'll end up inviting us to lunch."

Doug barely listened to what his partner was saying – he was wondering when Anne would call him with an update from the vet. They had dropped the stray dog that had found them the previous night off at the Foxcroft Veterinary clinic for an assessment first thing that morning and Doug was anxious to hear what they had found. Checking the addresses on the buildings they were passing, Doug sarcastically replied to his partner.

"Tom, I'm counting on your smooth chitty-chat and fancy duds to get her to spill everything she knows and to solve the case for us today. Don't let me down."

Tom nodded in agreement and paused to admire his reflection in a shop window. He had decided to celebrate the lifting of his suspension by turning over a new leaf, and as part of his new presentation of self he had invested in a new suit. It was dark blue with a subtle pinstripe, and was matched with a blue button-down shirt, a maize and blue striped tie, and glossy black wingtips. He was resplendent in comparison to Doug, who was wearing his standard work outfit –khakis, brown tweed sport coat, dress shirt and tie, and casual loafers.

In spite of Tom's new "pillar of the community" outfit, he still radiated the free-floating hostility of someone seemingly on the edge of violence, constantly scanning the street for potential danger and eager to confront it. Tom Richard was a lady's man who combined "bad boy" appeal with a dazzling smile and an uncanny ability to draw attractive women into conversation.

After a brief wait in the reception area of the fifth-floor law firm, Doug and Tom were escorted back to Rosemary Tremblay's corner office, which had a great view east across the Casco Bay ferry docks to the islands beyond. Tom casually moved in front of Doug as the secretary opened the office door, and he greeted Tremblay with a gentle handshake and a smooth "Bonjour."

Surprised, the lawyer responded in rapid fire French, to which Tom laughed, spread his hands wide in an expansive gesture, and responded at some length. Seemingly captivated, Rosemary invited Tom to take a seat, and then somewhat reluctantly acknowledged Doug's presence and waved him to a chair before retreating behind her desk.

Once seated, Rosemary turned expectantly toward Tom, and was surprised when it was Doug who opened the questioning.

"Thank you for meeting with us Ms. Tremblay. We're sorry for your loss. As I mentioned on the phone, we're hoping you can help us with our inquiry into the death of your late husband – Donald Robertson."

Tremblay was thin, with short black hair, brown eyes, and sharp, almost vulpine features. She wore a gray sweater set and knee-length skirt, little makeup, and no jewelry except for small pearl earrings. Doug noted the absence of a wedding or engagement ring. Gazing coldly back at Doug with ramrod straight posture, she projected a severe sensuality and a strictly business-like demeanor.

"I'm not sure I can be of much help Detective Bateman, and I'm somewhat confused. My husband has been dead now for several months, and the medical examiner ruled it an accidental death. So why an inquiry now?"

"New evidence has come to light Ms. Tremblay, that indicates that your husband's death was not accidental. We have good reason to believe that he was murdered."

Rosemary's mouth opened in surprise.

"Homicide? Who would kill him? And why?"

"That's what we're hoping to find out," Doug replied. "Can you think of anyone who had a reason to want your husband dead?"

"No, absolutely not. Don was not one to make enemies – he was, if anything, lacking in assertiveness and ambition. Weak, I guess you could say. That's one of the reasons we were getting a divorce. He was, truth be told, rather boring."

"Was it an amicable divorce process, would you say?" Doug asked, somewhat surprised at Rosemary's blunt assessment of her late husband.

"Pretty much," Rosemary responded. "We'd been separated for almost six months before his death – he'd moved out of my condo. I bought it before we got married."

"We have information of a conflict of sorts between your late husband and an individual named Lee Lamen. Can you tell us about that?"

Looking surprised, Rosemary paused before answering.

"Lee is a good friend and has supported me during a very difficult time. He defended me against Don's criticisms. And Lee actually liked Don. I think he was as stunned as I was when we heard about his death."

"How did you learn about it?" Tom asked.

"Lee and I were both at a dental convention in Las Vegas that week. Lee was on a panel and I tagged along to get a break from work and play the tables a bit."

Tom looked up from the notes he was taking and glanced at Doug. Rosemary noticed the interchange and smiled in comprehension.

"That's right, detectives. You can scratch us off your list of suspects. We were both 2,500 miles away when Don died and there are lots of people who can verify it. We had no opportunity and no motive. The divorce proceedings had started, and the financial disclosures showed I had nothing to gain from either his death or the divorce."

Leaning forward, looking directly at Rosemary, and speaking in a low, confidential tone, Tom asked his first question.

"Are you and Lamen romantically involved?"

Beaming back at Tom, Rosemary responded flirtatiously.

"Why detective, I didn't know you were interested. Lee's a good friend but that's it. We hang out together, but Lee's gay, detective Richard, so we were not in that sort of relationship."

Tom abruptly changed topics.

"Did your husband have any life insurance policies?"

Rosemary laughed out loud – a deep raspy cackle in sharp contrast to her professional demeanor.

"Yes, as a matter of fact he did – a nice one - $500,000. But shortly after he moved out he took pleasure in letting me know he had changed the beneficiary– as if I would care. I would have given up a lot more than that to be rid of him. Did I mention he was boring?"

"Did he happen to say who the new beneficiary was?"

"No, and I didn't ask. It was probably that slut he was seeing back up there in the sticks."

"What can you tell us about his investment consulting business? Did he have any disgruntled clients for example? Had any investments gone south? Did you have any investments with your husband?"

"Don and I kept all our finances separate and I would never have considered letting him play with any of my money. I'm an index fund kind of person when it comes to investments. I do like playing cards for money – blackjack and poker mostly – but that's different, and I only make small bets. I had nothing to do with Don's business, and judging from what I've learned since his death, he had few clients left and a pretty lackluster recent record of investment for himself.

Don made a reasonable income but nothing really impressive. He didn't leave any debts for me to clear up when he died, thank goodness, but there wasn't much for him to pass on either, other than maybe thirty thousand in his savings account."

"We'd like to look at his financials if that's possible," Doug responded.

Rosemary nodded agreeably.

"Sure thing. We filed our taxes separately. I can let you have copies of his returns for the past several years, and some of his old business files are also still boxed up at my condo. You can borrow them to look at."

Opening her hands out in front of her, palms up, Rosemary smiled again and continued.

"Come to think of it, I'll give you a key to the condo and you can take everything of his that's left. I was about to throw all that crap out anyway. Lee and I cleaned out his apartment the week after his death. Pretty much everything went to Goodwill except his files and a few computer components – a mouse and a side monitor, I think. Maybe a few other gadgets. All that stuff is in a few boxes in the front hall of the condo. Please, take it all away. Just give me an inventory at some point. I can't say for sure what you'll find. I haven't really looked at any of it in detail other than his active client accounts. Fortunately, those were all up to date and available in hard copy."

Fishing her purse out of a desk drawer, Rosemary rattled off the address of her condo while extracting a key from her key ring and handing it across the desk to Doug.

"Just drop the key off here with the receptionist when you're done – and there's no hurry on providing the inventory."

Tom and Doug exchanged a glance, and Tom asked the obvious follow-up question, while also deliberately trying out her first name.

"Rosemary. You mentioned taking computer peripherals from your husband's apartment – a mouse and a side monitor. Did you find his computer?

"No. Just an empty space on the desk where it should have been. He had a fancy laptop – an Apple Macbook Pro."

"Was there a break-in at your husband's apartment? Any police report filed?"

"No – everything looked normal when we went through the place. Not much to clean out."

"Do you have any idea of what happened to the laptop?"

"No. I asked the sheriff's office if they had recovered it at the cabin after his death, but they returned all his effects to me a few weeks later, and there was no MacBook Pro. I figured his white-trash girlfriend had taken it."

Pointedly looking at her watch, Rosemary stood up and placed both palms on her desk – a clear signal she was through answering their questions.

"If there's nothing else, I have clients waiting."

Doug glanced at Tom, who shook his head, indicating he had no other questions for Tremblay. They both stood, and Doug thanked the not so grieving widow for her time.

"Thank you for speaking with us Ms. Tremblay. And thanks too for providing your late husband's financial records. I'm sure we'll have more questions for you and will also need contact information for people who can vouch for your Las Vegas trip. One last question – Do you know how we can contact Nigel Underwood? He was a friend of your husband."

Rosemary blinked rapidly several times, looking confused.

"I can't say that I have ever met Mr. Underwood, and Don never mentioned him. I have no idea who he is."

Reaching out to shake Rosemary's hand, Doug thanked her again and moved toward the office door. Pausing at the threshold, he waited for Tom to conclude his animated conversation in Quebecois with Tremblay before the two men headed back to the elevators. As soon as she was sure they were out of sight, Rosemary picked up her phone and made a call.

Doug and Tom didn't speak until they were back on the street, when Tom broke the silence.

"Looks like Rosemary and her dentist mentor have a solid alibi if it checks out. What's our next move?"

"Let's pay an unannounced visit to this Lee Lamen character and see if their Las Vegas story holds up. He's supposed to be back in town today. We also need to pick up Don Robertson's financial records and computers. I'll call Peter Martell and have the evidence response team meet us at Tremblay's condo later this afternoon. But first, lunch somewhere. Any recommendations?"

Tom immediately set out at a brisk pace down Middle Street, calling back over his shoulder:

"The Thirsty Pig is just up here around the corner. You gotta have a few of their hot dogs – I recommend the Spicy McFirepants – that is if you can handle 'em."

Smiling at Tom's rapidly receding back, Doug responded to his jibe.

"But Tom – I thought your Quebecois patter was going to result in Rosemary inviting us to lunch. Now it turns out I have to settle for a few hot dogs. Nothin like living large down in the big city."

When they had reached the restaurant, ordered at the counter, and grabbed a table by the window, Tom sampled his beer and finally replied to Doug's crack about his failure to sweet talk Rosemary Tremblay.

"You're right Doug – I didn't manage to get a lunch invitation from Rosemary. Your pushy line of questioning squashed any chance of that. But my Quebecois patter, as you call it, rarely fails, and I deployed it successfully as we left. Rosemary and I are having dinner tomorrow night, and I know a small, very romantic French bistro - Petite Jacqueline, that I think she will enjoy."

Holding up his hands, palms toward Doug to hold off any objection, Tom continued.

"I know, I know. She's involved in our murder case and I should be avoiding any personal relationship. But it's just dinner, Doug – an opportunity for her to let her hair down and share her perspective on what might have happened with her late husband. I'm a good listener and my gently probing questions, along with the wine, should help Rosemary to share with me things that could be germane to our investigation."

Shaking his head in resignation, knowing it was fruitless to try to reason with his partner, Doug called and arranged for the evidence response team to meet them at Rosemary Tremblay's condominium that afternoon at three to pick up the orphaned boxes of computer components and paper files of the late Don Robertson. Witnessing the recovery and sealing of the boxes prior to transport back to the crime lab up in Augusta would be the initial steps in documenting an unbroken chain of custody for the evidence.

Doug then looked up Lee Lamen's office location and phone number on his iPhone and called to set up an appointment with the dentist for the early afternoon. He was surprised when Lamen's receptionist indicated that they had been expecting the call, and that Dr. Lamen was coming into the office from home to meet with them.

Neither Doug nor Tom knew exactly what to expect from the dentist when they arrived at his office, but they were not expecting the bundle of nerves who rushed out to greet them. Lamen reminded Doug of George Costanza from the Seinfeld TV show. Short, stocky, balding, outwardly anxious and insecure, with a pale, pudgy face, nervous chatter, and sporting a bow tie, Lamen led them back to his small cluttered office, scurried behind his desk, and started talking as soon as they sat down.

"Rose called me this morning and I've pulled together all the information you need to verify our conference attendance in Las Vegas – airline itinerary, hotel bills, conference registration receipts, and the names and contact information for six people who can confirm our attendance. Two of the people listed – I underlined their names, were panelists with me on the evening that Rose's husband passed away."

Lamen eagerly thrust the collection of documents across the desk toward the detectives. Tom reached out and took them, folding them into his jacket pocket without glancing at them, and smiling warmly at the dentist, thanked him.

"Thanks for these, Dr. Lamen, and sorry for disrupting your day. We've just a few additional questions and then will be on our way.

It's all just routine – checking off boxes and scratching names off our list."

Nodding vigorously and glancing back and forth between the two detectives, Lamen was clearly eager to please, and began to talk rapid-fire

"Sure, sure, detectives. Glad to help with your investigation. Terrible business. Rosemary and I were both shocked. Whatever I can do to help. Any questions, anything, just ask away."

Still smiling warmly, Tom took out a small notebook and pen. His first question caught Lamen off guard.

"What is your relationship with Ms. Tremblay?"

Looking puzzled, the dentist stumbled over his answer.

"Our relationship? We're good friends. I have been introducing her to people who share her desire to gain enlightenment, to live a rich and full life."

Tom's expression grew even more sympathetic.

"You and Rosemary are not romantically involved?"

Looking even more confused, and a little put out, Dr. Lamen sputtered.

"No, no – nothing like that. She's a wonderful woman, but we're just friends."

"You must be very good friends – spending a week together in Las Vegas."

Smiling now, Lee responded.

"You have the wrong idea detective. We had separate rooms. I had company every night, but it wasn't Rosemary, I can assure you. And in case Rosemary didn't mention it, I'm gay."

Tom nodded in understanding, his face registering even greater empathy, as he switched topics again.

"I see. Do you tithe, Dr. Lamen?"

"Tithe? What do you mean detective?"

"Tithe – you know – to pledge ten percent of your income to a church or religious body of some kind."

Guarded now, Lamen paused before answering.

"It's not technically tithing, since it's not a ten percent commitment, but yes I do contribute financially to the good efforts of my community of love and hope. It's all aboveboard and all legal."

Leaning forward, Doug picked up the questioning.

"And does your close friend Rosemary tithe too, Dr. Lamen?"

Frowning now, Lamen responded.

"No, she doesn't yet. Rosemary is still in transition."

Trying for a stern expression, Lamen continued.

"And what, exactly, do my charitable contributions have to do with your investigations of Rosemary's husband's death?"

"Just checking off the boxes Dr. Lamen. Just checking boxes," Doug replied. "Did you make any investments with Don Robertson? Did anyone you know invest with him?"

"No on both counts detective."

"Do you know of anyone who might have been a threat to him? Do you know of any threats made against the deceased, Dr. Lamen?"

Lamen paused, looking around the room for some way out of this interview. Spreading his hands wide, palms up, Lamen appealed for understanding.

"Threats? No, no threats. I might have cautioned him a few times about his uncalled-for harassment of Rosemary and her interest in reaching enlightenment, but that was just well-meaning advice, not threats."

Doug acknowledged Lamen's answer, and turning to Tom, asked if he had anything additional to ask. Tom shook his head, and standing, he reached out to shake Dr. Lamen's hand.

"Thanks for taking time from your busy day Dr. Lamen. We certainly appreciate your help in this manner. Good luck with your self-realization efforts. We will probably be back in touch with more questions later."

7.

Rosemary Tremblay's condominium was only a short fifteen-minute drive from Lamen's office, and Doug and Tom talked over the morning's interviews as they drove across town. Tom outlined his take on Rose and her situation.

"I think we can conclude that Rosemary and Lee Lamen are not the clever killer couple we suspected was a possibility," Tom surmised as Doug stopped for a light. "Our dentist, Dr. Lamen, is basically a convenient doofus - a safe harbor for the bored wife while she transitions to a new life. But it's a short-term solution, even though she may not fully realize it yet. Her husband's unexpected death has now shortened the timeline for her departure out of the safe harbor offered by her dentist mentor and the enlightenment quest. She may already be viewing the dentist as excess baggage to be cut loose and left bobbing in her wake."

Doug smiled at the nautical metaphors and continued the theme.

"I see the departing craft now Tom, as it sails out of the safe but boring harbor into the turbulent and exciting open sea, toward the romantic setting sun. And who's that I see at the helm, wearing a puffy shirt and an eye patch, with Rose gazing up at him with admiration and lust, and a little trepidation? Could it be Tom who rescues Rose from a boring humdrum harbor life?"

"Go ahead Doug, mock my theory. But look at what we just heard from Lamen. Rosemary won't commit to tithing, and I would guess she is dragging her feet on the enlightenment thing. And Lamen and his group don't appear to be much of an improvement over a husband she considered boring and lacking in initiative. Lamen's a dentist, Doug. By definition he's guaranteed to be brutally boring. Las Vegas conventions and a few nights of blackjack is as good as it's gonna get with him."

Doug nodded in agreement as Tom continued.

"And did you notice Rosemary's cackle when she told us about the beneficiary change in her husband's life insurance policy? She didn't show any anger or interest in the money. Just underneath her professional veneer, Rosemary is a woman desperate for a life – some excitement, some drama, some fun."

Tom's smile grew larger and he started humming a tune to himself as they entered Rosemary's condominium. Three cardboard boxes full of files and a few computer peripherals were on the floor right inside the front door, next to a scattering of mail that had been pushed through the mail slot. A few minutes after they arrived a knock at the door announced the arrival of the evidence response team, who quickly photographed and sealed the boxes of files and computer equipment and carted them off to the crime lab in Augusta. After they dropped off the condo key back at Rosemary's office, Doug and Tom drove back across town to where Tom had dropped his car that morning. As Tom got out of the car, he paused to offer another prediction.

"Don't be surprised if Rosemary decides to make some real changes in her life in the next week or so. That decision, I predict, will occur just before we start in on our crème brule at the Petite Jacqueline bistro tomorrow night."

Tom shut the car door before Doug could summon up a response and walked off toward his car with a spring in his step.

It took Doug a little over two hours to drive from Portland back to Dover-Foxcroft. As he pulled in the driveway of Anne's cabin on the south shore of Sebec Lake he could see Anne sitting on the end of the dock, with the Chinook that had befriended them the previous night stretched out at her feet, soaking up the sun. Anne turned and waved, and the dog jumped up and trotted toward Doug – head down and tail wagging. Doug was surprised, but the dog clearly remembered him, and demanded a serious ear snoozle before allowing Doug to join Anne on the dock.

Anne had grown to love her camp, which she had bought and renovated soon after she arrived in town, and as yet showed no interest in giving it up to move to Doug's place on the north shore. Sitting down beside Anne and accepting a glass of wine, Doug continued petting the dog, whose head was now firmly on his lap, and asked what the vet had to say.

"Well, it's all good news. He was neutered at some point in the past. They didn't find an ID chip, and there's no clue what his history is. Looks like he's been living on the street for a while. They treated him for fleas and ticks, started him on monthly heartworm pills, and gave him a rabies vaccination. Other than being malnourished they say he's in pretty good shape. I picked up a dog bed, water and food bowls, and some high-quality dog food at Bob's in town. He needs an ID tag, and most of all, a name. What are we going to call him?"

"I was thinking we might name him 'Jack.' Every time I see this pup I think of Melinda Blood's late great chinook named Jack. He was a wonderful dog. What do you think?"

"Jack it is," replied Anne, reaching over to ruffle the dog's fur. "That's a great name."

After a leisurely dinner – a curried scallop dish Anne had seen in the NY Times, they walked back out to the dock to enjoy the sunset. Doug filled her in on the Portland interviews, Tom's assessment of the not exactly grieving widow, and his upcoming dinner date with Rosemary Tremblay.

"Sounds like another dead end," Anne replied when Doug had finished, and then filled him in on her limited progress in the case.

"Nothing promising turned up here either. The unofficial analysis of the tarp and bungee cord we recovered from Wes Fuller's place indicated that they were similar in composition to the tarp and cord we pulled out of the Sebec River. But the paint spatter pattern on the tarp we recovered from the river is missing in the trap fragments recovered at Fuller's. And it turns out that both the tarp and the bungee are made in China and sold widely across the Northeast under a variety of different brand names. You could buy matching tarp and bungee items at both the Tru-Value and Ace hardware stores here in town. So the case for Fuller being the killer hasn't gotten any stronger."

"What about Ximena Lapointe?" Doug asked, "Anything new on her story?"

"Actually, yes," Anne replied. "I tracked her down at work and asked her straight out about where the money came from for her new truck. She had no hesitation in telling me she had been the beneficiary of Don Robertson's half-million-dollar life insurance policy. When I asked her why she hadn't mentioned it to us before she looked genuinely puzzled and told me it was personal, didn't seem relevant, and that she didn't want people in town to know."

Doug nodded and replied.

"I can understand her reticence, but the windfall payout does add a pretty sizable motive for killing her boyfriend to her column. We need to take a much closer look at her movements that night and the next morning."

"I was thinking about that," Anne replied, "and wondered if the long wire that was attached to the tarp has any significance. Why a wire rather than a length of rope?"

Puzzled, Doug turned to look at Anne.

"What do you mean?"

"Well, maybe the wire was dangled down the inside of the chimney and was used because a rope might catch fire from the heat generated by the space heater. Ximena could have set the chimney cover up the day before and dangled the wire down the inside. Then when she arrived back at the cabin the next morning, after Robertson was dead, she could have reached up the chimney, grabbed the wire, and pulled the tarp down into the cabin. A quick trip to the river to dispose of the tarp, and then she could have returned and called you, knowing that the undisturbed overnight snowfall surrounding the cabin would point toward an accidental death."

"What else did you get out of Ximena?"

"Oh, we talked a lot about her high school days. She told me about her various boyfriends. She talked about being sexually harassed by the Geometry teacher, getting mono, all kinds of things. I told her about growing up with two older brothers who were basketball stars, and about getting a scholarship to play basketball at UofM, how I got into law enforcement and the romantic breakup that lead me to apply for the job here in Dover."

Looking directly at Doug, Anne continued.

"We sort of girl-bonded, and then she mentioned that you were captain of the wrestling team, she was a cheerleader, and how the two of you had a hush-hush 'friends with benefits' sort of relationship for a while – that you were going steady with your future wife Beth, but that you and Ximena were hooking up pretty regularly, maybe once or twice a week for several months during your senior year. She seemed to enjoy telling me about your lack of faithfulness to your steady girl at the time, and how she seduced you."

Doug looked sheepish and nodded his head.

"Anne, I've wanted to tell you about Ximena ever since I avoided the topic at our meeting with Jack Walker and the sheriff a while back. It was high school. I was a horny teenager and Beth was still in her virgin purity phase. Ximena made it clear she was interested, and I can't say I resisted very hard. But that was a long time ago, and I'm a different person now."

Anne looked at Doug with a confident grin and reached over to grab his hand. She stood up from her chair and pulling gently, began to lead him back toward the cabin.

"Don't be so disappointed in yourself Doug – file it away as a youthful indiscretion. I know you, and I'm not that worried about you showing an interest in Ximena, or any other woman in town for that matter. I certainly don't take you for granted, but I think I can hold your attention pretty well."

Doug was about to reply when Anne let go of his hand and reaching up, unbuttoned the top button on her blouse. Turning toward the cabin, she looked back over her shoulder as she continued walking.

"Doug, I really think we need to be naked before continuing this conversation."

Doug quickly agreed, and Anne's suggestion proved to be brilliant. Their subsequent conversation in bed concluded on a very positive note after they had at length explored and rejected any possibility of Doug being distracted by Ximena or some other woman.

Just after midnight a heavy thunderstorm moved through the area. It failed to rouse either Anne or Doug from a deep sleep but did convince their dog Jack to once again jump up on their bed to seek shelter. He was still there, stretched out and snoring, when Jack Walker called at 3AM. Anne reached over Doug to retrieve her phone from the bedside table, eliciting a sleepy sigh of contentment as her breast brushed across his chest.

"Hey Jack, What's up?"

"Sorry to call you guys in the middle of the night, but we've got a suspicious death up by Willimantic. I'm on my way out to John Eastman's place – you know – the big place, near Earley Landing Falls, at the west end of the lake. We were up there last summer when they had some vandalism of their boats and boathouse."

"I remember. Who's the deceased?"

"It's John Eastman. His wife called a few minutes ago. She just found him crushed under his pontoon boat out in his boathouse."

"OK Jack – Doug and I are on our way – it should take a half hour or so once we get on the road. Keep everyone away from the garage – I'll call the evidence response team down in Augusta and try to get them up here this morning, if possible."

Anne had not met the dead man – John Eastman, when she and Jack Walker had responded to the Eastman's vandalism report the previous summer. He was away on business and his wife Elizabeth had made the report. Anne remembered Elizabeth as a quiet, serious person who had been quite upset – Anne thought unusually so, given the relatively minor nature of the damage to the boathouse and boats. She suspected that Elizabeth Eastman's anxiety was due not to the damage itself – several spray-painted obscenities, but rather to the reaction she expected from her husband on his return.

It was a big boathouse, with three mooring bays and Eastman's office above. There was nothing else like it on the lake, and Eastman had bought the three-acre property with its rundown Victorian cottage and collapsed boathouse expressly for the boathouse. New construction of shoreline structures of any kind, including boathouses, were not permitted under current shoreline zoning regulations. This one, however, had been built back around 1900, and had been grandfathered in as an exception. After his purchase, Eastman had torn down the Victorian cottage and replaced it with a new architect-designed summer residence. A new boathouse was also constructed on the footprint of the original structure, but with substantial upgrades, including a second story office and motorized lifts for Eastman's Chris Craft, Hacker Craft, and Gar Wood runabouts- classic wooden boats dating to the 1940s and 1950s.

Doug filled Anne in on what he knew about the dead man – John Eastman, during their drive west from her cabin over to Guilford, and then north to Willimantic. Their dog Jack, who objected to staying behind, slept soundly in the back seat.

"John built his summer place over by Earley Landing maybe five years ago. He and his wife come up here every summer. He was a real estate developer – hotels and strip malls. Made a huge amount of money and retired early. They spend their winters in California, I think – somewhere up north of San Francisco. He was a feisty sort of guy – short and stocky - a real fireplug of a man, but with boundless energy and enthusiasm. It didn't take him long to become involved in community affairs and local politics here in Dover, making big donations at the local and state level, and supporting a number of charities and good causes. He was used to getting his way, and could be pushy, but also generous with his contributions. He was generally liked around town."

Pulling Doug's Cherokee in next to Jack Walker's SUV, Anne and Doug were welcomed by the incessant pre-dawn calls of a Phoebe that had nested in the eaves of the Eastman's house. Walker met them at the front door to the Eastman's house, clearly concerned.

"I'm glad you're here. Just to be on the safe side, I think we need to get Mrs. Eastman down to the hospital in town. She's pretty much shut down – almost catatonic, which isn't that surprising after discovering her husband's body – it's not a pretty sight."

Anne nodded as she replied.

"Good idea Jack. See if you can contact a family member or close friend to be with her."

"I've already contacted her sister, who lives over by Monson. She's on her way."

8.

Peter Martell and the ERT arrived at the Eastman's place about ten that morning. A few minutes later the Lary Funeral Home vehicle out of Dover pulled up – it would transport Eastman's body down to Augusta for autopsy after Martell's team had finished processing the scene. Deciding not to enter the garage until the ERT arrived, Doug and Anne had searched the surrounding area for footprints or other evidence that might still be intact after the heavy rain the night before, with no success.

Martell and his team spent almost an hour in the garage before Doug and Anne were invited in to view the body of John Eastman. A bank of florescent ceiling lights harshly illuminated the interior of the garage. The floor was highly polished, perfectly clean concrete. Storage cabinets and workbenches covered with a variety of power tools lined the walls, and a massive pontoon boat dominated the center of the room. Four sturdy metal tripod stands had supported the boat, but it had somehow slipped off of one of them and pinned John Eastman beneath it.

He lay outstretched on his back, arms and legs akimbo, a wrench clasped in his right hand. His mandible was still intact, jutting upward at an angle, but most of the rest of his head was crushed flat and mostly hidden beneath one of the pontoon boat's massive hulls. Blood and brain matter formed a coagulating pool that had oozed out from underneath the hull.

Removing his crime scene coveralls, Peter Martell joined Anne and Doug next to the body and led them through what he suspected had taken place in the garage the preceding evening.

"First off – this was no accident, but it was staged to look like one. The killing was planned beforehand. It was premeditated but pretty poorly executed. We will have to check with his wife to find out what time he came out to the garage to work on the boat, but judging from the mud packed into the treads of his shoes, it was after it started raining last night. But that raises a question. If Eastman entered the garage with muddy shoes, why aren't there any muddy shoe prints on the floor? The floor is spotlessly clean – no prints for either Eastman or his killer. It's reasonable to conclude, I would say, that his killer waited for him outside, knocked him unconscious, and then carried him into the garage and positioned him on the floor where he is now. Removing their own shoes to avoid leaving prints that we could trace back to them, the killer made their first big mistake – forgetting about the missing footprints of their victim."

Pointing to the pontoon that had crushed Eastman's skull, Martell continued.

"The killer made their second mistake when they staged the crushing of Eastman's head by the boat's pontoon. It needed to be a direct hit, crushing the skull, in order to obliterate the evidence of the blow to the head they had delivered earlier, outside the garage. In spite of their efforts, and the crushed skull, I think there is a good chance the initial blow to the head will still be identifiable if the medical examiner knows what to look for. We'll make sure to preserve Eastman's crushed skull intact when they transport his body down to Augusta for the post-mortem."

Walking over to the boat stand that lay on the floor right next to the victim and pointing to it, Peter picked up the narrative.

"How did the killer make sure to get a direct hit on the victim's head? Simple really. They positioned Eastman's head directly under the pontoon, close to this support, and then took the support away. To accomplish this, they first placed a rod or pole of wood vertically right next to the support. Then, holding the newly placed rod in position, they cranked the support lower until the new rod, and not the support, held up the weight of the pontoon. Then it was a simple matter to slide the support out from under the hull, place it on the floor, tipped on its side as you see it, and proceed to pull the supporting rod out, dropping the hull straight down onto Eastman's skull."

Kneeling and pointing to a barely visible scrape mark on the floor, Martell smiled up at Anne and Doug.

"Judging from the mark the wooden pole left on the floor here when the killer pulled it away, you are looking for something maybe three inches in diameter and between thirty-seven and forty inches long."

Anticipating their question, Peter answered it first.

"There are two indicators of the killer's scheme to drop the hull directly on the victim's head, ensuring both the obliteration of his skull and, they hoped, the disappearance of any evidence of the blow he received outside the garage. The first of these indicators is the killer's failure to erase the mark the supporting pole left on the floor here when it was pulled away. The second is the length of the different boat supports. The support that's lying on the floor here by the victim measures 37 inches in length. The other three are all 40 inches long. This difference in length is because after positioning the wooden rod in place, right next to the boat stand, the killer cranked the support he wanted to remove down from its original forty inches to thirty-seven inches, and then slid it out and tipped it over. But the killer forgot to subsequently return the removed support back to its original forty inches or thereabouts. Pretty careless. All in all, it's a pretty poor attempt to cover up a homicide."

"Is there any evidence that might point to the identity of the killer?" Doug asked.

"Not so far," replied Martell. "We might get lucky with some prints we pulled from the boat support next to the body, but I doubt it. And the wooden support pole might give us something if we can locate it. I'm hoping the killer discarded it somewhere nearby."

A lengthy search of the area surrounding the garage, however, failed to turn up any likely candidates for the wooden pole used to temporarily hold up the patio boat hull. Doug's dog Jack was even enlisted in the search, and when let out of the car, he did show some interest in a location where the killer may have hidden waiting for his victim. He sniffed and scratched behind a bushy hemlock where the ground was flattened. No footprints were evident, but a raking of the leaf litter turned up a candy wrapper. Not exactly a case-breaking clue, but it was none-the-less bagged for further study at the lab in Augusta. Jack was no bloodhound, but he was a food hound, and Doug thought that the killer might have snacked on something the previous night while he waited in the darkness and the rain, and that Jack had homed in on the lingering molecules of something edible.

Peter Martell and the evidence recovery team stopped in Dover-Foxcroft on their way back to Augusta and joined Doug, Anne, and Jack Walker for a late lunch at Allie Oops Sport Bar. They avoided discussion of the Eastman killing, but the conversation was still understandably subdued. Katie waited on them and bustled around the table refilling drinks and sparring good-naturedly with the ERT members. She and Peter Martell clearly hit it off, and when Katie had disappeared into the kitchen with a stack of plates, Peter, clearly smitten, asked Anne about the redhead waitress. Anne smiled and patted his hand as she responded.

"She's a good woman Peter, and I get your interest. But I don't think you'll get very far with her. She's just survived two relationships that turned sour, one after the other, and has come home to Dover to get back on her feet. And anyway, she prefers women, not men."

Working on his third beer, an Alagash White, Peter looked puzzled, and then shook his head.

"Naw, I disagree. She's crazy about me. I can tell."

Just then Katie emerged from the kitchen and came over to the table in response to Peter's wave.

Motioning her closer, Peter, looking very serious, murmured something in her ear. Leaning back, Katie looked at him cautiously, then leaned in and gave him a single syllable response before turning on her heel and walking back behind the bar. Anne asked Peter what he and Katie had said to each other.

"Well, I am not usually so direct, but I've had a few beers. I asked if she was exclusively interested in women, and she answered 'Bye.' I'm not sure if she was telling me she's bisexual, or if she was telling me goodbye – basically blowing me off. What do you think Anne?"

Anne was pretty sure that Katie was not blowing him off but was surprised to learn that she was apparently bisexual.

"I'm not sure Peter. Maybe ask her out – that would clear up what she was telling you."

When Anne and Doug left Allie Oops a few minutes later, already late for an afternoon meeting with Sheriff Torben and Jack Walker, Peter Martell was still waiting for Katie to reappear from the kitchen so he could ask her for clarification, and maybe a date.

Sheriff Torben and Jack Walker were both looking at their iPhones when Anne and Doug entered Torben's office.

"Anything promising from the Eastman place?" the sheriff asked as Doug and Anne sat down and their dog Jack settled at Doug's feet.

Doug looked at Anne, who replied to the sheriff's query.

"Some good news and some not-so-good news. The ERT recovered enough evidence for us to be confident that it wasn't an accident. Someone waited for Eastman outside his garage, knocked him out, and then staged an accidental death, crushing his skull under the hull of his patio boat. We know it was a premeditated killing, but don't have any leads yet regarding who the killer is or what their motive was."

Jack Walker joined in.

"I just checked with the hospital and Elizabeth Eastman left a while ago with her sister. Elizabeth's not ready to go back home yet, so they're heading back over to her sister's place in Monson. But she's feeling somewhat better now and is willing to talk to us later this afternoon at her sister's."

"That's great Jack," Doug replied. "Anne and I can drive over to Monson right after we're finished here."

Sheriff Torben leaned forward in his chair and took a sip of coffee while opening the lid of a box sitting on the edge of the repurposed library table that served as his desk. He frowned at the few scattered crumbs - all that remained of the morning's dozen donuts from Elaine's Bakery over in Milo.

"Doug, I got a call from your boss Stan Shetler over in Bangor early this morning. He had already heard from several influential politicians and business leaders about the Eastman death, and he has decided that you should focus full time on solving his murder, assuming it was not an accident. He talked to your partner Tom Richard and directed him to take the lead on the Don Robertson case so you can be freed up for the Eastman investigation. I said I would let you know. Shetler and I agreed that you and Anne can continue looking into any leads on the Robertson case here in Piscataquis County, and your partner Tom Richard will handle the Portland end of the investigation."

"That sounds like a plan," Doug answered. "I hope Tom comes up with something, because we have no good leads so far. Maybe his follow-up with the widow, Rosemary Tremblay, will give us something to go on. And we might get lucky with Robertson's files – maybe a record of some disgruntled or scammed investors looking for a payback."

Jack Walker jumped in with a question.

"Is there any possibility the two killings – Robertson and Eastman, are linked?"

Torben looked skeptical.

"Why would you think they're linked?"

"Well, I'm just saying it's a possibility. Both deaths were set up to look like accidents and both victims had entries in the patio boat race. I checked with Bob Lutz this morning, and Eastman's fancy pontoon boat – the one that crushed his skull, was entered in the unlimited category, just like the boat that Robertson had entered along with his race partner, Nigel Underwood. Maybe someone is knocking off the competition."

"Good points," Anne agreed. "We need to ask Eastman's widow what she knows – was there any connection between Eastman and Robertson? We also need to take a much closer look at the Patio Boat race in general. Who's involved in organizing it? Is it all local people or are there outsiders running the show? Who's competing in the unlimited category? Is ESPN shelling out big bucks for the broadcasting rights? I find it hard to believe that someone is killing off the competition in a patio boat race just so they can win. But maybe there's more going on that we don't know about."

Doug replied.

"Anne and I will go over to Monson this afternoon to talk to the widow Eastman. Maybe Jack can look into this mystery man Nigel Underwood here in Dover, and I will get Tom to see what he can find out about him down on the coast."

Sheriff Torben looked up from his note taking.

"This all sounds good. I'll contact Bob Lutz and let him know that we will be meeting with the race committee. We need to be in the loop on this, and not just because of the Robertson and Eastman killings. The sheriff's office and the Dover-Foxcroft police need to be integrally involved in this undertaking. We should have been included from the get-go. There's sure to be traffic, parking, and crowd control issues, and all the other challenges that accompany an influx of visitors into our community."

Jack Walker had the final comment before the meeting broke up.

"I'll ask Bob Lutz, as well as a few other people, about Nigel Underwood, and I also want to get a better handle on the timeline for Ximena's Lapointe's movements on the night and next morning of the Robertson killing. The big payout she received from his life insurance policy still looms as a strong motive for murder."

Doug and Anne headed west out of town on route 6 toward Monson. Jack with his head out the window, gums flapping. As they drove over the Piscataquis River bridge, they noticed Katie and Peter Martell leaning on the bridge railing, deep in conversation. "Well," Anne thought to herself, "looks like it was 'bi,' not 'bye,' that Katie whispered in his ear at lunch."

9.

Following Route 6 to Guilford and then north toward Greenville and the Moosehead Lake region, it took Doug and Anne about half an hour to reach the small town of Monson. Marking the southern end of the Hundred-Mile Wilderness, Monson was an important waypoint on the Appalachian Trail, and Doug and Anne overtook half a dozen northbound hikers ambling down the hill at the southern edge of town. At the bottom of the hill, where Route 6 turns west into downtown Monson, a long defunct gas station stacked with pallets of slate for sale harkened back to when the town was a major center of slate quarrying in the late 1800s.

Turning right at the gas station onto the north Guilford Road, Doug continued for a half-mile before finding the house where Elizabeth Eastman's sister lived – a well-kept Victorian home with a wrap-around front porch and abundant gingerbread trim. Jack was sound asleep in the back seat, so they cranked the windows down a bit and left him in the jeep. The interview wouldn't take long.

Elizabeth Eastman, who looked to be in her mid-sixties, was tall and thin, with short gray hair and a resting frown face. She opened the front door of her sister's house, leaning for support on her cane, a clunky tree branch topped with a silver cap in the shape of what looked to be a loon's head. Liz surprised Doug and Anne with her greeting.

"You must be the police. Would you care for a glass of whiskey?"

As they followed Elizabeth into the front parlor, her sister Mary emerged from the back of the house. She was carrying a tray holding a coffee pot and mugs and hurried to explain her clearly tipsy sibling.

"Please excuse Liz officers, she's had quite a shock."

Mary's comment elicited a sad smile from Elizabeth as she wiped at her eyes with her free hand and settled in an overstuffed armchair. Anne and Doug took the sofa across from her and Mary sat in a second armchair. Doug was waiting for Mary to finish pouring the coffee before beginning the interview when Elizabeth started a quite candid but rambling monologue, pausing only occasionally to sip from her glass of amber liquid.

"We were married for forty-two years this past October. John was mostly a good husband to me. He had other women over the years, of course – part of his insecurity, but he never flaunted them, and I never brought them up. We had a solid marriage but weren't ever blessed with children."

"John built things," Elizabeth continued. "We first met in the mid-seventies down on the coast when he came north to Maine from New Jersey to work construction one summer. I was working as a waitress in a seafood restaurant in Belfast. We had it hard the first few years after we got married, but then John got involved in the real estate development side of things and managed to line up some bank loans to build small projects around town– apartments and retail space."

Liz paused, took a slow sip of whiskey and smiled wistfully.

"The projects got bigger, his company grew, and by the nineties they were building malls in Texas and town house developments in northern Virginia. Later, after we became really well-off, with more money than we could ever spend, John got bored with strip malls and started focusing on what he called "classy" projects - boutique hotels and luxury condos in destination cities – Charleston, Santa Fe, San Francisco."

Shaking her head, the widow continued.

"I never could understand why he kept striving, kept pushing. John couldn't seem to just enjoy his success. He always had to do more, accomplish more, and build something new, something different. I don't think he ever recovered from the abuse his father used to rain down on him – telling him how he would never amount to anything."

Elizabeth paused and glanced from Doug to Anne, seeing if they had any questions. Anne smiled back at her, Doug stayed silent, and Elizabeth returned to her narrative.

"After his second heart attack, six years ago now, John finally started to pay attention to what I had been telling him for years. He sold his company and seemed committed to enjoying our retirement, or at least trying to. We spent our winters in California and summers here on Sebec Lake. My family had a summer cottage here when I was growing up, and John went along with my interest in spending summers here again. He seemed to like the remoteness – it was so different from the coast of Maine. He often told anyone who would listen that Sebec Lake was undiscovered and undervalued."

Doug set his coffee cup down and took advantage of a pause in Elizabeth's narrative to ask a question.

"What interests did your husband take up in retirement? Did he stay involved at all in his former development projects?"

"No. Not really. John turned his back on all that and seemed to enjoy the planning and construction of our new summer place here. I wanted to look for a cabin closer to Greeley's Landing – something on the south shore, closer to Dover. But John for some reason decided that the remote northwest corner of Sebec Lake, way up by Bucks Cove, was where we needed to be. I didn't object too much – I was just thrilled he was willing to commit to spending our summers here. He spent endless hours on the internet looking for design ideas and high-end stuff for the house – a sauna and ofuro for the master bath, a top of the line Italian espresso machine and Smeg appliances in the kitchen – that sort of thing."

"But that couldn't have kept him engaged for long." Anne suggested.

"No. His interest in stuff for the house flagged pretty quickly. Fortunately, he discovered something new when we spent a weekend down on Lake Winnipesaukee visiting some friends. John fell in love with vintage wooden boats – old Chris Craft and Gar Wood gentleman racers. He searched all the web sites offering classic woodies and flew to Lake Tahoe and other places looking at runabouts for sale. He renovated the dilapidated boathouse here and ended up buying three boats. He added a second floor to the structure for his office, along with fancy boat lifts and a garage for working on them."

Doug interrupted again with another question.

"You had some vandalism of the boat house last summer. What happened? Were those responsible for the damage ever identified?"

"Oh, it wasn't much. Some spray paint cuss words on the boats and broken windshields. And they tried to set fire to the boathouse – stuck a rag into the gas tank of the Chris Craft and lit it. But it fell out into the water before anything caught fire. So there really wasn't all that much damage. John had a few guys from Hi Gloss Boat Restoration down at Lake Winnipesaukee drive up for a few days to make the repairs. The county sheriff's office looked into it for us, but never did figure out who did it."

Elizabeth paused for a moment, looking pensive, before continuing.

"It's funny in a way, I guess, that my husband managed to accidently kill himself with that stupid patio boat of his. He used to make fun of them all the time. He called them floating family rooms. Then all of a sudden he just had to have one. And it had to be big and fancy. And expensive."

Doug and Anne exchanged a glance, and Doug interrupted.

"Mrs. Eastman, we don't think your husband's death was an accident. It appears to have been a premeditated murder that was staged to look like an accident."

The widow looked stunned and her sister gasped in reaction to Doug's pronouncement.

"Murdered? Why would someone kill him?" Elizabeth asked.

"We're not sure. Do you have any idea who might have wanted him dead, or why?" Anne asked.

"No. I can't believe it. Are you sure it wasn't an accident? John didn't have any enemies, at least not since he retired and left behind all his fights with contractors and zoning people and local politicians. He was a different man the last few years. John had lots of interests and friends in the community here."

"When did he get interested in patio boats?" Anne asked.

"Oh, almost a year ago - early in the summer, right after they had that race for local pontoon boats. Someone he knew had a boat entered and he got to ride along. After that he decided he had to have one. He even got involved in the planning for this year's race."

"Was he looking forward to competing in the race?"

"Oh yes. He was eager to get his boat in the water and start getting ready for the competition. He and Nigel Underwood were constantly trash talking about who had the better boat."

"Your husband knew Nigel Underwood?" Anne responded.

"He did. John and Nigel were good friends. They were both active in the planning committee for the race, and Nigel often came for dinner after their meetings. A nice man - rather arrogant and a bit pompous, but nice."

"How about Don Robertson. Was he also a friend of your husband's?" asked Doug.

"Mr. Robertson. Yes, he was another friend of John's, and was also close to Nigel. I met Don a few times when he and his friend Ximena came to dinner along with Nigel. I think Don may have had a partial stake in the fancy patio boat Nigel has entered in the race, and Ximena was trying pretty hard to interest Nigel in buying a place here on the lake."

"Was your husband involved in any business dealings with either Underwood or Robertson? Did he have any investments with Robertson, do you know?" asked Anne.

"No. Not that I know of. But I never was much involved in John's business activities. He was always very circumspect when it came to his business interests, even with me. But you're welcome to take a look at his office. You might find something there. He would spend hours out there. It's the second floor of the boathouse. The key is hidden on top of the light next to the door. And take any computers and files you find that might be relevant. Just let me know what you take."

"Thanks Mrs. Eastman," Anne replied. "We'll head over there as soon as we finish up here. We have just a few more questions."

"Have you noticed anything suspicious lately?" Doug asked. "Anyone hanging around your place? Any incidents you thought unusual?"

"No. Nothing comes to mind. It's pretty quiet up at this end of the lake. One guy shows up early just about every morning through the summer in a bass boat and drops lines over toward Wilson Stream – but he's been doing that for years."

"Has your husband seemed distracted or concerned about anything recently – anything at all?"

"Well, not really, other than the boat race. But he has always been very focused, very invested, in whatever bright shiny object happens to have attracted his fancy. It used to be creating boutique hotels. Lately it's been patio boats."

Doug glanced at Anne to see if she had anything further to cover. She shook her head and Doug thanked Mrs. Eastman for answering their questions. As they stood to leave Doug gave the widow his card in case she thought of anything else, and said they would likely have more questions for her as the investigation developed.

Continuing east on the North Gilford road out of Monson, Doug angled left onto the Willimantic Road, and estimated it would take them a half hour or so to make it over to the Eastman house at the west end of Sebec Lake. He was eager to take a look at John Eastman's office above the boathouse.

Soon after the turn onto Willimantic Road, Doug's phone pinged, indicating an incoming text message.

"Yikes," Doug blurted out as he pulled over and opened the text alert from the Bowerbank Volunteer Fire Department.

"Structure fire at west end of Sebec Lake. Fire Boat dispatched. Can you respond? Map location below. What's your ETA?"

Doug texted a response: "ETA 30," and handed the phone to Anne as he pulled back on the road and floored the Cherokee, turning on the flashers. Looking at the GPS map image on the phone, Anne turned to Doug with concern.

"It's not good Doug. It looks to be the Eastman place, or close to it – what are the odds somebody decided to torch the boathouse and office before we could get to it?"

They could smell the smoke from the fire as they turned off for the Eastman's north shore camp and as they pulled up they could see orange flames reaching twenty feet above the boathouse and office structure's roof. It was clear that the structure was a total loss and that the priority now should be keeping the fire from spreading to the nearby garage or to adjacent vegetation.

The Bowerbank fire boat, a recently refurbished patio boat with fire hoses and pump installed, was already on the scene, and had maneuvered as close to the boathouse as was possible. It was obvious that there was no hope of saving the boathouse, and the steady stream of water from the fireboat was mostly directed at the surrounding trees and bushes. The nearby garage was beyond the reach of the patio pumper's hose, and as he saw Doug arrive, one of the firemen on the boat waved to him and yelled.

"Get their garden hose on the garage."

Doug ran back toward the house, looking for the garden hose outlet. Finding it by the vegetable garden that was located between the house and the garage, he directed a steady stream onto the garage roof and walls, slowly circling the structure and alternating his spraying between the garage and the smoldering underbrush between it and the boathouse.

While Doug manned the garden hose to water down the garage, Anne ran to the water's edge with the binoculars from the back seat of Doug's Cherokee. Standing upwind from the boathouse and the fire's dense cloud of black smoke that roiled east along the lakeshore, she quickly scanned the tree line both ways along the north shore. Seeing nothing, Anne then shifted her search to the west end of the lake on either side of the shoreline landmark locally called "The Castle." Built by a lawyer in the 1880s for his new bride, The Castle was a bright, white, three-story wooden confection with crenellated battlements. It had been a prominent landmark on the lake for more than a century.

Anne suspected that there was a good likelihood that the arsonist had approached from the water rather than either coming down the only road leading to the Eastman's isolated camp or emerging out of the miles of undeveloped forest that stretched east along the north shore. Her scan of the lakeshore didn't reveal any likely arsonists, just a number of curious locals watching the fire from their docks.

Switching her search from the shoreline to the open waters of the lake, Anne scanned for any boats that might be likely suspects. A half dozen watercraft had by now gathered just beyond the fireboat and their occupants were busy gawking and taking pictures of the blaze with their iPhones. Anne checked each of the gawker boats and took photos for later inspection, but nobody looked suspicious. It didn't appear that the arsonists had stuck around to watch the fire.

Anne then looked out beyond them for any boats at a greater distance, particularly if they were moving away from the fire, which would have represented an obvious attraction for anyone who noticed it. A few other boats were visible in the distance, but all but one of those looked to be heading toward the fire, and the single boat not heading toward the Eastman's camp was stationary, with its solitary angler occupant apparently dozing in the afternoon sun. Follow-up interviews of the spectators in the close-in boats and on the docks along the lake shore would be done in case anyone had seen anything, but it looked like the arsonist who had started the blaze had gotten clean away.

It didn't take long for the boathouse fire to burn itself out. Its charred remnants collapsed into the lake in a crescendo of sparks and smoke. The spectator boats started leaving soon after, with the Bowerbank fireboat continuing to soak the area for another half hour or so before departing.

Walking back from the burned-out boathouse toward their vehicle, Anne noticed a tree-mounted, high-end CCTV camera that had a clear unobstructed view of the boathouse. It might provide them with footage of the arsonist. Doug called Elizabeth Eastman to inform her of the fire and to ask about the camera. The widow uttered a few slurred swear words and then handed the phone to her sister Mary. Doug repeated his question about the camera and after a muffled exchange at the other end, learned that it had been installed after the vandalism the year before and was connected to a hard drive in the house.

Their initial viewing of the footage from the boathouse surveillance camera, surprisingly, showed nothing – no boats or individuals could be seen approaching the boathouse in advance of the fire. The video showed calm water with a few ducks swimming by, and then a sudden small explosion followed by flames bursting out of the boathouse door and obscuring the transoms of the three vintage wooden boats stored inside.

Later, on the larger computer monitor at the sheriff's office in town, however, Jim Torben took a closer look and found the CCTV evidence they were looking for. It wasn't much – just the momentary but distinctive surface bubbling up of expelled air from someone using a SCUBA breathing system to swim into the boathouse underwater a few minutes before the explosion, and then exiting just before the initial burst of flames.

10.

Following the first interview he and Doug Bateman had conducted of Don Robertson's widow, Tom had been diligent in his continuing investigation of any potential role she might have played in her husband's death. He was now confident that she was innocent of any wrongdoing.

His in-depth investigation of Rose had begun with their dinner together at Petite Jacqueline, a small French bistro in Portland. Doug had objected to the idea, but Tom had justified the dinner invitation as giving Rose an opportunity to let her hair down in an informal setting and share her perspective on her late husband's murder. Tom was a good listener and he assured Doug that his gently probing questions - purely professional, along with candlelight and wine, would help Rosemary to share things that could be germane to the investigation.

Tom had not been particularly attracted to Rosemary during their initial interview. She was three or four inches shorter than he was, thin, with short black hair, brown eyes, and sharp features. And she was a lawyer – smart, highly educated, self-confident, with strong opinions and a sharp wit – not Tom's type at all. Taking her to dinner was just part of the job.

Soon after they were seated at a red leather banquette in a quiet corner of the bistro, however, Tom's perception of Rose began to change. They had chatted about mundane things on the drive to the restaurant, continuing in the Québécois that Tom had tried out on Rose during their initial interview. Perhaps it was the lyrical nature and undertones of intimacy inherent in their casual conversation in French that affected Tom, or maybe the invisible influence of pheromones in the enclosed space of his car on the drive over, but by the time they had reached Petite Jacqueline, Tom's indifference had vanished, replaced by a growing interest in this high-energy gamine.

In contrast to the business attire Rosemary had worn when they first interviewed her, tonight she was wearing a heather green Meghan Markle sweater and a short black pleated skirt. As the maître d pulled the table back and Rose slid onto the banquette, Tom couldn't help but notice her finely shaped legs. When he sat down next to her, he also couldn't miss her amused, rather smug expression, and realized that she had seen him admiring her legs and was enjoying the attention.

Tom had planned on getting right down to business with a series of questions about the murder of her late husband, her relationship with Lee Lamen, and her meditation group. But once they had agreed on steak frites paired with an inexpensive Merlot, and had started with flash fried calamari, he realized that they should first get to know each other better. He needed to loosen her up a bit.

Curious about her tendency to toggle back and forth between Québécois and proper Parisian French as they sampled the squid, he learned that her parents were from Montreal and that she had grown up speaking Quebec French. She had layered standard French on top of the Québécois during her junior year at the Sorbonne. After law school in Boston she had joined the large law firm in Portland where she still worked.

It was then Rosemary's turn to ask Tom about his childhood, and he surprised himself by telling her things he had not talked about, or even thought about, for years: growing up poor in Fort Kent, just across the St. John's River from Canada, his father abandoning the family when Tom was twelve, having to work long hours at the local market and other jobs after school to help with the bills, and going off to college at the University of Maine on a hockey scholarship. Tom even told Rose about the rape and murder of his ten-year old sister, and how the event shaped his decision to go into law enforcement.

Rose wore little makeup – a subtle lip-gloss and some eyeliner, and Tom became fascinated by the light scatter of freckles across her face as she laughed and reached over to touch his arm, sipped her merlot, and encouraged him to open up about himself. Dinner was over far too quickly, Tom thought, when the waiter brought the dessert menu. As they pondered their choices, Rose gently raked the fingernails of her left hand along the inside of his thigh, and in a throaty French whisper suggested they skip desert and instead go back to her place to continue his investigation.

Rosemary's idea of what Tom's continuing investigation should focus on became clear soon after they walked through the front door of her condo. She shyly took his hand in hers and led him back to the bedroom.

They had made love, dozed off, and briefly emerged from the bedroom to forage in her fridge before returning to bed and sleeping soundly until mid-morning. Rose's exploring hand woke Tom out of an intense dream, but he was instantly awake as she whispered endearments in French in his ear and slowly eased on top of him. When Rose got up a little later to forage again in the kitchen, Tom Richard lifted his head from the pillow slowly and stretched. He began to hum a tune from his childhood and realized that he had not felt this relaxed and content for years. He also acknowledged with a low whistle that during dinner and through the night, he had not asked Rosemary a single question directly pertaining to the murder investigation.

Any concerns Tom might have had about his lack of progress in pursuing the case evaporated as a naked Rosemary returned to bed and handed him a cup of coffee before shyly pulling the sheet up to cover her breasts. They had not spoken more than a dozen words of English since he had picked her up for dinner the night before, and neither one of them seemed inclined to stop communicating in French. The continuing use of the language created an intimacy that both relished, and neither wanted to break the spell.

By the time they got up, a little before noon, Tom had agreed with Rosemary's suggestion that what they needed was a long car ride, during which Rose could answer all of Tom's questions about the case in as much detail as he required. The question of where they would go was easily agreed upon. It would take them a little over five hours to drive from Portland up to Quebec City. They could be there in time for dinner. Perfect. And returning the same night to Portland really made no sense – much better to stay over for a night or two before heading back. Tom called in and took several days of annual leave as Rosemary started packing an overnight bag. Tom always kept several changes of clothes and a dopp kit in his car for cases that kept him overnight somewhere across the extensive territory covered by the MCU North unit stationed in Bangor.

Once they got on the road the first half hour was devoted to a discussion of where to have dinner when they arrived in Quebec City. When that was decided – they agreed to try Arvi – a new restaurant with solid reviews, Tom put on his detective hat and began asking questions. Rosemary, it turned out, had a far different take on the breakup of her marriage than the version Don Robertson had recounted to Jack Walker during karaoke night at the Bear's Den. She had met Don soon after she moved to Portland for her new job. At the time, he was bursting with confidence and riding high on a remarkable recent record of investment picks for a rapidly growing group of investors. Rosemary was impressed with this brash young man from the boonies who had little formal education but a seemingly unerring ability to pick investments that yielded impressive returns. After dating for six months or so they got engaged, and a few months later were married in a simple ceremony at city hall in Portland.

Rosemary was reasonably content early in the marriage. She was doing well at work and all the signs were favorable that she was on track to become a partner in the firm. Don's investment company continued to flourish, at least according to what he was telling her. But he had always been somewhat secretive about his business, keeping all his finances in separate accounts from hers and filing his tax returns separately. They also kept separate checking, credit card, and savings accounts.

She didn't really mind the secretive side of Don's business dealings all that much. After all, she made a very good living, owned her condo outright, and could maintain a high standard of living on her own. Don always picked up the bill when they went out and he was invariably generous with gifts at Christmas and her birthday.

But several years ago, Rosemary started hearing intimations from her co-workers at the law firm that all was not well with her husband's investment portfolios. Several indicated that they had shifted their holdings to other firms due to Don's increasingly poor investment choices. Don laughed it off when she asked about these defections, writing his critics off as weak-willed, sunny day investors without the vision and commitment to stay the course. But Don started smoking weed more frequently and occasionally would light up a fatty first thing in the morning. He called it "wake and bake" and claimed it helped him to focus on his investment research.

They slowly drifted apart - Don talking more and more about his desire to move back to Dover-Foxcroft, and Rosemary spending more time at work and climbing the ladder of success toward a partnership in the firm. Rose also found friendship and support in an unexpected place – an informal mindfulness movement in Portland that attracted a wide range of people from different walks of life, all looking for more meaning in their life, for ways to fully engage in the world around them.

Rosemary laughed out loud when Tom told her that Don had said that she was romantically involved with Lee Lamen.

"Don didn't have a clue. Lee is a very sweet man who is openly gay and still searching for Mr. Right. We have fun together and compare notes about what we are looking for in a man. Lee and the meditation group he introduced me to have helped me a lot in sorting out what my priorities are in life, and what will make me truly happy."

Surprised by Rosemary's openness and candor, Tom's next question went in a direction he hadn't expected until he voiced it.

"Have you reached any conclusions, Rose, about what you want from life?"

Rose stayed quiet, and after almost a full minute had passed, Tom looked over to see her looking out the window, avoiding his glance.

Tom reached over, put his hand on hers, and apologized.

"I didn't mean to pry Rose. Sorry."

The silence in the car stretched another long minute or so before Rose responded with a deceptively casual expression and a toss-away tone of voice.

"That's OK Tom. I'm happy you asked. I'm still searching for answers, but I think I've found some solid ground."

Lacing her fingers through Tom's, Rose quickly changed the subject back to the case.

"Do you think Don was killed because of his investment business?" she asked.

"Could be" replied Tom. "But it's still early in the investigation, and we still don't know that much about what he was up to and who his business partners were."

"Well now that you have gotten me thinking about it, there were times when he was pretty secretive about who he was talking to on the phone. I figured it was probably a woman, but it could have been business, I guess. And he had security protection out the wazoo on his MacBook Pro. It still hasn't turned up?"

Tom frowned and shook his head, and as they approached the border crossing, he and Rose both thought about her late husband's missing computer – where it might be, who might have it, and if its files might provide an explanation for his killing. Tom checked his Glock service weapon with Canadian Customs, and after they crossed over into Canada, their conversation turned back to what they would do in Quebec City. Once they had checked into a small boutique hotel that was one of Rose's favorite places to stay in the city, they still had several hours to kill before their dinner reservation. Tom was tired from the drive and thought a nap would be a good idea, but after a quick shower, Rosemary easily convinced him there were better ways to spend the time.

Dinner was a huge success. Arvi had a great menu and very personal service, as the chefs came out of the kitchen to serve the dishes, offering information on the locally sourced ingredients and how they were prepared. Tom and Rose struck up a lively and warm back and forth with the staff and were in excellent spirits when they left the restaurant. Arm in arm, they strolled back toward their hotel through the narrow streets of Old Port Quebec City, discussing the rabbit with smoked mustard, and the P.E.I. oysters they had for dinner.

They had turned a corner onto a quieter street when Tom heard footsteps rapidly approaching behind them. Without conscious thought Tom's military training and years of police work kicked in and he pivoted toward Rose, pushed her roughly to the side with his left hand, and then continued the turn, instinctively swinging his left arm up and back, into the space where Rose had been a second before. The blade of the knife that had targeted her back got caught in the sleeve of his coat and clattered to the ground as Tom squared on their assailant and buried his right fist in the man's face, knocking out several of his teeth.

Tom kicked the knife away and turned to Rosemary, who still lay crumpled on the sidewalk, her legs akimbo, and swearing like a French sailor. Pulling her up, he held her, apologizing for the push and asking if she was OK. She gave him a confused look, and glancing past him, saw their attacker staggering away down the street and around the corner.

"What was that Tom? What just happened?"

Tom frowned, reached down and picked up the knife. Shielding it from her view, he closed it, quickly slipped it into his pocket, and then replied.

"My guess would be an attempted mugging. Looks like he was going for your purse. We can report it when we get to the hotel."

Rosemary had seemingly mostly forgotten the incident by the time they had reached the hotel. Tom paused at the front desk to report the mugging attempt while she headed up to the room to look at the scrapes she had gotten when Tom pushed her out of range of the knife attack. Following her up a few minutes later, Tom checked his left arm, relieved to find only a shallow cut where he had blocked the knife.

He was not convinced it had been a simple mugging. Rose had clearly been the target, and he believed that it had been meant to seriously injure or kill her. He wondered if the assault was tied to the killing of her husband. It would mean that someone had followed them all the way to Quebec City and then waited for the right time to make an attack look like a street crime gone wrong.

Tom was worried that Rosemary would be totally freaked by the assault, and that he would find her huddled in a chair trembling in fear or packing her bag and insisting they leave immediately. Instead, when he opened the door to their suite, Rose was sitting up in bed, wrapped in a bathrobe. She had lit several candles on the side tables, dimmed the lights, and poured them each a glass of wine. He paused just inside the door as she rose from the bed, picked up the two glasses of wine, and walked slowly toward him. Her bathrobe fell open and she smiled as she handed him a glass and pressed up against him, looking directly into his eyes from only a few inches away.

"Tom, will you show me the knife?"

Feigning ignorance, Tom looked puzzled as he replied.

"What knife?"

"The knife that guy was trying to bury in my back. The one you picked up off the sidewalk and slipped into your coat pocket, thinking I didn't see it."

Surprised, Tom retrieved the knife from his pocket and held it out to her. Rose took the knife and sat down on the bed. Setting down her wine glass, she opened the blade and looked at it.

"I think he tried to kill me Tom. Why would he do that?" Rose asked, seemingly unfazed.

"I'm not sure Rose. He was probably after your purse."

"You're not a very good liar, Tom. This looks like a four-inch blade at least, and he was going for me, not you. If he had gotten to me with this I would have bled out on the sidewalk. I bet it has something to do with Don's death and the police getting interested in the case. Somebody thinks I might know something, and they want to shut me up in case I do. That scares me, but probably not as much as it should. Mostly it makes me curious – I think my ex was probably involved in some shady stuff with some shady people."

Rose leaned back and looked at Tom with a now dead serious expression.

"More importantly, you saved my life tonight and that confirmed the feeling I have had since you first started chatting me up at our initial meeting in my office. I checked up on you, and I know your history. You're a tough guy. You hurt people now and then. I'm sure they likely deserved it. But you're also sensitive and smart and loving – and a good man to have nearby in case of trouble. I'd like to keep you around." As she finished the sentence, she shifted her shoulder slightly, and the bathrobe slipped off her shoulders.

11.

The next morning Tom and Rosemary met with several detectives from the Quebec City Police Service in the hotel lobby. The team interviewing them quickly concluded, once they found out that Tom was a detective with the Maine State Police, that he, and not Rose, had been the intended target of the night before. Tom could see that they thought someone from one of his past cases with a score to settle had most likely followed them north from Portland to carry out the attack. Tom didn't press the issue with them, realizing that any follow-up investigation on their part would be a waste of time. They weren't even interested in the knife, which they decided that Tom should keep and investigate when he returned to Maine.

After a leisurely breakfast of beignets and coffee at the Café du Monde in the Old City, Tom and Rosemary drove back south to Portland. It was mid-afternoon when they arrived back in the city. As Tom pulled up in front of Rosemary's place, she asked him to come up for a moment – she had something to show him that she had been thinking about on the trip back from Quebec. Hoping they might hop back into bed, Tom accompanied her up to her condo. Rosemary immediately went to her walk-in closet, leaving Tom to fantasize about her reappearing in flimsy lingerie. Almost immediately, however, she reappeared holding what looked to be a beat-up small pink plastic laptop computer bearing a well-worn Flying Spaghetti Monster decal. Holding it out to Tom, she explained.

"When Lee and I cleaned out Don's place after his death I also found this. It's my old computer from when I was in law school – I used it for lecture notes. I didn't put it, or my old printer- which was also at Don's, in with the boxed-up stuff I let you guys take. I don't know why Don took them with him, and neither was on his desk with the other computer stuff. This computer was in with a stack of books on his bedroom floor, and I found the printer in the back of the closet."

Tom opened the pink laptop and glanced at its dilapidated keyboard and cracked screen.

"Is there anything on the computer?" Tom asked.

"I have no idea. The battery is dead on the computer and I couldn't find the power cord for it or for the printer, which I am pretty sure stopped working a few years ago."

"OK, let me take both of them to our computer crimes unit office here in Portland, and I'll see if their forensic examiners can find anything."

Several of the officers in the computer crimes unit had played on the state police hockey team with Tom, and with a little cajoling, he was able to get them to look at Rosemary's pink laptop soon after he arrived. Laughing loudly, David Rosenthal, a rough and tumble defenseman on their hockey team who Tom knew well, called out to the other officers scattered around their sprawling office:

"Check this out you guys, Tom's brought in his pink Little Pony laptop for us to play with."

After a brief delay looking for a vintage power cord, Rosemary's laptop was logged in and powered up. The results were disappointing.

"Well, it's pretty much hollowed out," David muttered. "And I don't think any deleted fragments can be recovered from the hard drive. Documents haven't just been deleted; the hard drive has been wiped."

"Look again Dave – there's got to be something," Tom urged. Frowning with concentration, David busily looked for something, anything, of value on the cracked screen of the laptop. After a few minutes of silence broken only by the sound of the keyboard, David looked up.

"There's nothing Tom. It looks like it was just used for word processing. There's no search engines, nothing in the way of external connectivity except a printer link for a printer that was discontinued long ago."

Looking at the laptop's screen, Tom replied.

"I think I might have the printer in question in my car. I'll be right back."

Tom retrieved the printer Rosemary had given him, and after another search for a power cord for the printer, as well as a cord to connect it to the laptop, David was able to open communication between the two.

"Let's see what we have on this antique printer. Nothing in the print queue. Not surprising – all the volatile memory is lost when power is interrupted."

David paused, called over another forensic geek, and they muttered to each other and pointed at the laptop screen.

"This is weird – there's a document file stored in the printer – separate from the print queue. That's not supposed to be there. It's a new one on us."

"What's in the file? What's it called?" Tom asked.

"The file's labeled 321A."

David clicked twice on the file icon, and the screen filled with three long columns of numbers. Once the file had been copied to the pink laptop and from there to an external thumb drive, David transferred the thumb drive from Rosemary's laptop into his computer.

"I'll print out a hard copy of the file for you," David said as his printer came online. "We can also see what the nerds here and at the federal level can tell us about these columns of numbers, but my best guess is that we are looking at records of electronic funds transfers. Let's hope the financial analysts can tell you if that's indeed the case, and the origin and destination of the funds. Who knows, we might get lucky."

Leaving the forensic examiners to continue their recovery efforts, Tom called his partner, Doug Bateman, catching him in the middle of a late afternoon meeting at the sheriff's office in Dover Foxcroft. Glancing around the table at Sheriff Torben, Anne Quinn, and Jack Walker, Doug looked at the screen on his vibrating phone.

"Finally. Tom, or should I say Romeo, is checking in."

After answering the call, Doug listened in silence for what seemed like a long time, then responded briefly before hanging up.

"O.K. Sounds good. I will let her know. Good work Tom."

Setting his phone down, Doug filled the others in on what Tom had told him.

"It looks like we can take Rosemary and her dentist friend off our list of suspects. But the forensic examiners have found some hidden files on an old printer of Rosemary's that her husband had been using. They appear to be encrypted and suggest he may have been into some shady dealings. It's a promising new lead on a possible motive. They'll be sending us copies of the files once they work around some security hurdles, and Tom thought that Anne's contact at the FBI – the profiler who helped us a few years ago with our murder case, might be able to get someone at Quantico to pitch in with deciphering them."

Anne nodded.

"I'll give my FBI contact a call first thing tomorrow and see if she can help."

The mood in the room noticeably improved with the promise of a new line of inquiry, as all of their current suspects appeared to be dead ends. Jack Walker's interview of the babysitter, Susie Arter, had backed up Ximena Lapointe's account of the night of Don Robertson's killing, and his follow-up conversations with Ximena hadn't turned up any discrepancies or loose ends. Wes Fuller and Gary Crite's stories also continued to check out, and nothing new had turned up on the murder of John Eastman.

Anne gathered up her notes and phone and looked around the table.

"We still need to locate this Nigel Underwood character - the guy bankrolling the patio boat that he and Don Robertson have entered in the Sebec Lake race. There's a race committee meeting tomorrow morning that Doug and I have arranged to attend, and maybe he'll show up there. If not, we'll have to track him down."

Anne left her truck in the parking lot and she and Doug took his well-used Jeep Cherokee and headed back up to his place on the north shore of Sebec Lake, with Jack hanging his head out the window, jowls flapping.

It was clear, in the mid-70s, with a light breeze. After an early dinner they took Doug's vintage Chris Craft out for a late afternoon cruise. Jack had initially been skittish about going for rides in the boat, but now jumped in with no hesitation, hopping up on the engine box cover behind the front seat and settling in. The 250-horsepower inboard, nicknamed "old reliable," started right up when Doug turned the key, and they slowly rounded Otter Point and then turned west toward Pine Island. Doug slowed as they passed the south end of the island and they caught a glimpse of the two baby eagles perched high above on the edge of their nest.

Doug reminded Anne of the warning she had offered to a family who had been staying at the rental cabin on the island the summer before. Oblivious to the threat posed by the hungry fledglings and their predator parents, the renters had allowed their small fluffy dog to play on the dock, drawing the attention and seemingly casual circling of the island's eagles. The renters, from away, at first laughed at Anne's idea that their dog represented a tasty snack for the eagles. But after taking her suggestion that they check out the bone pile at the base of the eagle's nesting tree, they appeared to keep the dog inside for the rest of their stay on the island.

Skirting the deceptive shallows just west of Pine Island, Doug continued west along the south shore of the lake, heading toward the point with the tall pines and cluster of cabins dating back to the 1920s and earlier. From there it was only a mile or so to Merrill's Marina at Greeley's Landing. Doug was going to stop at Merrill's to gas up the boat and then continue west through the narrows and on to the South Cove and Peaks-Kenny State Park. The wind was freshening as they rounded the point and the roller rink at the marina came into view, its metal roof reflecting the late afternoon sun. Anne noticed a pair of loons on the surface at 2 o'clock, fifty yards or so away, and indicated their presence to Doug by pointing to her eyes with two fingers, then pointing downward, then toward the location of the birds – the silent signal they used when kayaking to indicate the presence of the birds without disturbing them.

Doug nodded, located the birds, slowed, and angled the boat to port to avoid them. As he changed course he saw something just below the surface, maybe ten yards in front of them, and abruptly swerved further to port to avoid it. The vintage boat's throttle lever was mounted in the center of the steering wheel, and as Doug turned the wheel counterclockwise with his left hand, he rapidly turned the throttle clockwise with his right, dropping the engine speed to idle. The boat slammed into a large log at an angle, with the bow's steel shearwater strip absorbing most of the impact. Jack slid onto the floor from his perch on the engine cover and Anne blurted out an expletive as Doug shifted the boat into neutral, glanced over at the log, now bobbing some distance away, and remarked on their good luck.

"That was a close one. If we hadn't slowed for the loons and changed course, I never would have seen it in time. We would have hit it head on at a good speed and likely sunk like a stone."

Reaching over and pushing the floor mounted gear shift into forward, Doug slowly circled the boat and came up alongside the large log. Reaching under the dashboard he pulled out a towline and tied it around one end of the log, which looked to be about two feet in diameter and thirty feet long. Tying the line to the boat's rear tow ring, Doug continued at a slow speed on into the marina, pulling up at the dock next to the gas pump.

An older man with a white beard walked over from the marina's office and caught the aft mooring line from Anne, tying it off while glancing over at the log.

"Can't say that I have much use for a log, Doug. There's plenty around here, in case you haven't noticed."

"Very funny Tim. We hit this a few minutes ago – it was floating loose out toward the point."

Walking around to the bow of the boat, Tim looked closely along the waterline.

"Looks OK – I'd say the bow shield saved your ass this time."

Smiling in response, Doug pulled the log up next to the dock and looked at it more closely, noting the trimmed limbs and orange symbol spray painted on its end.

"That's no dead tree that fell in the lake," Tim remarked. "That's off a logging truck. How the hell did that happen?"

"Must be deliberate," Anne suggested, puzzled. "Why would anyone do that? It looks like somebody's got it in for boaters."

Tim frowned as he unscrewed the gas cap and started fueling the boat from the dockside pump, looking over at Doug.

"I didn't think it was worth bothering any of you law enforcement types, but we have been having problems the last several weeks or so with pranksters. Last weekend someone untied a bunch of the boats here in the middle of the night. Fortunately, there wasn't much wind so they all just floated around the marina without doing much damage. But people were pissed. Then a few nights ago two boat trailers disappeared from the parking area over by the roller rink. I mean who steals a boat trailer?"

Jack had regained his place on top of the engine box, and reaching over to scratch his offered belly, Anne recalled something she had heard the week before.

"They've been having problems down at Bear Point Marina too – a bunch of boats untied, and a few drain plugs pulled. Nothing funny about waking up early for a good morning of fishing only to find your boat on the bottom."

Rather than continuing on as planned to the South Cove and Peaks-Kenny State Park, Doug headed north toward the narrows and then turned east and followed the north shore of the lake back toward home. Anne stood next to him in the fading daylight, scanning the waters ahead of them for any more floating hazards. As soon as they docked Doug lifted the floorboard just behind the front seat and checked the bilge to see if the boat had taken on any water. The mahogany bottom was original, and almost seventy years old, but still in good condition. It didn't appear to have sprung any leaks. He would come back out before they turned in for the night and check again. In the morning he planned on pulling on his swim goggles for a closer underwater inspection of the bottom to look for damage.

12.

Jack, as usual, woke Doug up just before six the next morning with a gentle nose nudge to his foot, which was sticking out over the end of the bed. This maneuver usually did the trick, but if not, it would be followed after a few minutes by a shaking of his head and rattling of his dog tags. If that failed Jack would eventually invoke his default ploy – barking to alert his slugabeds that something serious was occurring close by – perhaps a fisherman cruising past in a bass boat, or some raucous loons yodeling in celebration of the sunrise.

After his morning bowl of food and a leisurely walk with Doug and Anne, Jack took up his usual position on the screen porch. He would spend the morning napping in the sun and watching the red squirrels in their invariably unsuccessful attempts to access the bird feeder, while Doug and Anne headed off to the meeting of the patio boat race committee. The meeting was to be held at the old roller rink at Merrill's Marina next to Greeley's Landing, which had stood empty and unused for a number of years but was now serving as the command center for the upcoming race.

By race week one half of the roller rink would be restricted access, housing monitors and several technicians handing the different video feeds from stationary cameras along the racecourse, as well as the cameras mounted on patio boats and drones. The other half of the space would be occupied by a registration and local information desk for race entrants, as well as a number of picnic tables and couches for people to congregate.

None of this was set up yet, however, when Anne and Doug arrived a few minutes early for the 10AM meeting. The large space was empty except for a 4x8 sheet of plywood set up on sawhorses in the center of the room, surrounded by a number of folding chairs. Bob Lutz, a member of the race committee who was responsible for maintaining the data base of information on race entrants, was alone at the table, busy with a laptop computer. Light streamed in from a series of windows high up on the long wall of the roller rink, illuminating small explosions of dust that rose from the floor with each step Doug and Anne took. Their footsteps echoed through the room, and Bob looked up and smiled as they approached the table. He stood and shook hands, inviting them to sit.

Lutz, who had worked at Dave's World, the appliance store in Dover, for more than a decade, was an outgoing, up-beat individual and active in a range of community activities.

"Thanks for getting here a little early. It will give me a chance to bring you up to speed on how everything is organized, and the timeline for the weekend of activities. It's a lot more complicated than you might think, with lots of moving parts and challenging logistics. Being law enforcement, I would guess you probably are most curious about how all the parts fit together, so let's start there."

Anne and Doug took seats across the plywood table from Lutz and waited for him to continue.

"OK, first off, The Bureau of the Warden Service, part of Maine's Department of Inland Fisheries and Wildlife, is in charge of keeping everyone safe on the water. They only have 125 wardens statewide but are willing to assign up to a half dozen officers to us for the race weekend. The wardens will have overall responsibility for keeping the course clear of interlopers – boaters and others that might stray into harm's way. Obviously, they can't do it all on their own, and will be overseeing Kiwanis volunteers who will be stationed around the routes the race will follow – from Greeleys Landing east around Pine Island and back for the Friday preliminary time trials, and then on Saturday west from Greeleys through the narrows into the west basin and Bucks Cove, then back to Greeleys Landing."

Lutz paused and glanced at Doug and Anne, who both nodded for him to continue.

"OK, turning to the situation on terra firma – Sebec Lake extends across four different town boundaries – Dover-Foxcroft, Bowerbank, Sebec, and Willimantic. Each town has agreed to provide people to manage the boat ramps within their jurisdiction and to oversee the smooth launching and pull-out of patio boats for the race, as well as coordinating trailer placement and other related tasks. Willimantic is responsible for monitoring the new boat ramp up at the west end of the lake, Sebec the Cove Road ramp down at the dam, Bowerbank the Newell Cove Boat Ramp, and Dover-Foxcroft the launching ramps at Greeleys Landing. The Bowerbank Fire Department will also be deploying their fire boat in case there are any race related mishaps."

Looking concerned, Doug broke in.

"You're using all four boat ramps – how many entries will you have?"

"Yeah, that's turning into a bit of a potential problem. So far, we have 120 or so confirmed, paid-up entries, and the way things are going we could hit 200, which is the cutoff. More than that would be too many, but it's going to be hard to turn people away."

"Two hundred?" Anne blurted out. "Are you insane? Can you imagine what this lake will be like with two hundred crazed patio boat racers flying around?"

"It will be amazing," a voice behind them boomed out, followed by a loud laugh. Anne and Doug turned to look at a tall older man in a dark suit striding across the roller rink. Behind him, two beefy men in suits took up positions on either side of the door. Reaching the table, the man who had called out to them took a chair and reached across the table to shake hands. Ignoring Bob Lutz, he flashed a remarkably white set of teeth at Anne and Doug.

"Nigel Underwood here. You must be Investigator Anne Quinn and Detective Douglas Bateman. Sorry we have not been able to connect before now, but I have been quite busy lately, planning for the race and all."

Looking at Underwood's dazzling smile, Doug raised an eyebrow and turned to Anne.

"I thought you said he was British."

Nigel laughed good naturedly and responded.

"Yeah – not sure where that got started. My mom thought the name Nigel sounded upper class, but I've never claimed to be

British. And as soon as I open my mouth, my smile and my New Jersey accent remove any question of my origins."

Careful to dust off the plywood tabletop before resting his bright white shirt cuffs on it and clasping his hands, Underwood continued with deliberate casualness.

"I have a very full calendar of meetings and events today, so I won't be able to spare any time to talk with you about the unfortunate demise of Don Robertson, or the death of John Eastman – both fine gentlemen who will be sorely missed. But you can contact my lawyers to set something up – maybe next week?"

Underwood raised his hand and snapped his fingers. One of the men stationed by the door hurried over and handed Doug a business card – "Redman and Spencer, Attorneys at Law."

Clearly enjoying the little performance Underwood was putting on, Doug responded in kind.

"That would be most excellent Mr. Underwood, we shall contact your legal representatives forthwith and schedule a time, at your convenience of course, for you to come down to the sheriff's office here in Dover-Foxcroft and be interviewed. It should only take a few hours or so, and your lawyers are, of course, welcome to attend as well."

Clearly getting the import of Doug's reply – that rather than being interviewed on his own ground he would be compelled to come in and be questioned in a formal setting, Underwood frowned as he turned toward the sound of several new people entering the roller rink.

"Here they are," Underwood said loudly, raising his hand in greeting as Lou Binford and an older man in jeans and a "Whoopie Pie Festival 2010" t-shirt took the remaining seats at the plywood conference table. Doug recognized the older man as Don Wilson, a prominent and long-standing officer with the local Kiwanis Club.

"What about ESPN. Aren't they coming?" Anne asked.

Underwood laughed. "ESPN puts their name on the race when it airs, but it's my baby, my idea, my up-front money. That's what I do Anne - package junk sports events and pitch them to ESPN and other broadcasters. ESPN liked this idea, and we're going to try it one time, see if it catches on. Don't misunderstand. I'm not badmouthing patio boat racing when I call it junk sports. Lots of now very popular sports started out being viewed as marginal and laughable. The first triathalons were mocked, and how about snowboarding – it was banned from most ski resorts for years – now look at its popularity. And have you seen the junk events they are adding to the Olympics? Patio boat races may seem silly, but there are lots of people who own them and would enjoy watching them compete. We could well be on the cusp of a very popular new sport. Sebec could become the center of the Patio Boat racing universe."

Doug looked at Underwood across the table with a quizzical expression and asked another question.

"Surely other places have patio boat races?"

"We looked into that Doug," Nigel replied. "It turns out there are patio boat competitions, like the Shootout at Lake of the Ozarks, but those are just individual speed runs on a straight timed course. They don't involve head to head competition between boats."

Doug moved to the question he had been most interested in.

"How does the financial arrangement sort out between you and ESPN and other stakeholders?"

Underwood gave Doug and Anne another thousand-watt smile.

"That's the genius of it. Without going into the boring details, I can tell you that my company, Underwood Events, has donated a good-sized chunk of money to the Kiwanis Club up front. For this contribution they will be providing all the logistics and volunteers and lining up all the necessary buy-ins from law enforcement and the four towns involved. The Kiwanis Club also gets all the entry fees from the race, and of course will be running hotdog stands and other concessions throughout the weekend. I've also arranged an umbrella insurance policy to cover any claims made against the race organizers. ESPN, in turn, will provide all the necessary media marketing for the races. In fact, later today we'll be filming some promotional footage for ESPN. I'll be taking my patio boat on a high-speed run through the narrow entrance into Bucks Cove, around a small island, and back out again. You're welcome to come along for the ride if you want. It should be a blast."

Bob Lutz cleared his throat and changed the subject.

"I have to be at work in less than an hour, so let's work though what we need to get accomplished. I can start by summarizing where we stand on contestants. Registrations continue to come in at a steady pace, and we could hit our ceiling of two hundred entrants by race day. Participants are required to check in on Thursday, the day before the preliminary time trials around Pine Island. We'll have information packets for each registrant ready to pick up starting on the day before race day. Included will be boat bibs showing their race number, bright red commemorative t-shirts indicating their race participant status, and instructions for staging areas and race day procedures. Race participants have been divided into four different groups and assigned to one of the four different boat ramps at Newell Cove, Greeley's Landing, Willimantic, and the Cove Road ramp at Sebec Village by the dam."

Lutz paused, looked down at his laptop, and continued.

"Each entry will pass through two inspections at the boat ramps prior to being launched – first to ensure that the boat and trailer are free of any unwanted invasive aquatic plants, and secondly to make sure the boats conform to regulations regarding limitations on structural modifications below the waterline. All the volunteers are lined up and all the forms and procedures are ready to go. We anticipate smooth sailing, so to speak, on race weekend."

Lutz closed his laptop and turned to Don Wilson, who scratched his head and nodded before picking up the narrative.

"No problems so far on the Kiwanis end of things. We'll have concession stands at each of the boat ramps and at the Piscataquis Valley Fairgrounds, where we will provide facilities for RVs and campers. Peaks-Kenny is also keeping some of their campground reserved for race participants that weekend. I'm sure we'll encounter some problems along the way, but that's to be expected. That's about it – we're pretty much ready to go."

Anne looked across the table at Wilson and questioned the rosy picture being painted.

"I wonder what the level of support for this race is among Sebec Lake property owners. There are not all that many summer weekends in Maine to enjoy. Are people going to be happy with getting their lake activities shut down for a whole weekend? What does the Sebec Lake Association have to say?"

Nigel sat forward, placed his palms down on the table, and interrupted.

"Everybody's on board with these plans – let's not start making waves here."

"So, let's be clear on this," Anne replied, "The recent boat vandalism here at Merrill's Marina and at Bear Point, as well as the burning of John Eastman's boats and boathouse has no relationship to the upcoming race? And what about the recent floating of logs as boat hazards on the lake?"

Nigel looked puzzled and looked at Don Wilson and Bob Lutz for an explanation.

"Ya can't please everyone," Wilson responded. "Sure, we've had some complaints, but we just have to press forward – this will put Sebec on the map, and we sure as hell need the publicity and the economic boost."

Lutz stayed silent, pointedly gazing at his laptop with feigned concentration.

Nigel Underwood broke the silence.

"There you have it. The dogs bark, but the caravan moves on. Ms. Binford, what can you tell us about your plans for video coverage of the race?"

Louise Binford smiled at Underwood and started in on an oleaginous update.

"First let me say how thrilled I am to be a part of this exciting event Mr. Underwood. It's a real honor to be involved in one of your productions. A real honor."

Louise paused momentarily for Underwood to nod in acknowledgement of her abject ass-kissing and then continued.

"I've gone over our proposed coverage with ESPN and they have signed off on it. For the Friday time trials to determine which boats will qualify for the match races on Saturday we'll have a total of three drone-based cameras in rotation. They will follow the boats around Pine Island. There will also be a stationary camera suspended from a balloon tethered above Pine Island, and several other boat mounted cameras will roam the course, catching shots of boats as they go past. For the match races on Saturday we'll have the same trio of drone cameras and the balloon mounted long-lens stationary camera will be shifted to the narrows where it can provide coverage at a distance of most of the match racecourse. In addition, we'll have cameras on the race boats, providing close-up views of the competitors. Footage from all cameras will be monitored on viewing screens and stored on hard drives here at the roller rink. We'll be running some boats around the course this coming week and working on camera angles and coverage, but that should be straightforward. That's all I have. Any questions?"

Nigel gave the group at the table another of his thousand-watt smiles and pushed away from the table.

"Well, I guess that does it. If there's nothing else, I have to get back down to the coast. Let's meet again in a week – same day, same time. And get in touch if there's anything I need to know in the meantime."

Doug stood as soon as Nigel pushed his chair back and circled the table to stand next to him. Reaching out to shake Nigel's hand, Doug reminded him of their upcoming interview.

"We'll need you back up here to be interviewed in the next few days, unless right now works. No? Well talk to your lawyers then. You can bring them along if you want, but make sure you don't avoid us any longer Nigel. It's in your best interest. Two of your close associates have been murdered, and I don't think you can count on your two bodyguards by the door to keep you safe."

Pulling his hand away, Underwood managed a curt nod in reply before heading for the door, where his two shadows flanked him for the walk to his waiting town car. Anne and Doug headed back into town, stopping at the Spruce Mill Farm and Kitchen for an early lunch. Reaching over to wipe a spot of mustard from Doug's chin, Anne offered her depressing take on their cases.

"We've got two murders, both staged to look like accidents, and so far, no good leads. The Eastman murder is a complete blank as far as I can see, with not even any suspects or motives coming into focus. And none of our leads on the Don Robertson killing have panned out. His widow Rosemary seems to be in the clear, at least according to Tom, and Wes Fuller and Gary Crites never were very promising candidates for the crime."

Nodding, Doug responded.

"I think we can close out those possibilities and focus on Nigel Underwood. He's a slippery character and I think he has quite a scam going with this patio boat race. Everybody else is doing all the work to make it a reality and based on a small initial outlay of money to the Kiwanis, probably a bank loan, he stands to make a bundle when the race airs on ESPN."

Anne agreed.

"He may not be directly involved in the killings, but I'd put some money on the two murders being linked. And it's lookin like Nigel and his patio boat race are right in the middle of whatever's going on. Robertson was entered as Underwood's co-pilot in the race, and both Robertson and Eastman appear to have had lots of involvement with Nigel on planning the event. And I think Ximena Lapointe is also potentially in the mix. She was Robertson's lover, beneficiary of his life insurance policy, and is also directly linked to Nigel. She had dinner with him the night of the killing, supposedly to discuss selling Nigel a lakeside home, but then nothing ever came of it. And remember what John Eastman's widow Elizabeth mentioned – Don and Ximena and Nigel all were dinner guests as a group at the Eastman's home on a number of occasions."

"Nigel's the key," Doug agreed. "He might be behind the killings, or he might be next in line for someone intent on keeping the race from taking place. The sooner we get him in for an interview the better."

13.

Nigel Underwood's patio boat mishap at the entrance to Bucks Cove was a popular topic of conversation around Dover-Foxcroft's watering holes for the next several weeks, and accounts of those who had witnessed it firsthand were in high demand. "Nigel's mishap," as it was soon labeled, had all the elements necessary to give it legs – a rich arrogant fool from away, ignorant and disrespectful of the local environment, destroys his ultra-expensive boat and lands himself in the hospital in spectacular fashion. What could be better?

The eyewitness accounts were quite colorful and tended to become more embellished over time, but the footage captured by Lou Binford's drones provided a crystal-clear high-resolution record of what actually happened. Nigel's Manitou tri-hull patio boat could be seen approaching the narrow entrance to Bucks Cove at an estimated speed of 35 to 40 MPH. The boat's massive wake washes the rocky shore on both sides as it roars into the narrow opening, and Nigel and his boat appear to have successfully cleared the narrowest part of the entrance when the boat suddenly jerks violently as the stern is lifted high above the water line. The boat's large outboards break loose and spiral wildly through the air as Nigel is launched high over the bow, landing hard in the rock-strewn shallows a good thirty feet away.

The next morning at the roller rink, as he and Anne watched the drone footage, Doug knew what was coming before it happened. He had been through that opening into Bucks Cove many times growing up on Sebec Lake and knew that a massive boulder lurked just below the surface on the left side of the channel a little past the entrance. The boulder was clearly marked by a large white hazard buoy and Doug couldn't understand how Nigel hadn't seen it and angled off to starboard to avoid it. The boulder, not visible from an approaching boat, could be clearly seen in the drone footage, a large dark shape directly in the path of the boat.

When Doug mentioned his puzzlement regarding Nigel, the boulder, and the buoy, Anne's response surprised him.

"What buoy Doug? Run the tape again. I didn't see any buoy."

They ran the footage several more times, and the clear calm water of the lake revealed the hazard buoy. It was there but submerged under water about ten feet to the left of the boulder. A bright blue line could be seen running underwater from the buoy toward the shore. Someone had apparently tied a second line to the buoy and, leaving its anchor line intact, had pulled it sideways until it disappeared below the lake surface. Then they tied it off. In the aftermath of the crash it would have been a simple matter to remove the blue line and let the buoy pop back up to its proper place above the boulder, which was now known locally as "Nigel's rock."

Anne and Doug hitched a ride to the crash scene on the Bowerbank fire boat, which was dispatched to haul Underwood's patio boat and outboard engines up from their resting place on the bottom. As they anticipated, the buoy was floating in its proper place right above Nigel's rock, with no sign of the blue line that had pulled it below the surface. A small flotilla of boats as well as a collection of onshore people from nearby camps had gathered, and several uniformed officers from the Warden Service were busy canvasing them for any information or leads about the accident. There was a festive atmosphere, and although the onlookers were friendly enough and forthcoming, none appeared to have anything relevant to offer. It took a little over an hour to drag first the patio boat and then each of its engines up onto shore, where Underwood's insurance company could decide what to do with the mangled wreckage. Having cleared the passage into Bucks Cove, the Bowerbank fire boat carrying Anne and Doug headed back to Greeleys Landing.

In the moments after the crash several of the boats that had been filming Nigel's ill-fated run quickly arrived on the scene. Nigel was carefully loaded onto one of them and rushed back to Greeleys landing, where a waiting ambulance took him first to the Mayo Regional Hospital in Dover-Foxcroft for initial assessment and stabilization, and then on to Northern Light Eastern Maine Medical Center in Bangor.

Underwood had several broken ribs, a fracture of his left femur, and a sprained wrist. By far his most serious injury, however, was a fractured skull and concussion. A craniectomy to relieve pressure inside his skull had been performed soon after Nigel arrived at Northern Light, and the swelling had come down overnight. All his vital signs had remained stable since his arrival, which was encouraging, but Nigel had yet to regain consciousness.

Doug and Anne were meeting with Jim Torben and Jack Walker that afternoon at the sheriff's office when Tom Richard called in to report on his meeting with Underwood's physicians and to update them on what little the computer technicians had learned about the 321A file hidden on Rosemary's old printer. There was no firm estimate of when Underwood would regain consciousness, Tom reported, but they thought it would be a matter of days, perhaps weeks. Access to the ICU where Nigel was being treated was tightly restricted, and Doug and Tom agreed he would not need any additional protection.

Offering more bad news, Tom passed on the results of the analysis of the computer file found hidden on Rose's printer. Rather than being revelatory it looked as if it was going to turn out to be another dead end, even though they were able to identify in general terms what it showed. The file's columns of numbers listed a series of deposits flowing into a Deutsche Bank account over a period of several months the previous fall. The deposits could be traced back to a half dozen accounts in overseas financial institutions of sketchy reputation, often linked to Russian oligarchs involved in money laundering. Just over fourteen million dollars had been deposited in the account, in total. The identity of the account holders on both ends of the money transfers could not be determined, and when queried, Deutsche Bank provided a curt reply- the account in their bank into which the funds had been deposited was no longer active.

The funds had been transferred. Deutsche Bank declined to indicate where the funds in the account had been transferred. Don's widow Rosemary was stunned when Tom told her of the existence of the account and the amount of money involved, which was far beyond what Don usually dealt with, and far outside his normal realm of funds management.

For the investigators sitting around the table in Jim Torben's office, Tom's account of the computer file and the financial transaction records opened up an entirely new avenue of possible suspects and motives for the series of crimes they were pursuing. While they were waiting for Underwood to wake up, if he ever did, Tom Richard would take on the task of tracking down and talking to his relatives and business associates, as well as taking a closer look at the ESPN deal Underwood had put together.

Tom also reported an additional item of bad news that sobered his colleagues in Dover-Foxcroft. He had received a phone call from one of the detectives that had interviewed he and Rose after the knife attack in Quebec City. Doing a routine follow-up on the case, not really expecting any results, the detectives had contacted local hospital emergency rooms asking about any reports of someone seeking treatment for mouth trauma and missing teeth on the night of the attack or the next day. They were surprised to find out that a hospital not far from the hotel where Tom and Rosemary had been staying had treated someone for a battered mouth within hours of the attack. The man had given what turned out to be a false name and had abruptly left halfway through treatment when several uniformed police officers brought in a prisoner in need of medical attention. The man, in his haste to leave, left behind his coat. In one of the pockets of the coat they found a recent photograph of Rosemary, with the name of their hotel written on the back in Cyrillic. It had not been a random attack. The knife-wielding assailant had clearly been targeting Rose. Tom would have to stay close to Rose for the foreseeable future – a responsibility he willingly took on.

On the Dover-Foxcroft side of the investigation Jack Walker was going to circle back and interview the Eastman widow again to see if she had remembered anything relevant, and to press her harder both on her late husband's recent activities and contacts, and who might have harbored a grudge from his long career in property development. Did she remember any recent altercations or local disagreements he had experienced, even of a seemingly minor nature? Was her husband seeing another woman? Had any disputes occurred with contractors they had employed in their house construction? Had there been any unusual encounters or unexpected appearances of individuals from his past life?

When Nigel's catastrophic attempt to run the narrow entrance to Bucks Cove was added to the Don Robertson and John Eastman killings, which had also been set up to look like accidents, it was a no-brainer for Doug and Anne to decide to take another look at Ximena LaPointe, this time as a possible target. If her babysitter hadn't had an SAT test the next day, Ximena would have been in the cabin with Robertson all night and would have died alongside him. She had escaped that night, but three people she had been closely associated with had since either turned up dead or ended up in the ICU. Jim Torben ended the meeting by underscoring their need to cast a wider net and follow up with the other individuals that were at the roller rink meeting – Louise Binford, Bob Lutz, and Don Wilson.

Anne called Ximena as soon as the meeting was over to set up another interview with her. The call went right to voice mail and Anne left a message saying that they needed to talk to her as soon as possible.

They needed a few things for dinner, and rather than going all the way out to Shaw's Supermarket, Anne and Doug stopped at Will's Shop 'n Save in town. Will's was a local landmark of sorts because of the large mural painted on the side of the building that featured several hot air balloons. The Dover-Foxcroft Hot Air Balloon Festival, like the upcoming pontoon boat race, had been an earlier effort to draw attention and visitors to Piscataquis County. The festival had deflated after just two years and about the only remaining record of it was the Will's Stop 'n Save mural, several abandoned web sites, and an occasional vintage T-shirt seen around town. Anne and Doug were loading groceries into the back of Doug's Jeep Cherokee when someone called to Doug from across the parking lot. Turning to see who it was, he recognized Ted Height hurrying toward them.

Ted had been a childhood friend of Doug's late son Eric and had been with him on the day Eric drowned jumping off the dam in Sebec Village. Ted and Eric had belonged to the "Water Rats" - a very loose assemblage of maybe a dozen or more boys, and a few tomboys, who, following a tradition reaching back generations, spent a lot of their free time on Sebec Lake during the summer months – exploring every cove and stream with their small outboard motorboats, pirate flags flying. They would share cigarettes snagged from their parents, seek out the best fishing spots, have impromptu obstacle course races through shallow rocky waters, and try to sneak up on the river otters that frequented Seymour Cove. They weren't a formal club or anything, and as you might expect, exhibited a wide range of personalities and interests.

Ted Height was one of the serious ones, more interested in studying the carnivorous aquatic plants by the beaver dam in Flag Cove than pranking adults, which was not an uncommon activity for some of the Water Rats. Pranks varied in severity, depending on the perceived degree of disrespect shown either to them or to what some of them considered the very sanctity of Sebec Lake itself. They thought of themselves as protectors of the lake – stewards of its plant and animal communities and arbiters of appropriate behavior toward the environment. Their pranks would most often involve a stealthy approach under cover of darkness by one or more swimmers to the target's shorefront and dock area. Minor insults might call for turning the offender's flag upside down on their flagpole, or perhaps lobbing the offender's life preservers up into the trees, or loosening the sparkplug wires on their outboard. Things that could easily be reversed with no lasting damage.

Pranks could be more serious, however, particularly if it appeared that a major crime against nature had taken place. Someone who recklessly disturbed a nesting loon, or cut down trees within the shoreline no-cut zone, for example, could wake up to find that while their boat was still moored securely to their dock, it was also resting solidly on the bottom of the lake due to the simple overnight removal of a boat's drain plug.

There was no formal membership list for the Water Rats, and the size, composition and degree of internal communication and integration of the group varied considerably over time. Each year some of the older members would be drawn to other pursuits and would be replaced by younger, newly joining members, eager to become part of a long established, if never explicitly formalized, tradition.

Ted Height had aged up and out of the Water Rats, but his interest in the environment and threats to Maine's freshwater lakes and waterways grew and matured. After graduating from the Foxcroft Academy he had gone on to attend the University of Maine at Orono in Ecology and Environmental Sciences. He was back in town this summer working part time at Will's and spending long hours helping to organize and supervise the Foxcroft Academy student research teams carrying out systematic surveys of Sebec Lake's aquatic plants. For the past several summers they had been using kayaks and a glass bottomed boat to search the shallow shoreline habitats of the lake, carefully documenting aquatic plant communities and looking for any of the dozen or so exotic invasive species that were turning up in an alarming number of lakes farther east and south in the state. The exotics – Eurasian and variable leaf watermilfoil being the most feared, could be carried in on boats and boat trailers.

"Hi Anne, Hi Doug. Glad I caught you." Ted greeted them. "I heard you were up at Bucks Cove where that fool from away crashed his patio boat. Does that mean that stupid boat race has been cancelled?"

"No such luck Ted." Doug responded. "And it looks like they are expecting two hundred patio boats to descend on us for the race that weekend."

"Not good, not good at all." Ted mumbled as he pushed his thick glasses back in place. "Fuckin Kiwanis sold us out. And I'm not the only one who thinks so. There was no public meeting, no chance for anyone to object. People are pissed. We don't get all that many summer weekends to enjoy the lake, and now they're gonna shut it down for patio boat races? Patio boats? Whose lake is it anyway?"

"Ted, who's pissed?" Doug asked.

"Oh, you know – people." Ted answered evasively. "Still a few weeks until the race – lots of things could happen between now and then."

With a smug grin he abruptly turned away, grabbed an abandoned shopping cart and headed back toward the entrance to Will's. As Ted walked back in the store, Anne turned to Doug.

"Doug, did you notice the tattoo on the inside of his forearm?"

"No. What about it?"

"It looked like an outline of Sebec Lake. What's that all about?"

"Oh, that," Doug replied, looking concerned. "Not sure. Back when I was a kid if you were really into the Water Rat scene, lake tattoos were a way to show your dedication and commitment. Hard core pranksters would get the tattoos. Usually they would be pretty well hidden under clothes, but occasionally they're right out where you can see them. Ted must have gotten that one recently. I don't remember seeing it before."

On the drive back to his place in Bowerbank Doug filled Anne in on the long local tradition of the Water Rats – their environmental stewardship interests and their pranking activities.

Anne's response was quick.

"It sounds to me like the Water Rats, or maybe some radicalized Water Rat alumni like Ted, might be behind the recent spate of incidents. The untied boats at Merrill's Marina, the problems at Bear Point Marina, the floating log we hit, and Nigel's Bucks Cove mishap would all appear to fit comfortably within the Water Rats prank profile. But the torching of John Eastman's boats and boathouse seems a bit out of character, and the killing of Robertson and Eastman would be quite extreme – don't you think?"

Doug nodded and replied.

"If Water Rats or their alumni are responsible it's going to be really difficult to track them down. There's no membership list, no centralized authority structure, no meetings or blogs or anything, as far as I know. Pranks were usually conceived and carried out by one person or a few individuals, on their own. Part of the fun was the anonymous nature of the pranks and the subsequent slowly spreading accounts of what had transpired – the offhand acknowledgement months later at a party, or the floating of unsubstantiated rumors of who had pulled off a particular attack."

"So, what's our next step?" Asked Anne.

"Our next step, lover, is to get home and feed our hungry dog." Doug answered. "Then I can pour you a glass of wine, we can start thinking about dinner, and I will call a few people who might have some insights and some leads for us."

14.

The next morning, after taking Jack the dog for his daily walk, followed by a leisurely breakfast – Anne's "eyeballs" concoction of soft-boiled eggs, arugula, blueberries, blackberries, chunks of bacon and toast, and a little olive oil, Doug and Anne headed into Dover-Foxcroft. They had just crossed the dam in Sebec Village and were headed up the hill past the Reading Room and old post office when Anne's phone rang. Jack Walker's name appeared on the screen.

"Hi Jack. What's Up?"

"Where are you? Is Doug with you?"

"Yes. We're just passing through Sebec Village, heading into town."

"You and Doug were going to follow up on interviewing Ximena Lapointe, right?"

"Yes. I called yesterday and got bumped to her answering machine. Why?"

"Well, she's available for interviewing now. Someone ran her over with a boat early this morning – she's banged up pretty bad and being worked on now at the Mayo emergency room in town."

Ximena had been moved to a private room and given a mild sedative by the time they arrived at the hospital. The emergency room physician who had treated her was waiting to brief them.

"What the hell's going on out on the lake? This is the second serious boating casualty we've gotten in the last two days. Fortunately, this one isn't as bad as yesterday. Ximena doesn't remember anything that happened, so she won't be much help, I'm afraid. You can't see her right now, but this afternoon would be possible." The doctor paused, and Anne jumped in with a question.

"Who brought her in?"

"A couple of men showed up with her about an hour ago. The two had been fishing early this morning in the South Cove, by Peaks-Kenny State Park. They saw the whole incident and were able to get to her quickly. Fortunately, she had some sort of a yellow buoy tied to a strap around her waist, and it kept her afloat until they got to her. She was breathing but unconscious when pulled out of the water. They bundled her into their truck and by the time they got here she had regained consciousness. She's pretty beat up and has a mild concussion. That should resolve in a day or two. Otherwise she has a bunch of bruises, and I stitched up several lacerations on her ass from where she was grazed by the boat's prop when it went over her."

Doug handed the doctor his card with contact information.

"Thanks doc. I'll check back in this afternoon to see if she's up for an interview. How about the two men who found her. Are they still around?"

The doctor fished around in the pocket of his white coat and pulled out a scrap of paper.

"They headed back over to Greeleys Landing to do some more fishing. Here's the phone number of one of them – Kevin Laland. He said to call him, and they can meet you back at the marina."

Anne made the call and the two fishermen were waiting for them when they arrived at the marina. Laland, a trim man of perhaps sixty, with an easy smile, introduced himself and his nephew, who looked to be in his early twenties.

"Detective Bateman, Investigator Quinn, I'm Kevin Laland. This is my nephew Andrew. How's Ximena?"

"She's got a concussion and lacerations, but thanks to you two she should be back on her feet in a few days. Kevin, I'm pretty sure I should recognize you, but can't remember from where."

Anne answered before Laland had a chance to respond.

"Kevin delivers your mail Doug. You've probably seen him a hundred times up on Bowerbank Road in his red Honda Element. Looks like you might need to brush up on your detective skills."

Laland and his nephew joined Anne in chuckling at Doug's expense, and Kevin, speaking in a calm scholarly voice, started right in on an account of their rescue of Ximena that morning.

"We were on the west side of the South Cove, over among the scattering of large boulders, casting for bass. We'd been there for maybe a half hour and not having much luck. It was maybe eight o'clock when we heard a boat at low speed, and saw an eighteen-foot Lund with red sides, close to the shore on the east side of the cove, heading toward the beach at Peaks-Kenny. I didn't pay much attention to it until it suddenly turned west toward us and really picked up speed. That's when I noticed the yellow float directly in the path of the Lund. I couldn't figure out what the yellow thing was at first, then saw the swimmer right by it."

Anne interrupted Kevin's narrative.

"Did it look like the boat deliberately targeted the swimmer?"

"No question about it." Andrew answered. "And it was going quite fast when it ran right over her. We could hear the thump when it hit her."

"Did you get a look at who was in the boat?" Doug asked.

"Not really." Kevin replied. "The sun was pretty low on the horizon and we were looking right into it. There was one person in the boat, standing at the wheel, and all we could see was a black silhouette. I'd say maybe six feet tall, thin – dark clothes, maybe a hoodie – hard to tell. After the Lund ran over the swimmer it turned north and sped off around the point, heading east back toward the narrows. One of the boulders blocked our view of the boat at that point, and anyway, we were focused on the person in the water."

"Was she conscious when you pulled her into your boat? Did she say anything?"

"She was unconscious but breathing when we got to her," Kevin replied. "There was a lot of blood in the water and her swimsuit was shredded. I recognized her right away and realized she was probably doing a training swim for the YMCA's upcoming triathlon. She did well last year, certainly posted a much better time than I did, and I've seen her cycling and running pretty frequently lately on my mail route. Lots of open water swimmers use the yellow floats like the one Ximena had attached with a strap around her waist. They wear them to alert boaters to their presence, so they won't get run over. This time it did just the opposite – it helped someone locate her and run her down."

Doug turned to Andrew.

"What did you see?"

"I didn't recognize Ximena right away, but I think I know the boat that hit her. It belongs to the people who bought the old cottage that was owned by either the Peaks or the Kenny's – I forget which family. It's the one on the south shore not too far after you round the point toward the narrows. It's the one that has the big stone blocks protecting their boat slip."

Kevin offered to ferry them over to see if the boat Andrew had identified was at its mooring, and twenty minutes later they pulled up next to a red-sided Lund outboard. High above them, unnoticed, a drone had followed their trip over from the marina and watched as they checked out the boat. The outboard engine was warm to the touch and the windshield still had a scattering of water droplets, indicating the boat had recently been used. Anne walked up to check on the cottage – a large turn of the century shingled landmark, and found it locked up tight with no indication of recent occupancy.

"Nobody's home Doug. It looks like somebody took advantage of the owners being away and borrowed their boat to run down Ximena."

"I doubt we'll find anything, but I'll call Augusta and have the evidence response team go over the boat," Doug replied. "Maybe we'll get lucky."

Doug called the ERT number when they were on their way back to town and was surprised to learn that Peter Martell, commander of the evidence response team, was already in Dover-Foxcroft. He had taken a few days annual leave, but no one in Augusta knew why he was in Dover-Foxcroft.

"I bet I know," Anne responded with a snort when Doug told her. "He's up here to see Katie."

Anne called Katie, who was working a shift at Allie Oops, and her suspicion was confirmed. When Peter came on the line Doug was able to cajole him into checking out the suspect boat right away. Peter always carried some of his basic gear, including a fingerprint kit, in the trunk of his car, and Kevin and Andrew, who were still at the marina, agreed to ferry him back over to the Lund. Before she hung up, Katie asked Anne and Doug to stop by Allie Oops. She had something serious to discuss, she said, but wouldn't say more.

When Doug and Anne arrived at Allie Oops they stopped briefly to talk with Peter, who was just leaving to check out the Lund as they walked in the front door. Then they joined Katie, who was having a quick lunch in a back booth. The bar was mostly empty, but Katie still kept her voice low.

"You guys know that Louise Binford and I were a couple for several months. We split up because it became clear to me that she was a pathological liar, and she got tired of me calling her fantasies into question. What I didn't say was that I'm still pretty uneasy about her and what she might do. I freaked when she showed up in town again for this Patio Boat race. So far, I've been able to stay off her radar. But if she finds out that Peter and I have really hit it off, she might come after us."

"Why?" Anne asked.

"I'm no psychiatrist, so I can't give you a sound medical diagnosis. But based on what I saw when I lived with her, I'd say that Lou Binford is, in technical terms, batshit insane. She moves back and forth between reality and a fantasy world. A lot of the time she seems fine – outgoing and a bit aggressive, but outwardly normal. And then out of the blue she will spin these elaborate fantasies and start telling me about all the people who are laughing at her behind her back – people who have wronged her or abandoned her. She's paranoid and talks a lot about settling scores with people for perceived wrongs. At the time I tried very hard to make her believe that it was her that dumped me, and she seemed to accept that. But she could easily change her mind if she sees that Peter and I are a couple and gets it into her head that we're laughing at her."

"Do you want us to talk to her?" Doug asked.

"Jesus no, Doug. That wouldn't help. It would only make things worse. That's not why I'm telling you this stuff. It's about what happened to Ximena. From what Lou told me late one night last fall after way too many margaritas, she was furious at how Ximena behaved toward her when she was up here working on the serial killer case. She was pretty vague about what happened, but my guess is that she tried to seduce Ximena, who always seemed solidly cisgender to me, and Ximena must have blown her off. I tried asking Lou about it again a few weeks after she first mentioned it, and she wouldn't say anything, just smiled and said all that would be taken care of."

"You think she might be behind the boat attack on Ximena?" Anne asked.

"That's exactly what I'm saying. Maybe it isn't her, but it's worth looking into. And Peter said I needed to tell you two what my suspicions were."

"He's right," Anne replied. "And we're definitely going to follow this up."

"Peter also wants me to come down to Augusta and stay with him until you guys sort this all out. He's concerned I might be at risk. What do you guys think?"

"That's a good idea Katie," Doug said. "I trust Peter to keep you safe, and maybe you can smooth out his rough edges a bit while you're down there."

Katie smiled in relief and pumped her fist.

"I'm halfway out the door. As soon as Peter gets back, I'll pack a bag and we'll be on our way south."

"What now?" Anne asked as they left Allie Oops and turned up the alley that led to the parking lot in the back. Doug paused, squinted as he briefly looked up at the narrow slice of sky that was visible between the buildings on either side of the alley.

"Don't look up Anne, but I think we are being watched by a drone. It seems that Lou Binford may be monitoring more that patio boats."

Once they were in Doug's Cherokee, he continued.

"I don't know all that much about Binford, other than what we know from her work on the serial killer case back a few years ago. But I think Tom Richard might have information about her time in the military, and why she later left the state police. I'll check with him. For now, let's go slow and careful, and not give her any indication of our suspicions while we see if there's any hard evidence we can work with. Her fingerprints on the Lund that ran over Ximena would be nice, for example. First thing we need to do, though, is to try to allay any concerns she might have about us focusing on her. It's not a good sign that she's tracking us with a drone."

Louise Binford sat in front of a large video monitor at the Greeleys Landing race command center, watching the feed from the drone high over Dover-Foxcroft that showed Anne and Doug exiting the parking lot behind Allie Oops and appearing to head her way. She didn't turn when she heard Anne and Doug come through the front door of the roller rink a quarter of an hour later, but smiled and stood up as they approached.

"Greetings, officers of the law. What can I do you for?"

"Well, we're hoping you can help us with something," Doug began. "There was a serious boat accident over by Peaks-Kenny State Park this morning. We're hoping you might have captured it if you had any drones up over the South Cove at the time."

"No, I don't think so. I got in a little late this morning – car trouble, and have been going over footage from poor Nigel's crash, so didn't have any drones running this morning. But I can check with my new intern, Rebecca Hull, she might have had something up over the South Cove. She's at lunch right now."

"That would be great," Anne replied. "Can you also check to see if you have any footage just east of the South Cove, by the Peaks-Kenny cottage. We think there's a boat there that was involved in the accident. We already got a lucky break on that – one of the guys from our evidence response team was in town, and is checking out the boat now. But any video would be excellent."

"Sure," Lou responded. I'll check with her when she gets back from lunch."

After a few more casual questions Anne and Doug thanked Binford and headed back into town. On the way Anne suggested enlisting Binford's intern, Rebecca Hull in their efforts to learn more.

"Becky Hull played basketball for the Foxcroft Academy before going off to the University of Maine. She often joined our informal pickup games on the weekends and after school, and I got to know her and her family really well. Becky is usually quiet and doesn't say much, so people tend not to notice her. But she's very sharp and doesn't miss much. I can talk to her. What do you think?"

"As long as she's very clear that all we want is for her to keep her eyes open and let us know if anything seems off. If she's willing, make it clear that Binford could be dangerous, so she should not take any chances. No snooping around, no Nancy Drew fantasies – just doing what she's supposed to do as an intern, and talking to you when it's safe, about what's going on."

Anne looked up Becky's number and called her when they got back to town, and she quickly signed up to be their eyes and ears inside the race control center. Becky had already picked up on Binford's mercurial mood swings and had decided to keep a very low profile. She had considered quitting but needed the internship experience for college course credit. And Becky already had some interesting information to pass on. Binford had just told Doug and Anne that she had spent the morning reviewing footage of Nigel's crash at the entrance to Bucks Cove, but Becky said Lou had arrived late that morning and ever since she got in had been piloting drones and appeared to be tracking something or someone.

15.

Peter Martell stopped by with disappointing news later that afternoon.

"Sorry Doug. I didn't get any usable prints off the Lund. Looks like they wore gloves. I did get a partial footprint on one of the seats – probably someone stepping into the boat. We'll see what we can do with it back at the lab, but don't hold your breath."

"Sounds good Peter. Anything you can come up with on the footprint would be great."

Reaching out to shake Doug's hand, Peter replied.

"Katie is packing a bag and we're out of here. Thanks for encouraging her to stay with me in Augusta until this is all sorted out. From what she says this Binford woman is unhinged."

Later that night, Tom Richard returned Doug's call from earlier in the day.

"Hey Doug, I'm still waiting on a callback from someone who served with Binford in Iraq, so no info on that yet. But I have talked to a buddy in HR about why she left the state police, and it's pretty creepy. Apparently Binford decided that her lieutenant, Marge Johnson, was not treating her with sufficient respect, or maybe didn't respond in the way she wanted to her flirting. So late one night Louise unexpectedly showed up in Marge's bedroom and wanted to talk it over. Fortunately, Marge is a hostage negotiator and knows all the right moves in such situations. She was able to sweet talk Louise out of her dark mood, and they ended up having a few beers at the kitchen table and then Louise left."

"What happened then?" Doug asked.

"I'm not sure about the exact sequence of events, but Binford was quietly reassigned to an obscure job in the cold-case records archive, and after a few months she realized she would be stuck there forever and quit."

"OK – thanks Tom. Any update on Nigel Underwood's condition? Still in a coma?"

"As of late this afternoon, there's no change – stable but comatose. And Doug, getting back to Binford for a minute – we need to look at the possibility that she was behind the murder of Don Robertson. What if she was trying to kill Ximena, and Doug was just collateral damage? Maybe we have been looking at the wrong suspects and the wrong motive all along? Maybe Robertson's murder was the result of Binford's scheme to knock off Ximena and didn't have anything to do with the patio boat race, Nigel Underwood, or that other killing – John Eastman."

"You're right Tom. Anne and I talked about it a bit, and Binford definitely moves up in our list of suspects. Maybe tomorrow you could go around to where Louise lives – I think she has a house up by the university in Orono, and take a look around. Peek in some windows, check out the garage, that sort of thing. Maybe we'll get lucky. But no clandestine B&E Tom. Let's avoid any fruit of the poison tree problems down the road."

"The mere suggestion offends me," Tom replied with mock outrage. "I would never consider such a thing, particularly in daylight hours."

The next morning, after a leisurely breakfast with Rosemary, who had slept over at his place, Tom checked in at the Maine State Police barracks in Bangor and looked up Louise Binford's home address in Orono. Cruising by the house first to make sure there was no one about, he continued on to the end of the block, turned the corner, and parked by the alley that ran behind Binford's house. Walking down the alley until he reached her backyard fence, Tom pulled a spotting scope from his jacket pocket. Crouching down, he scanned Binford's small two-story brick house, looking for security cameras. Not seeing any, he opened the unlocked gate and cautiously approached the house, checking for any tripwires or other surprises that might have been set for unwanted guests. Although he still hadn't heard back from his source about Binford's military record, Tom knew that she had served several tours in Iraq with special forces units, and was very careful as he conducted the reconnaissance. Slowly circling the house, checking for any opportunity for access through unlocked windows and doors, Tom came away disappointed. The house was locked up tight, shades were drawn, and there were few bushes or other plantings to shield him from view.

He walked back toward the alley, pausing by the ramshackle garage to look in the door, which was partially ajar. It was dark in the garage, with the only illumination coming from the gap between the doors where Tom was looking in, and from a small side window that was partially painted over. Pulling one of the doors open wider, Tom could see that the space was mostly empty. A rusted lawnmower and assorted yard tools – a hoe, rake, and axe, were piled haphazardly in one corner. In the other back corner, a vintage Triumph motorcycle missing its front wheel was partially covered by what looked to be a worn tarpaulin. Seeing the tarp, Tom perked up. If the tarp covering the motorcycle in Lou's garage was a match with the tarp fragment that had been used to block the air flow up the chimney in the cabin where Don Robertson was found dead, it would be the hard evidence needed to charge Lou Binford with murder.

Under the legal concept of "curtilage," the garage, like the house, could not be legally entered and searched without a court approved search warrant. Tom could not resist a closer look at the tarpaulin, however, and entering the garage, took several closeup photos of it from different angles. Stepping back through the door he had pulled open, Tom swung it back to its original location and then took a photo of the motorcycle and tarp through the gap. Checking to make sure he had left no footprints, he then exited Binford's back yard and returned down the alley to his car.

As soon as he got back to the office Tom uploaded the photo he had taken of the cycle and tarp through the open garage doors and sent it to both the evidence analysis lab in Augusta and to Doug. Then he sent Doug the additional photos he had taken of the tarp from inside the garage, knowing that Doug would understand their problematic nature. Since they were not obtained in a legal manner the inside-the-garage photos Tom took could never be used in court. But if the closeups suggested that the tarp was a good match to the fragment recovered at the Robertson murder scene, they would just have to figure out a way to get a search warrant for the garage so the tarp could later be legally "discovered." Maybe with a better camera, long lens, and bright lights they could go back and take more photos through the open doors to get what they needed for a search warrant. And if the tarps didn't match, based on the photos, then they needn't waste any time following up.

At the same time that Tom was sending out the photos from her garage, Louise Binford was sitting in front of her computer at the roller rink, listening to her intern giving an account of the previous morning's boat accident in the South Cove.

Listening to Becky drone on, Binford couldn't help returning once again to the memory of how Ximena had humiliated her at the Bear's Den over a year ago when she and Katie had come up for the weekend. Katie had been visiting her mother, who didn't think much of Lou, so Lou went for a beer at the Bear's Den. Ximena had been sitting at the bar that night when Louise took the empty seat next to her and struck up a conversation. They seemed to hit it off right away, and after buying each other drinks and getting more and more friendly, even flirty, Lou thought, Ximena got up to use the restroom, and Louise followed her.

Ximena was at the sinks, washing her hands when Lou walked up and embraced her from behind, nuzzling her neck and whispering a few explicit endearments. Ximena immediately broke the embrace, laughed drunkenly, and good-naturedly told Lou to "fuck off" before pushing past her and exiting the bathroom. Lou took a piss and then followed her out. Ximena had moved to a table where she was excitedly talking to three men sitting with her. They were all listening to her with rapt attention. As Ximena caught sight of Lou coming out of the bathroom, she blurted something out to her companions and wagged her thumb in Lou's direction. As the men looked up at her with mocking leers, hand gestures, and raised glasses, Lou turned and stormed out of the Bear's Den.

The humiliation of that moment, with drunken losers laughing at her, had remained raw for Louise all these months, and her frustration was bubbling up again when she received a call from her next-door neighbor in Bangor.

"Hey Lou. You told me to call if I ever saw something suspicious at your place while you were out of town. So get this. Just a little while ago me and Alison were upstairs watching TV and smokin some weed when I saw this big guy slinkin across your backyard toward your house. He went all the way around the house, checkin doors and windows, and then went back to the garage. He peeked in the doors, which were open a bit, then went in the garage. I saw some flashes in there. I figure he probably took some photos. After he came out he took a few more shots through the open doors, and then went back out to the alley and walked away. I know you ain't got shit in that garage, so I got no idea what he was takin photos of."

Lou listened with growing anger and apprehension, and after thanking her neighbor for the heads up, she quickly ended the call.

"Fuck me," she thought. "That had to be Tom Richard, the sneaky prick."

Becky had resumed her long boring monologue, but Lou ignored her and decided to get some fresh air and think this through. Exiting the roller rink, she walked over to a bench by the water and sat, looking out across the lake toward Borestone Mountain looming on the horizon to the north.

"What was he looking for?" she thought. "What would he find worth photographing in the garage?"

She tried to think of what all was in the garage, which she rarely used. Lou could remember a few rusty garden tools left behind by the previous renter, and her old Triumph Bonneville motorcycle, which had a blown engine. And the tarp covering it. Then it dawned on her. Tom had been photographing the tarp left behind by the previous owner. The one that she had used to cover the Bonneville. The story about a tarp being used to cover the chimney in Robertson's death was all over town by now, and Lou realized they were hoping they might be able to match the tarp in her garage to the murder weapon.

"Well, well," she thought. "Fuck me. Maybe they also suspect me of running over Ximena in the South Cove."

Lou was briefly tempted to call Tom Richard and tell him that he had her permission to take all of the photos he wanted in her garage, but immediately decided not to. Better to act as if she didn't know what they were up to. Let them simply flail away. At the same time, Louise was insulted that Tom and Doug considered her stupid enough to hold onto a piece of evidence that could so easily link her to a murder. Gazing out across the calm surface of the lake, Louise also began to suspect that it was Katie that pointed Doug and the others in her direction.

"That bitch," she thought. "She's gonna regret ratting me out."

Tom's hope that the tarp photos would provide hard evidence linking Lou Binford to the murder of Don Robertson were soon dashed. When Doug checked Tom's incoming photos on his phone, he quickly sent a text in response.

"No match – different color, wrong grommets, no paint spatter."

"Oh well," Tom thought, "It was worth a try."

Back in his office at the Maine State Police barracks, Tom checked to see if his special forces source had emailed him anything new about Binford's service records, but nothing had come in. There was, however, an email response with several attached files to the initial inquiry he had made to New Jersey authorities regarding Nigel Underwood. They confirmed that there was an LLC company registered under the name "Underwood Events" in the state. But no one named Nigel Underwood was associated with the company. Adrian Capler was listed as the registered agent for the firm, and very little other information was provided in the certificate of organization filed by Underwood Events with the state.

Curious now, Tom settled in for an on-line search for information on Adrian Capler in a number of different law enforcement data bases. In a little over an hour he had found two other aliases associated with Underwood/Capler. According to arrest records and court records from jurisdictions in New Jersey, New York, and Pennsylvania, Underwood had also used the names Edward (Ned) Unger and Andrew Conan at various times. In the last two decades Underwood had been the subject of a string of fraud investigations, a few of which had resulted in fines, but he had never served jail time. There were no outstanding warrants for him or any active ongoing investigations, but it was clear he was a con artist with a long record of scams he had pretty much gotten away with.

Tom emailed Doug and Anne summarizing what he had found, and attached files detailing a number of Underwood's arrest records and court proceedings. He then called Northern Light Eastern Maine Medical Center to check on Underwood's status and was surprised to learn that he had woken up from his coma a few days ago and was showing rapid signs of improvement. Nigel was now responsive and had been moved out of the ICU that morning. After checking with Underwood's physician, the nurse Tom talked to indicated that he could interview Underwood that afternoon.

Located right on the Penobscot River at the northeast edge of downtown Bangor, the EMMC was a sprawling red brick complex that had clearly grown incrementally over the years. Tom flinched at the familiar smells that wafted over him as he walked in the main entrance. He had spent far too much time in hospitals, both as he grew up and during his time in the military. Tom's mother had spent the last few years of her life in hospitals and hospices in northern Maine as she battled cancer and Tom had always dreaded having to visit her – watching her slowly waste away, the antiseptic smells and scuffed linoleum in the hallways, the careworn nurses, and the seemingly endless moans of people in pain. His time in military hospitals had only added to his hospital aversion. When an IED blew up his Humvee during his second tour in Iraq, Tom had escaped with only a concussion, ruptured eardrum, and leg burns and lacerations. But he saw too many much more serious injuries among his fellow war wounded patients to ever be able to erase them from his dreams.

Passing the nurse's station on Underwood's third floor ward, Tom noticed a large man in a rumpled dark suit sitting in a chair halfway down the hallway.

"Must be one of Nigel's bodyguards," he thought, approaching the man.

As he got closer he realized the bodyguard was fast asleep, his chin resting on his chest and a "Guns & Ammo" magazine open on his lap. Deciding against waking up the dozing guard – no point antagonizing the man, Tom quietly slipped past him, opened the door to Underwood's room and entered. Nigel was watching TV, his head wrapped in bandages and his elevated right leg encased in a bright green fiberglass cast.

Nigel looked startled and let out a weak bleat as Tom entered the room. Dropping the TV remote, he tried to grab the nurse call button to summon help. Taking several quick steps, Tom moved the call button out of reach and with a friendly smile, introduced himself.

"Don't be concerned Mr. Underwood, I'm not a threat. My name's Tom Richard. I'm with the Maine State Police, and I'd like to talk to you for a few minutes. It won't take long, and then you can get back to your TV show."

Taking out his state police identification, Tom held it up close in front of Nigel's face. Underwood, displaying a remarkable spectrum of yellow to red to purple bruises down the right side of his head, stared back at Tom with an addled expression.

"You can't be in here. Get out."

"It's OK Nigel. The doctors say it's OK. And your guard is still right outside the door."

Tom decided it was better to not further alarm the patient by mentioning that the guard in the hallway was fast asleep and drooling.

"How are you feeling Nigel? Have they told you when you'll be released?"

Underwood gazed back at Tom but said nothing. Tom tried again.

"Do you remember anything about the crash?"

Still no response from Underwood, who shifted his gaze to the door, silently urging it to open and for someone to rescue him.

"Apparently, Nigel, someone removed the buoy that marked the rock you crashed into. We're thinking they tried to kill you, and that they almost succeeded. Any idea who would want to harm you?"

Tom waited for an answer, but Nigel rested his head back on the pillow and returned to watching the TV, acting as if Tom wasn't even there.

"Nigel. Pay attention. You already know that Don Robertson was murdered. You also know John Eastman was murdered. But you might not have heard this yet – someone also tried to kill Ximena Lapointe a few days ago. Ran her down with a boat. So, let's see – the four of you knew each other. You all had dinner at Eastman's place a number of times. Four fast friends, it seems, all apparently tied in somehow with the patio boat race. And now two of these four friends are dead, and attempts have been made on the lives of the other two. What do you think Nigel? Maybe you need to start talking to us."

No response from Nigel.

"OK Nigel, let me try some other names out on you."

Doug took out his notebook, flipped through it quickly, and found the page he wanted.

"How about Adrian Capler? Does that ring a bell, Nigel? Or maybe Edward Unger or Andrew Conan?" Surely you remember those – you used them often enough. Does ESPN know about your storied - or maybe checkered is a better term, past?"

Tom was impressed by Nigel's continued façade of interest in the infomercial that was now on the TV. So far he had shown no visible reaction to Tom's questions. That was about to change.

"What happened to the money, Nigel? You know, the millions Robertson had stashed in overseas accounts? Where did it come from?"

Nigel continued to keep his gaze fixed on the TV, but his hands were now clenched on top of the bedcovers, and Tom could see a vein pulsing in his neck.

"OK, you won't say where the funds might have come from. What were they for, and who has them now? I'm betting that right now, Nigel, the oligarchs want their money back if you can't launder it."

Leaning over Nigel now, Tom continued.

"The way I see it, if you don't know where the money is, you're in a bit of a pickle. And if you do know where it is, you better clean it quick, or you're still in a pickle. I hear the Ruskies have lots of inventive ways to get rid of people who cross them."

Dropping his voice to a whisper now, Tom leaned in close to Nigel's ear.

"OK Nigel, that's enough for now. I'll let you rest. One last question – What's 321A?"

Nigel turned his head to the side, away from Tom, and closed his eyes.

16.

It was one of those perfect mornings on Sebec Lake. While such days were more frequent after Labor Day, when boat traffic dropped way off and the summer people started closing up their camps, they could also surprise you earlier in the year.

Anne was up early, eager to get out on the lake to enjoy what was shaping up to be a beautiful day. Leaving Doug and his dog Jack snoring away contentedly, she quietly crept out of the bedroom, and after pulling on her kayaking clothes and fixing a quick cup of coffee, slipped out of the cabin. The air was crisp and a slight fog drifted along the water's surface in shadows near the shore. The lake was perfectly still. Anne heard a raucous loon call from a nearby cove and the laughter of small children playing on a dock some way down the shore. Otherwise it was silent.

Grabbing her life vest and carbon fiber paddle from a hook on the porch she tucked her water bottle under her arm and walked down to a small sand beach. Picking up her kayak with her free hand, she lifted it free of the canoe rack. The kayak, a surprise gift from Doug on her last birthday, was light enough to be carried in one hand. Its distinctive orange and yellow hull was bright enough to be seen by other watercraft from a considerable distance. Manufactured in Portugal, Anne's Nelo Viper was extremely light and fast, and also easily tipped over. Doug had tried paddling it once. He had only gone about twenty feet before suddenly flipping over and sliding right out of the kayak. Anne, on the other hand, immediately took to the Viper, and after several years had yet to match what they referred to as Doug's "almost Eskimo roll."

Stepping over to the water's edge, she slid her kayak into the shallows. She was careful to avoid disturbing the dozen or so sunfish nests– shallow bowl-like depressions in the sandy bottom, each with a male aggressively watching over it. Pushing off, Anne could feel the sun on her back as she headed west toward Pine Island. On most mornings, if the wind was not too strong, she would paddle west down the middle of the lake until Borestone Mountain came into view over the tree line to the northwest. Then she would turn around and paddle back, usually doing the round trip in about an hour.

Anne was about twenty minutes into her paddle and had settled into a smooth, powerful rhythm that moved her kayak through the water at a deceptively fast pace. She always watched for flotsam as she paddled – and would later add whatever she picked up to the large collection of stuff that had floated ashore at Doug's camp and was exhibited on the side of his woodshed. Seeing something small and pale green floating on the surface of the lake off to her right, she slowed and turned toward it.

It was a moth wing. Just one. Floating alone in the middle of the lake, a good two hundred meters from shore. Slipping the blade of the paddle under the wing, Anne lifted it out of the water and lay it on the flat surface of the kayak's deck, just in front of the cockpit. She recognized it as being from a Luna moth, although she had only seen them illustrated in books. Luna moths, also called giant silk moths or moon moths, have vibrant lime green wings, each with distinctive eye spots or "moons" that are thought to confuse predators. Their long feathery hindwing tails also serve as a defensive mechanism, confusing the echolocation efforts of bats - their prime predators.

Excited about showing this delicate, beautiful moth wing to Doug, Anne started paddling again, confident that the still wet wing would stay stuck to the kayak's surface. She was surprised a few moments later to notice another lime green moon moth wing floating on the lake surface. Pausing, Anne added it to the one she had already recovered. Then she saw several more wings and a complete intact moth just ahead. Over the next ten minutes or so, Anne collected more than a dozen additional partial and complete specimens of Luna moth.

"What the hell are all these moths doing in the middle of the lake?" she wondered.

The sound of a small outboard motor had been steadily growing louder as Anne circled to collect her prizes, and just as she lifted the last of the wings from the water a beat-up ten-foot aluminum boat painted flat black drifted to a stop a little way off. A girl, maybe thirteen or fourteen, killed the motor and reaching up, pulled her hoodie farther forward, mostly shielding her face from view. Anne was looking into the sun and couldn't see the girl's features very well, or tell her hair color, but the purple edging on her hoodie and her light green nail polish on the fingers of both hands drew her attention. Pointing at the impressive collection of moth wings, which were a similar shade of green as her nail polish, the girl asked Anne what she was doing.

"Why are you collecting the Lunas? Did the Moon Mother give you her blessing?"

"Who's the Moon Mother?" Anne replied.

Ignoring her question, the girl continued in a scolding voice.

"You shouldn't be picking those up. You're disturbing things. Who are you?"

"I'm Anne Quinn. Who are you?"

Laughing now, the girl answered.

"We all know who you are. You're the deputy with the silver pinkie. But if you're collecting moth wings you must have a lake name. What is it?"

"Lake name?" Anne wondered. At a momentary loss for words, she asked the girl a question in reply

"What's yours?"

Looking at Anne from the shadow of her hoodie, the girl responded.

"Oh, I don't have a real lake name yet, I'm still a fledgling."

Anne suddenly realized that this must be one of the Water Rats she had heard about.

Quickly running through a list of possible lake names that might satisfy the girl, Anne settled on what she often thought of as her spirit animal.

"I don't have a lake name yet. But if I can ever get one, I want to be called Kingfisher."

"Oh, that's beautiful. When I get my imprint and take my name, I'm going to ask to be called Phoebe. Like me, phoebes are up before dawn, guarding their territory and waiting for the sunrise."

"When will you get your name, fledgling?"

"I'm not exactly sure – it depends on the dark of the moon and how well I do with my tasks."

"How are your tasks coming along?"

"Good actually. So far this morning I found five more boats to tag."

Sneaking a quick glance into the fledgling's boat, Anne saw a box of rectangular reflective stickers and a computer printout of what looked to be a long column of numbers.

"What's tagging mean?"

Realizing she might have said too much, given Anne's lack of a lake name, the fledgling stayed quiet, and Anne rushed to fill the silence. She was pretty sure what the fledgling was referring to with her use of the term "imprint," and decided to see if she was right.

"When you get your imprint, where will it go – on your forearm?"

"Naw. That's too hardcore for me. I'm gonna get a small Luna moth on my inner upper arm. That way it's easy to conceal, but I can flash it when I want to."

Anne had been asking a lot of personal questions and could tell the girl was getting skittish. She quickly backtracked.

"I shouldn't have picked up the Lunas, fledgling. Can you help? What do you think we should do to restore the balance? Should we take them to the Moon Mother?"

Suddenly suspicious, the girl replied. Her tone now decidedly less friendly.

"Nobody approaches the Luna. Even fledglings know that. You want to restore balance? Return the eye wings to mother Sebec."

Anne cradled her paddle in her lap, and as the fledgling watched approvingly, she delicately peeled the Luna moth wings and body parts from the deck of her kayak, one by one, and returned them carefully to the surface of the lake.

As soon as the last wing had been returned to the water the fledgling girl abruptly started her outboard and pulled away from Anne's kayak. Without a backward glance she headed off toward the narrows. Too late, Anne realized, she had not managed to take note of the registration number on the fledgling's boat. She knew she would have a hard time making an identification of either the girl or her boat. All she had to go on, really, was Luna green nail polish.

After the strange interaction with the mystery girl in the middle of the lake, Anne had a hard time getting back into the smooth unconscious rhythm of paddling.

"Who was that girl?" she wondered. "What was she tagging and why? What was all that about lake names and the Moon Mother?"

It took her another quarter of an hour to reach her turnaround point, and Anne was still thinking about the moth wings and the girl with the unusual nail polish as she turned her Viper back east into the morning sun and started home. A slight breeze had picked up and the lake was now a zigzag display of diamonds as the sunlight bounced off the water's surface. She had just passed Pine Island when the silence of the morning was broken by the roar of a powerful and poorly muffled outboard. Looking to her right, Anne saw a bizarre-looking patio boat veer around the south side of Pine Island at a high rate of speed. She stopped paddling and watched as the boat slowed and pulled up to a dock on the north shore. Curious now, Anne turned her kayak around and after a short paddle, pulled up next to the patio boat.

A lean man in his fifties wearing shorts, sunglasses, flip-flops and a t-shirt was tightening a bolt on what looked to be a large wing that had been mounted on the bow of his boat. Clearing her throat to announce her presence, Anne asked the obvious question.

"What's that thing?"

The man looked around, and seeing Anne, turned back to his task.

"It's an airfoil. An upside-down airplane wing. Theoretically it keeps the boat from going airborne when I hit a wave at high speed. But I'm not sure how well it's going to work. It doesn't seem to make much difference."

"Getting ready for the big race?"

"Ayup. I still have lots to do and not a lot of time. And it's getting difficult to keep all my modifications under wraps. I saw someone just this morning, right at dawn, in a little black boat, checking out my airfoil."

Anne could guess who the early morning visitor had been, and glancing over at the patio boat's hull, recognized one of the fledgling's reflective stickers attached to its stern. The airfoil wasn't the only unusual addition to the patio boat. In the bow she noticed a bright red Weber kettle grill.

"How come you have a charcoal grill if you're modifying the boat for racing?"

"Oh, that's just to distract and confuse people. I welded it to the deck and wired on the top so it doesn't fly off at high speed. Might fool some people into thinking I'm just playing around."

"You're not in this for fun?"

"Sure it's fun. But it's still serious fun. I've been working on the boat in my garage all winter. See those brackets welded to the deck right by your kayak? They're for the two outriggers I'm having built. They'll fold up out of the water when not needed, and I can lock them down when I need one or the other for going through tight turns."

Anne was warming to the man. His enthusiasm for his project was contagious.

"What changes have you made below the waterline?"

The man stopped working on the airfoil and looked directly at Anne. Bending down to shake her hand, he introduced himself.

"Hi. I'm Dave Oliver. We've never met, but I know who you are – Anne something... Doug Bateman's partner. You're with the sheriff's department. I see you go by in that fancy kayak some mornings. How's Doug doing these days? Haven't seen him in quite a while. When are you two getting married?"

Suddenly flustered, Anne had no quick response to the marriage question – which she herself had been mulling over for the past several months. She was saved from having to come up with a response as the man continued talking.

"Below the waterline? I can't do any changes underwater – it's not allowed. I had thought about trying to hide some hydrofoils in the pontoons, but they could easily be detected once the boat rose out of the water on the foils – not exactly stealth technology."

The man paused, looked around in a dramatic fashion, and then whispered conspiratorially to Anne.

"I'll let you in on what is stealthy though, if you promise not to tell anyone."

Anne nodded her assent, and the man continued, clearly eager to brag about his hidden modifications.

"I'm in the twenty-two foot and under category. That's a Yamaha LF150XB outboard I got mounted on the boat. It has a manufacturer's stated one hundred and fifty horse power rating, which is the max allowed in the twenty-two and under class. But that little baby you're lookin at right there is far from a stock one hundred and fifty horsepower. It's bored and stroked. You wouldn't notice any difference unless you took it apart, but it puts out a bunch more horsepower. It's gonna be shock and awe time when this baby gets going."

After a few more minutes of back and forth Anne could tell that Dave Oliver was eager to get back to working on his boat so she said she would be sure to say hi to Doug for him and turned to head for home. The wind started to pick up out of the west, as it often does mid-morning, making the last part of her paddle almost effortless. Doug was up and had walked Jack by the time she returned, and over their standard breakfast of soft-boiled eggs, greens, bacon and blueberries, Anne filled him in on the two boaters she had encountered during her morning paddle.

Doug at first suspected that Anne was pulling his leg - making up the part about finding the Luna moth wings and the subsequent encounter with the fledgling girl. It had to be a joke, he figured – a whopper she was throwing out there to see if he would swallow it.

Maybe she was trying to balance things up a bit. Early in their relationship, when Anne was still new in town, Doug had on occasion trotted out some plausible sounding tales about Dover-Foxcroft that were completely made up, and Anne would invariably believe them, only to learn later that they were fictitious. Doug came to realize pretty quickly, however, that entertaining himself with made-up stories at her expense was not a good idea. Anne's older brothers had teased her constantly when she was a girl, and she found little humor in Doug's fabrications.

Once he realized she was serious, Doug asked Anne to recount her conversation with the fledgling girl several more times, focusing on the Moth Mother, aka the Luna, and the reference to "mother Sebec." It almost sounded like a cult of personality with magical overtones. It also reminded Doug of the elusive command and control structure often employed by right wing domestic militias. A leader would voice general opinions and statements of purpose, often by encrypted social media messages, and individuals and small isolated bands of followers would then act on the wishes of the leader without the need of any direct face-to-face orders or instructions.

"This girl you met – the fledgling. From what she told you it sounds like the Water Rats have been become much more cohesive and likely more radicalized. When I was a teenager, not all that long ago, the name "Water Rats" was mostly just a blanket term, shorthand for kids pulling pranks – randomly messing with people they didn't approve of. Now it seems they're more organized, and apparently have a leader of some sort, as well as a more focused and aggressive plan of action – one which appears to target patio boats with the goal of disrupting the upcoming race."

Doug paused to take a sip of coffee and then continued.

"Whoever this Luna character is, the Moth Mother, it sounds like she's come up with a compelling story line for the Water Rats. And I think your interaction with the fledgling on your morning paddle brings it into better focus. This Moth Mother is smart. She's taken the preexisting informal attitude of Water Rats - their pranking of people, and recast it as enlightened stewardship. This Water Rat stewardship encompasses protecting the lake and its ecological community from bad behavior and embraces a more sophisticated worldview that integrates humans more closely and more responsibly in the natural world."

Anne slipped Jack a piece of bacon under the table, and ignoring Doug's frown, continued with his line of speculation.

"You suspect the Water Rats are like child eco-soldiers – enlisted now in the perennial struggle in Maine between protecting the natural world and the constant pressure for development."

"That's basically it, but Luna's spiritual enhancements are a powerful addition. She's borrowed a lot, I think, from the world view of indigenous groups in Maine – reverence for the natural world and recognition of the important role that humans should play in protecting it."

They headed into work, and by the time they had joined the sheriff and Jack Walker for their morning progress meeting, Anne's internet search during their commute had yielded a pretty good picture of the key role of the Luna moth in transforming the Water Rats into eco-activists.

"I think the Luna moth is their totem, their spirit emblem. It's a quite large and stunningly beautiful insect, but like the Water Rats, it's rarely seen. Lunas are a pale lime green and have distinctive purple edging on their wings, which the fledgling mimicked with her nail polish and hoodie edging. Like Luna moths, Water Rats are also mostly nocturnal. Both deflect unwanted notice– the moths employ eye spots on their wings as well as hindwing tails to distract predators, and the Water Rats use the simple camouflage of blending into the background. The small outboards they move around in are ubiquitous on the lake, and don't draw much attention."

Anne paused to grab a donut from the box on the table and motioned with it as she continued.

"It might be pushing the metaphor too far, but Luna moths and Water Rats also appear for just a short time and then disappear. From what I've read, adult Luna moths only live a week or so, and then disappear for another year. Water Rats only come out on occasion, for short periods, and then disappear back into the background of everyday life."

Jack Walker added to Anne's speculation.

"Maybe that's what was so upsetting to the fledgling – you were disrupting the natural order of things – keeping the moths from disappearing back into the sacred lake, and in doing so somehow interfering with the Water Rats' ability to stay undetected."

Tapping on the table to get their attention, Jim Torben, the sheriff of Piscataquis County, summarized their predicament. His slow measured delivery made it clear to the other three people around the table, who knew him well, that he was not happy.

"This is great news. Really great. Let's see – we have two unsolved murders that may or may not be related to each other. A real estate agent has been run down by a boat. A prominent businessman bringing much needed visitors to our town has been lured into totaling his expensive boat and has ended up in a coma. All of our initial suspects for these crimes appear to have turned out to be dead ends. Our colleague Tom Richard is falling in love with one of our suspects and wasting his time sneaking around another suspect's garage. We have five thousand people coming into town this weekend for the Whoopie Pie Festival, and two hundred or so patio boats will soon start descending on us for the race scheduled just a week later. And now, our latest breakthrough in the case appears to involve a big green moth and a mysterious leader of an eco-terrorist cult. Sounds to me like we are well fucked."

17.

The silence in the room after Jim Torben's summation was finally broken as Jack Walker leaned forward and lifted the lid on the donut box, selecting a traditional cake donut as he added to the sheriff's perspective.

"That pretty much sums things up, boss. Just about everybody will be busy with traffic flow, setting up street closures, and monitoring the crowds and the cash boxes at the Whoopie Pie Festival this weekend. That won't leave a lot of manpower for our murder investigations. But then we don't have all that many leads to follow up on anyway. I think we can parcel up the workload between us and still make some progress."

Doug nodded in agreement.

"Tom can continue drilling down on Nigel's background. If Jack will keep on with the monitoring of Lou Binford, Anne and I can focus on the Water Rats. I have a few pretty good contacts with people who used to be involved in their pranks back when I was a teenager, and I am sure Jim and Jack do too. We should be able to make some headway with the Water Rat alumni. For the younger folks we can start by talking to the Foxcroft Academy students involved in the summer monitoring for invasive aquatic plants. They might have some leads if we can get them to talk. We also need to circle around and have a long talk with Ted Height. Anne and I ran into him in the parking lot at Will's the other day, and he seemed quite worked up about the patio boat race."

Looking around the table, Anne added to Doug's assessment.

"I've been thinking about the Water Rats. They have got to be a quite diverse group of individuals with different degrees of understanding and commitment to what they're involved in. I bet a lot of the younger Water Rats, like the fledgling I encountered, see their little pranks as noble and exciting contributions to the effort to preserve their lake environment and their way of life from harm, from unwanted change. But the pranks are different now. Up until recently their mischief has taken the form of individual isolated acts unrelated to each other except in the most general way – educating people regarding the mores – the customs and conventions, of the local community - teaching people the right way to act.

But now the pranks are coordinated and focused, although the pranksters probably don't perceive much of a change. They are getting guidance from others, and quite probably don't know the identity of the individuals instructing them, other than under the guise of the Luna moth totem."

"And it's the youngsters, the fledglings and recently tattooed," Doug added, "doing all the small stuff, similar to what they've always done – flagpole mischief, unmooring of boats, that sort of thing. Sometimes those fairly innocent pranks are tied to more serious acts, but mostly the other group, the adults, I would bet, are using this background of petty pranks as a cover to carry out more serious stuff – dumping logs in the lake, setting fire to boathouses, luring a fool to crash his expensive patio boat."

"Sounds possible," added Sheriff Torben, "but what does all this pranking, naively innocent and otherwise, have to do with our two murders?"

"Oh, I bet it's all connected," Anne replied. We don't have a clear picture yet, but I think this is all tied into the boat race somehow."

When the meeting concluded Doug called the Foxcroft Academy and got the contact information for the staff member who was directing the summer aquatic plant survey. A dozen students, along with a few older volunteers, had been working the lakeshore habitats in the South Cove that morning, and Doug arranged a lunchtime meeting with them at the beach at the Peaks-Kenny State Park.

They had no difficulty finding the Foxcroft Academy group, who were lounging in the shade, just finishing up their bag lunches. Doug shook hands with Dan Grant, their faculty advisor, and he and Anne both joined the circle of students sitting on the grass. They had agreed to approach the topic of Water Rat pranking indirectly with the students, while at the same time underscoring the seriousness of some of the recent escalations. Doug did the talking.

"I'm Doug Bateman, and this is Anne Lapointe. The state police and the sheriff's office are looking into the recent serious turn vandalism on the lake has taken, and we wanted to ask for your help."

Doug looked around the circle of curious faces, making sure he had their attention.

"I'm passing out business cards with my cell phone number. We're hoping you'll think about contacting us with any leads or ideas you might have about the recent incidents of a serious nature. These incidents are not like the pranks that occasionally occur. I was born and raised on the lake, and I've seen and heard about lots of pretty good pranks that have been pulled off over the years."

Doug recounted a number of his favorite pranks, emphasizing that the perpetrators were never identified: there was the monstrously large inflatable pink swan, an eyesore visible for miles, that had been coated with grease, making it impossible to climb on; the loud late night partiers whose found their lawn chairs high up in the trees the next morning; and his personal favorite – the obnoxious hotdogger who woke one morning to find his jet ski perched precariously on top of his garage. Doug's recounting of past pranks accomplished his goal of relaxing the circle of teens a bit before he turned serious.

"But those pranks, and Water Rat activities in general, are entirely different from some of the recent events that have occurred. Burning down a boat house with classic boats inside is not a prank – it's a felony with jail time attached. A few days ago, a swimmer was deliberately run down with a stolen boat. That's attempted murder, not a prank. And the patio boat crash up at Buck's Cove is also being investigated as an attempted murder. These are not pranking. They're not funny."

Doug paused, saw that most of his audience was no longer smiling, and continued.

"We're also investigating two homicides and are not yet sure how they may fit in with the recently escalating incidents. But we need to talk to anyone who might be able to tell us anything. And just as importantly, we need to get the warning out to the Water Rats to not get drawn into doing things that are suggested by others, even if they seem innocent enough."

While Doug was talking, Anne looked around the circle. She identified the fledgling immediately. She was an attractive girl with short blond hair, blue eyes, and a nervous expression. The girl had buried her hands in the folds of her sweatshirt, but not before Anne had glimpsed her distinctive green nail polish and noticed the purple trim on her hoodie. Anne decided to keep the fledgling's identity to herself. No point in embarrassing her. The girl risked a quick glance at Anne, who smiled back at her and gave her an exaggerated wink.

Anne also noticed that several of the young men in the circle were displaying lake tattoos on their forearms similar to the one that Ted Height had shown them. The teens with lake tattoos didn't seem all that concerned by Doug's admonitions, and were the first to jump up, casually dropping Doug's business cards on the ground as they walked away. Anne also saw a few Luna moth tattoos – a small one on a girl's ankle, and a larger one on another girl's shoulder.

Driving back into town, Anne and Doug stopped at the Bear's Den for lunch and considered their next moves over burgers and beers.

"We're not going to get much out of that group," Doug observed. "They seem pretty set on keeping quiet, even your fledgling had the zipped lip."

Seeing Anne's surprised expression, Doug laughed.

"What? Didn't you think I would notice her hidden hands and the purple trim on her hoodie? Jeez Anne, I am a detective. Good move not calling her out, by the way. She might be able to help us out down the road."

"OK Doug, Mr. All-seeing. How many tattoos were there?"

'That's an easy one, Anne- two lakes on the surly young men, one moth on the short brunette."

"Not bad – you missed a second Luna moth tattoo, but it was a small one and you were pretty busy trying to scare them straight."

Doug took a sip of his Allagash White and replied.

"Tattoos. That's what we're missing. We need to canvas all the tattoo parlors from here to Bangor at least – see if they have any sort of list of customers who got Sebec Lake or Luna moth tats. It might give us a membership list of sorts for the Water Rats."

"Sounds like a plan, Doug. If we get lucky the tat lists might include some of the Water Rat alums – the older ones like Ted Height who would more likely be into the serious stuff."

They stopped at Will's Shop 'n Save to see if Height was working, only to learn that he had decided to take the week off to go canoeing up north of Baxter State Park. Doug got Height's contact phone number from the manager at Will's and tried it several times, but his calls went straight to voice mail.

Jack Walker was waiting for them when they arrived back at the sheriff's office.

"I think I have something for you on the Eastman killing. I know his widow said that he didn't have any problems or run-ins locally, but I figured it wouldn't hurt to check our county court records, and it turns out someone filed a civil suit against him a while back. It was apparently settled out of court a few weeks after his death, but might still be worth a look. The company that brought the suit against Eastman was Ostrum Enterprises."

"That would be Gary Ostrum," Doug replied. "He runs a small construction company out of his home over on Boyd's Lake. I'll bet Gary built the boathouse."

Doug called Ostrum, who chuckled when Doug identified himself. He confirmed the civil suit had to do with construction of the boathouse and wanted to know what had taken them so long to contact him. Ostrum didn't sound at all concerned about their interest. He and his crew were putting an addition on the Hollister place on the south shore of Sebec Lake, close to Parson's Landing. It took twenty minutes for them to drive out to Hollister's camp, and when they arrived Ostrum shook hands and led them over to a picnic table in the shade of several white birches. Ostrum started talking as soon as they sat down.

'Can't say as I'm sorry that the man's dead. He was a real prick. A penny-pinching prick, and a cheat."

"How so?" asked Anne.

Doug broke in before Ostrum could reply to Anne's question.

"How about we start at the beginning. How did you first hear about the job?"

"It was Bob Lutz. He works at Dave's World. I was in there looking at their refrigerators, and he had heard from Mary Payne - she's the sister of Eastman's wife, that the Eastmans were looking for a local contractor to build a boathouse. That sounded like my kind of construction, so I called him up, and he invited me over to look at his plans and discuss the project."

"When did the problems start?" Doug asked.

"Almost immediately. I knew pretty quick that I should just walk away, but he had a big budget, and I needed the work. So I talked myself into believing I could control things once we got into it."

Shaking his head ruefully, Ostrum continued.

"The first disagreement was over the footprint. In his plans, which he had drawn up, the new boathouse was almost twice the size of the original. I told him it had to stay within the original dimensions of the old structure. It could go up. I could build the second story he wanted but couldn't expand the horizontal footprint of the boathouse. He said he was confident he could work something out on the bigger size with Bowerbank officials, maybe after the fact."

Ostrum smiled and continued.

"I laughed out loud at that, which he didn't like, and I pointed out that probably most of the people living in the thousand or so cabins on Sebec Lake would like a nice boathouse too, but they couldn't have one – it's against statewide shoreline building regulations. The only reason he could build one was because there was already one there – he could rebuild, but it had to stay the same size. If he built larger, other people living on the lake would be falling all over each other rushing to complain about his project to not only Bowerbank but to county and state officials. It wouldn't end well for him. He thought I was wrong, but he must have checked with some of his influential buddies after our meeting because he called back a few days later and hired us to do a two-story structure that stayed within the boathouse's original footprint."

One of the men fastening a new red metal roof on the cabin addition called over to Ostrum, who excused himself and walked over to confer with him briefly before returning to the picnic table.

"They gave us the wrong screws for the roof. It's been that kind of a week. Where was I?"

"Boathouse footprint," Anne offered.

"Oh yeah. Things went smoothly at first. Eastman seemed to be always hanging around, checking our work. He was mostly satisfied, I would say. But after the old structure was cleared away and the foundation was in and we started framing, he started doing a constant stream of change orders – adding considerable time and expense to what should have been a straightforward project."

"Let me guess," Doug offered. "Then he refused to pay for all the overruns."

"That's exactly what he did," Ostrum replied. "When it came time for the final payment, which was a big one – almost forty thousand dollars, he stiffed me – refused to pay any of it. I guess that qualifies as a pretty good motive for murder, so I was expecting a visit from you guys. But I wouldn't kill a man for being an asshole – otherwise I'd end up being a serious serial killer, given the number of assholes around these days."

With that witticism, Ostrum began to get up from the table, but Anne stopped him with a question.

"Did you think you were going to win your lawsuit?"

"I was looking forward to it, actually. Eastman probably stiffed a lot of people during his days as a cut-throat developer. He could count on his lawyers to make it so difficult that his victims just gave up as the legal fees mounted. But a jury trial in Piscataquis County would have ended up with a different outcome, I think. Here I am - an honest, hardworking businessman with lots of ties to the local community and a solid reputation as a straight shooter, who gets cheated by a rich prick. Did I mention he was a real prick? And I was asking for a little over a million, the emotional stress it caused and all. I thought I had a good chance of winning."

Anne abruptly changed topics again.

"Mr. Ostrum, do you ever do any SCUBA diving in the lake?"

Smiling again, Ostrum leaned over and placed his hands palm down on the table.

"I heard you guys think someone swam in underwater to torch his boathouse. But it wasn't me. To answer your question – no I don't do SCUBA diving. But my son does. We've been thinking about trying to bring up hundred-year-old waterlogged timber resting on the lake bottom from the logging days. Reclaimed timber is in high demand these days."

"Is your son around. We'd like to talk to him," Doug asked.

Ostrum's smile broadened.

"I can give you his phone number. He's been in California since last fall – he calls it a gap year, I call it surfin, smokin weed, and generally fuckin off. But he's twenty-one and he's a good kid. His SCUBA gear is in the garage at home gathering dust if you want to investigate it."

Anne asked the next question.

"What happened after Eastman was killed – there was an out of court settlement of your suit?"

"Ayup. Elizabeth, who I remembered vaguely from high school, called me up about a week after her husband was killed and apologized for the misunderstanding. She asked how much I was owed, and I got a certified check from her a few days later."

"Were you surprised?"

"No, not really. Elizabeth impressed me as a good person, but I think she had it pretty rough at home."

"How so?"

"Oh, I think she was a handy punching bag for that prick. She kept to herself mostly, but I heard him screaming at her a few times when we were working on their boathouse, and when she did appear at the job site, I saw bruises and once she was sporting a split lip. Like I said, the guy was a prick."

"Did you ever see him hit her?"

"No, I never did."

Doug had the next question.

"Have any idea who might have torched the boathouse or been involved in the Eastman killing?"

"Nope. I haven't a clue."

"One final question Gary, do you have any tattoos?"

Ostrum laughed again, clapping his hands. Several of the workers looked over at the sound.

"You might be on to something there. The only one I have is an old Marine Corps Semper Fi tattoo," Ostrum replied, pulling up his shirt sleeve to display the faded eagle, globe and anchor symbol. "But my son got a Sebec Lake tattoo last summer. A lot of the crowd he hangs out with have gotten lake tats lately. It's a fad I guess, but I have no idea why they're getting them."

Anne and Doug finished up the interview, recognizing already that the Ostrum lead Jack Walker had provided looked to be another dead end. And in what was becoming a frustrating pattern, while Ostrum dropped way down their list of suspects, their interview with him surfaced another line of inquiry to pursue – Eastman's abuse of his wife could be a motive for her or someone close to her to have punched his ticket. They would have to follow up by interviewing his widow and her sister again and pressing the two women harder on their accounts. Maybe Jack Walker had more background on the sisters. They also needed to check with him on how his surveillance of Lou Binford was progressing.

Anne and Doug decided to call it a day, and were looking forward to a quiet evening watching the sun go down and enjoying whatever other entertainment might be on offer – a mother merganser leading her dozen young in parade past the dock, or kingfishers chittering as they prowled the shallow waters, or maybe a low flying float plane eliciting angry objections from resident loons.

When they got back to Doug's Bowerbank cabin on the north shore there was a succinct handwritten note tucked into the screen door. Judging from the purple ink, Anne thought it was probably from the fledgling, and likely foreshadowed a coming uptick in pranking and worse by the Water Rats.

"Best store your kayak in the house from now on."

18.

Jack Walker's surveillance of Louise Binford had so far yielded bupkis. He had focused on trying to match her boots to the print they had recovered from the boat at the Peaks-Kenny cottage after it had been used to run over Ximena in the South Cove. Jack knew that Lou always wore the same footwear - vintage combat boots, and he found a pair like hers on craigslist. Their tread pattern was a match with the boot print found on the boat. He was close, he thought, but needed her boot imprint to provide an exact match. He had tried following her at a distance for several days and waiting for her to walk on soft soil or across a hard surface with wet boots. He knew he had to be circumspect, however, to make sure she didn't catch sight of him. After several days of fruitless following with no success, he devised another way to get her boot prints. Arriving at the roller rink early in the morning, he first soaked the ground at the bottom of the steps leading up to the front door with water, creating an impressive mud puddle that was impossible to avoid. He then replaced the worn carpet scrap on the roller rink porch with a new light-colored piece of carpet that should capture good impressions of any wet footwear that crossed it. It was then a simple matter of watching the roller rink from a distance, waiting for Lou to arrive for work and lay down some nice boot prints as she walked across the new carpet. Jack was optimistic that his plan would work, but halfway expected her to show up wearing flipflops, or to wipe her feet at the top of the stairs just prior to stepping on the waiting carpet.

Lou arrived a little after eight o'clock, and Jack was relieved to see her splash right through the puddle climb the stairs, and then take a few firm steps on the carpet, as if she was deliberately making sure to provide clear prints of her boots for Jack.

Jack waited a few minutes to make sure Lou was settled in front of her computer before slipping up to the side of the porch and recovering the carpet. Taking it back to his SUV, out of view of the roller rink, he was excited to see clear prints of Lou's boots, and took several photos of the muddy patterns. Jack then sent the photos as email attachments to both Doug and to Peter Martell, head of the state police evidence response team, asking for a comparison of the boot imprint he had just recovered with the print found in the Lund boat used to run over Ximena Lapointe.

It took less than a half hour for the text reply to come back from Martell – it was a match. They now had solid evidence that Lou had run over Ximena with the borrowed boat and could be charged with attempted murder. That in turn would give them grounds for obtaining a search warrant for her truck and house in Bangor, which could turn up evidence that she was behind the earlier attempt on Ximena's life that resulted in the death of Don Robertson.

Soon after he had received the text from Martell, Jack's phone rang– it was Doug.

"Great work Jack. Where are you, and where's Lou right now?"

"She's alone inside the roller rink. I'm watching the front door from the parking lot."

"OK. Stay there. Don't take any action. I repeat – watch but don't approach. We need to pull together a team to take her down. And don't let anyone else gain access to the roller rink."

Jack confirmed he had heard Doug's instructions, and looked down at his phone as a follow-up text from Martell popped up.

"Distinctive cut marks on the bottom of the left boot are a clear match with the print lifted from the boat. No question."

Looking up from his phone, Jack was surprised to see Becky Hull, Lou's intern, come around the corner of the roller rink and splashing through the puddle, start to climb the stairs. Jumping out of his truck, Jack ran toward the girl, calling out for her to stop. She stopped on the top step and he motioned her over to the side of the building, out of view. Sensing that something was up, Becky listened as Jack asked her to get back in her car and leave, and then with a quick nod, trotted to her car and drove away.

Inside the roller rink, Lou had stepped over to the window, wondering where her intern was. They needed to go over several of the drone camera flight programs. With a growing sense of alarm, she watched as Jack exited his truck, rushed over to Becky, and sent her on her way.

Lou realized the local yokels must have found some hard evidence for either the run-down of Ximena or the killing of her boyfriend Robertson. Soon they would come for her. Walking back and sitting down at her computer, she said a few "fucks" under her breath and started going down her mental checklist of preparations for a quick disappearance if she ever got in trouble. She had to move quickly, that was obvious. The first problem would be getting past the deputy lurking outside before the cavalry arrived. Once that was accomplished, she would be most vulnerable during the drive back down to Bangor. But once she reached her rented garage over by the airport and exchanged her truck for the pickup truck she had hidden there – the one registered to her new identity, it would be smooth sailing. She had plenty of cash, along with a new passport, driver's license and other identity papers stashed under the spare tire, and a very healthy online bank account linked to her new persona. A quick dye job to get rid of her distinctive purple hair and she would head out west. But first, she needed to pick up a few things from her motel room at the Peaks-Kenny motel and take care of a loose end – Katie.

Outside, Jack stood next to his truck, watching the door to the roller rink, and thinking about how he would probably take shit from his friends for waiting around for a SWAT team. Why not just walk in and take her into custody? As far as he knew she wasn't armed, and anyway, he would be ready if she went for a weapon.

Lou was thinking over her options for how to get by the deputy lurking outside the roller rink when she heard the front door open and turned to see who had just come in. She was momentarily stunned to see Jack Walker in his Piscataquis County Sheriff's uniform letting the screen door slam behind him as he walked toward her. The sun was behind Jack, and Louise couldn't see the expression on his face, but she decided it was not a good idea to take any chances. He had started to ask something about Rebecca Hull when Lou casually slipped her hand into her coat pocket, thumbed off the safety on her Colt 45, and without removing the gun from her coat, shot Walker, hitting him in the right side of the chest. "Nice shot," she thought to herself.

Jack fell backward and was knocked unconscious when his head hit the floor, hard. Lou considered a second shot to finish him off but had seen enough sucking chest wounds during her time in the military to know that even with prompt medical attention he was most likely a goner. And while one shot might not draw much notice, she figured a second shot would definitely draw unwanted attention.

Moving out the door, Lou held the gun down at her side and looked quickly around. There did not appear to be anyone nearby, other than a canoe coming into the marina, so she pocketed the Colt, walked over to her truck in the parking lot, and headed back into town.

Tim Wakeland, who was walking back from the marina office toward his truck, heard the shot, and rounding the corner of the roller rink, noticed Lou's purple hair as she drove out of the parking lot. Curious, he opened the door to the roller rink and saw Jack Walker's body sprawled motionless on the floor. Stepping quickly inside, Wakeland approached Jack, saw the blood, and tore his shirt open to check the wound. Tim immediately recognized the seriousness of the situation. Quickly placing his hand over the hole in Jack's chest, which was oozing bloody froth and producing an audible whistling noise, Tim Pulled out his phone with his free hand and called 911.

"911. What is the nature of your emergency?"

"My name's Tim Wakeland. I'm taking a gunshot victim to the Mayo hospital in Dover-Foxcroft. Let them know I'm maybe twenty minutes out. Chest wound. Unconscious but breathing."

Grabbing both arms of the wounded man, Tim slid him out the door, leaving a wide bloodstain on the floor. Several fishermen rushed over when they saw Tim pull the wounded man out through the front door of the roller rink, and with their help Jack was loaded into the bed of Tim's pickup truck. One of the fishermen drove while Tim knelt next to Jack in the bed of the truck, sealing off the chest wound with a plastic bag.

Just up the road a bit, Louise stopped briefly at the Peaks Kenny Motor Lodge on the way into town, packed up her stuff, and checked out. Glancing up as she paid her bill, she caught a quick glimpse of Tim's truck fly past the motel but thought little of it.

She had driven by Ximena's house on the way into work, and not seeing her truck parked outside, had no idea where she was, and wasn't going to waste time looking for her. She didn't have much time. Her only stop would be Allie Oops in town, where she was hoping to confront Katie and find out if she had ratted her out.

A doctor and several nurses met Tim's truck with a gurney outside the emergency room entrance, and Jack Walker was rushed inside and straight back to an operating room. It wasn't long before several police vehicles pulled up outside the front door and a small crowd began to gather. Sheriff Torben was the first in the door, soon followed by Anne and Doug. They took Tim into a nearby conference room to wait for news on Jack's condition. Tim had just started his account of what had happened when a nurse poked her head in the door and gave them an update on Jack's status.

"He's stable right now, but he'll be in surgery for another hour at least, and he's lost a lot of blood. Another few minutes and he wouldn't have made it."

"When can we talk to him?" Doug asked.

"I'm not sure," replied the nurse. He'll be transferred over to Northern Light in Bangor as soon as he's able to make the trip, and I'm not sure you will be able to interview him before that."

"Is he going to make it?" Anne asked anxiously.

"He was shot once, in the right chest. It's a serious wound but the bullet doesn't appear to have hit any major blood vessels or any internal organs other than his right lung. Otherwise he would have bled out before you got him here. We'll stop the bleeding and see how it goes from there."

"It shouldn't be too hard to find the person who shot Jack," Tim interjected. "I saw them driving away after the shooting, and they have purple hair."

"That's Louise Binford." Doug replied. "I guess Jack decided to take her on by himself."

After the nurse left Anne pulled Doug aside.

"Doug, I think Binford might try to find Ximena and Katie before leaving town. It would be really stupid, I know, but she's crazy enough to try it. I'm going to swing by Ximena's place and Allie Oops to see if anyone has seen Binford, and I'll call Peter Martell to make sure Katie is still down in Augusta."

After Anne headed out, Doug got Tim to run through his account of the shooting, and then followed up by asking him what he might have heard about Water Rat pranks that had been escalating recently. Tim had been a Water Rat growing up in Bowerbank, not too far from Doug, and was able to add to their list a few more recent incidents that had occurred along the north shore of Sebec: patio boats untied from their docks, missing spark plug wires, and life preservers in trees. Nothing really serious, but still more vandalism than usual. Doug asked Tim to keep his ears open and let them know if he heard anything else of interest.

After interviewing Tim Wakeland, Doug called Tom Richard and filled him in on the shooting of the sheriff's deputy. Given the statement by Wakeland that it was Lou Binford that he saw driving away from the scene of the shooting, they now had more than enough for a search warrant of Binford's garage and house. Tom agreed to set up surveillance on her house, put out a bolo for Binford and her vehicle, and get the search warrant application going. The net was closing.

Anne called Katie as she jogged out to her truck, but her call went to voice mail. Next she called Peter and was stunned to learn that Katie had driven back up to Dover-Foxcroft that morning to pick up her paycheck. Anne replied, her anxiety level suddenly increasing.

"Listen, Peter. Lou Binford shot a deputy here in town less than an hour ago, and she's still at large. She may have skipped town already, but it's possible she stuck around and is looking for Katie. I'm on my way right now to Allie Oops. I tried calling but she doesn't pick up. Get on your phone and call and text her and tell her to turn around. Keep at it till you contact her."

There were several cars and a logging truck backed up at the stoplight by the civil war memorial in Dover-Foxcroft, and Anne turned on her blue flashing grill lights as she snuck around them on the right and turned to cross the bridge over the Piscataquis River. Once past the traffic backup she turned off her blue flashers and intently scanned traffic for any sign of either Lou Binford or Katie. Rather than continuing on Main Street, Anne turned left into the parking lot entrance by the Center Theatre. The lot stretched for several blocks behind the buildings on Main Street, and driving slowly through it, Anne could approach Allie Oops from the rear. She was hoping to enter the bar through the rear door but found it locked. Staying close to the wall, she walked quickly down the alley at the side of Allie Oops, and reaching the sidewalk at Main Street, peeked around the corner. There were a few people looking in the window of the hardware store across the street, but otherwise no pedestrian traffic. Anne froze, however, when she saw Katie's truck parked on the other side of the street. Right behind it was Louise Binford's pickup.

Anne called Doug, who told her to stay where she was. "Don't pull a Jack Walker here Anne. This woman is a trained killer."

Doug was on the way – maybe five minutes out, and quickly alerted the sheriff's office to dispatch deputies from the other end of town. It looked like they might have a hostage situation.

Anne risked another look around the corner of the building just as Katie came out the front door, followed closely by Binford, who had a firm grip on Katie's belt with one hand, and held a Ka-Bar Marine Corps fighting knife in her other hand. Judging from the knife's bloody blade, Lou had already used it on someone inside the bar that morning. Katie appeared unhurt but seemed in shock.

Thinking back on it later, Anne wasn't sure why she did it, exactly, but she suddenly stepped out of the alley into view and caught the attention of Binford and her hostage. Binford smiled warmly when she caught sight of Anne, and turning toward her, let go of Katie. Katie slowly slid along the front of the building away from Binford, whose attention was now locked on Anne. Binford, whose smile was now more of a rictus of rage, waved her Ka-Bar at Anne, and crouching into a fighting stance, began to close on her.

Anne reached for her sidearm, but it slipped from her grasp, clattering on the pavement. Lou snarled when she saw this. Rather than retreating, as Lou no doubt expected, Anne flexed her knees, extended her right foot forward, toe pointed toward Binford, and slid her back foot sideways, perpendicular to her forward foot. As she positioned herself in a classic fencer's stance, with her trailing arm cocked up at a jaunty angle, Anne pulled out her steel baton, extended it with a quick snap of her wrist, and leading with her forward foot, took two quick steps and lunged.

Reacting to the lunge, Binford anticipated a high outside attack by Anne, targeting the knife arm. Instead, Anne attacked high inside, thrusting the baton like a foil directly at Binford's chest. The strike was off a bit, with the baton tip catching Lou squarely in the throat.

Given Anne's strong lunge, and Lou's corresponding move toward her, the baton struck with considerable force. Letting out a harsh squeak of surprise, Lou dropped her weapon. Falling forward, she did a face plant on the sidewalk. Anne quickly cuffed her before rolling her over and checking the extent of the damage to her throat. Ignoring for a moment Binford's difficulty breathing, Anne leaned down and spoke softly into the woman's ear.

"Looks like that fencing class my sophomore year ended up paying off after all."

19.

Jack Walker was still in intensive care when they were allowed in to see him the following day at the hospital in Bangor. The surgery had gone well, and he was expected to make a full recovery. He was still quite groggy and disoriented, and Doug and Anne avoided pointing out what a stupid move it had been for him to take on Louise Binford without any backup. Jack had no memory of the shooting or its aftermath, and they gave him a brief recap, describing the race to the Mayo hospital in Dover-Foxcroft and how Tim Wakeland had no doubt saved his life. Jack dozed off a half hour or so into their visit, and they quietly stepped out.

Louise Binford had also been transferred down to Bangor for surgery on her crushed larynx. Stopping on the second floor, Anne and Doug identified themselves to the state trooper standing guard outside Binford's room and briefly looked in on her. Lou glared back at them from her bed. Her neck was wrapped in thick bandages and she was unable to speak. Binford's face was beet red and she writhed under the sheets in rage. Her mouth moved but no sounds came out. Anne managed to lip-read several of the silent curse words and winked at her in response. One of Lou's hands was handcuffed to the bed frame, but she raised her free hand and offered an enthusiastic middle finger to her visitors, who both smiled broadly back at her.

Unfortunately for Anne, one of the clerks at the True Value Hardware store across the street from Allie Oops had caught her takedown of Lou Binford with his iPhone and quickly posted it to his social media accounts. The video soon went viral with the hashtag "Touché," and it made the national news that evening. At first Anne was able to avoid much of the resulting attention by taking a few personal leave days, turning off her phone, and spending a lot of time on the water and with their dog Jack. But as the Whoopie Pie Festival weekend arrived, and everyone at the sheriff's office was needed to help with crowd control and security, Anne was forced out of hiding and for a few hours on Saturday morning had to endure a seemingly non-stop onslaught of well-wishers, reporters seeking interviews, and people wanting photo ops. The University of Michigan, Anne's alma mater, even got into the act, using footage of her fencing lunge to feature the skills she learned on campus and to highlight the real-world applications of the U of M student sports programs.

Anne hadn't slept well the night before. Lying awake in the dark next to Doug, she kept replaying the encounter with Louise Binford over and over again in her mind - the look of calm calculation on Louise's face as she moved in her knife fighter's crouch toward her and the large bloodied blade of the Ka-Bar in Lou's hand. The sound of Katie shuffling away down the sidewalk, and the country music drifting out of Allie Oops. Anne couldn't remember making the conscious decision to take a fencer's stance and to lunge – there hadn't really been time.

For once the weather cooperated for the Whoopie Pie festival weekend, with temperatures in the seventies and clear skies. Doug had never particularly been drawn to whoopie pies – circular slabs of cake, traditionally chocolate, with a marshmallow fluff filling. They were too rich, too sweet for his taste, but lots of people would converge on Dover-Foxcroft in June every year to enjoy a wide variety of creative flavor combinations and vote for their favorites. Bakers from across Maine and beyond were increasingly being drawn to the competition and the crowds of Whoopie Pie Festival weekend. The festival had started out small in 2010, but had grown each year, and now drew more than five thousand people, making it the largest event in Piscataquis County, outdrawing even the Piscataquis Valley Fair. And it wasn't just whoopie pies. A 3K race was held early Saturday morning, a number of bands from around the state provided constant musical entertainment, and the streets were lined with more than a hundred vendors hawking various crafts and food items. There were also rides and games for the kids, a best-dressed pet contest, and of course a whoopie pie eating contest.

Anne was getting increasingly freaked out by all the unwanted attention, all the people who would grab their necks in faux fear when they saw her, and finally found a pretty good hiding place. She sat in the deep shadows at the rear of the main entrance tent for the festival, watching as Kiwanis Club volunteers took festival goers' entrance fees in exchange for the wooden tokens that they could in turn use to purchase whoopie pies from the various vendors. It was a logical place for Anne to be positioned. A lot of cash was coming into the entrance tents for the festival, where it was kept in metal boxes and periodically shuttled under guard up the street to the Bangor Savings Bank. And although she was mostly hidden from view, Anne enjoyed a good vantage point from which to watch the passing parade of people intent on trying the different whoopie pie flavor combinations on offer.

It was getting warm in the tent and Anne was struggling to stay awake when a familiar face came into view at the festival ticket counter right in front of her. Nigel Underwood, fresh out of the hospital and sporting crutches, a bright green leg cast, and two bodyguards, reached the front of the line and handed the cashier his credit card, asking for three admissions, each of which included a set of wooden tokens and a hand stamp. Moving up beside the cashier, Anne caught Nigel's attention, curious to see how he was going to address the loss of his drone queen.

"Nigel. Great to see you up and about. What are your plans for finding someone to take over for Louise Binford? Is there a replacement being flown in from somewhere?"

It took Nigel a moment to place Anne, and he frowned when he did.

"No thanks to you – we've had to scramble. Nobody of Lou's skill level is available for next weekend, but I am hoping that Lou's intern, Becky Hull, can fill in adequately. I've talked with her, and I think she's up to the challenge. What can I say – the show must go on."

Anne had more questions for Nigel, but he quickly moved away into the crowd, flanked by his two bodyguards. She would have to check in with Becky to make sure she was OK, she decided. Scanning the crowd, which was growing larger by the moment, Anne briefly caught sight of Bob Lutz just before he disappeared from view in the crowd. He was saying something to the woman next to him, who looked familiar to Anne, but she couldn't quite place her. The crowd cleared and Anne recognized the women next to Lutz – it was Mary Payne, the younger sister of Elizabeth Eastman. Laughing at something Lutz said to her, Mary leaned up against him affectionately and they again disappeared into the moving mass of festival goers.

Anne thought again about Tom Richard's call late last night. He had information his contact had provided about Louise Binford's military career. She had quite an impressive record, it turned out, of targeted drone attacks on enemy combatants, as well as several commendations for bravery in close combat situations. Her weapon of choice apparently was a Ka-Bar knife, and she was known to be quite good with it.

Along with Lou's prowess with a knife, Anne also thought about just how lucky her baton lunge had been. She had aimed for a center of chest strike - her biggest target area. But Lou had crouched lower as Anne lunged, turning sideways and leading with her knife hand. Anne's planned chest strike ended up hitting Lou higher up than she expected - square in the larynx. It was, Anne knew, an incredibly lucky blow. If the baton, or Lou's larynx, had been just an inch or so to either side, her baton would have slid by harmlessly, and Lou would have quickly closed and buried the knife at the base of Anne's neck, or maybe between her ribs. She would have bled out in a matter of minutes – all caught on camera and uploaded to the internet.

The close encounter with Louise Binford's Ka-Bar had also resurfaced Anne's deeper ongoing worry with what she was doing with her life. Dover-Foxcroft had been a new start for her – and in the time she had lived there, more than three years now, she had grown to feel comfortable in the community. She now knew a lot of the townsfolk, at least to wave to from her truck or to say hello to in passing on the street. Anne also had a group of close women friends, including the sheriff's wife June Torben, along with several of the mothers of the girls Anne helped coach on the Foxcroft Academy basketball team, and a group of women she regularly cycled with.

And then there was Douglas Bateman – her best friend and the love of her life. She and Doug had built a solid relationship – one that was easygoing and full of laughter and far more silliness than one would expect from law enforcement professionals. She had long been confident that they were a pair bond for life. Anne and Doug had never broached the topic of marriage, however, and Anne knew that Doug was understandably gun shy after his first marriage fell apart. She had decided early on to take their relationship slow and steady, and to trust her instincts that while it might take a while for Doug to take the next step, it was only a matter of time.

But last night, lying awake in the early morning hours, having just dodged death in front of a sports bar, Anne realized that her dreams of a bright future with Doug could go off the tracks any time, in the blink of an eye. Slow and steady didn't seem like such a good idea anymore. Anne didn't ask for her current celebrity status, and didn't want it. She didn't want children to shy away from her, or teens to choke themselves and fall down in mock agony when they saw her. Admiration, sure. Respect, of course. Being treated as a solid citizen and a valued member of the community. Absolutely. But right now she felt like a sideshow freak at the Piscataquis Valley Fair – step right up, see the tall woman with a silver pinky where a serial killer cut off her finger. The one seen scuffling in the street with a killer in that YouTube video.

That's the last thing Anne wanted. She didn't want Jim Torben to look sideways at her, wondering if she might be thinking about parlaying her notoriety into running against him for county sheriff next time. She didn't want to have to worry about whether other deputies thought she was somehow special - better than them. She didn't want nut cases seeking her out to try their luck. Things would have been so much better if that stupid clerk at the hardware store hadn't caught her lunge on his camera. And lying in the dark next to Doug, listening to Jack's snores from the foot of the bed, Anne also faced up to the reality of her biological clock, which was ticking away. She wanted kids. A family. A real life.

Hearing a commotion over by the long picnic table where the whoopie Pie eating contest was going on, Anne looked over in time to see a pretty young girl pull her blond braids out of the way as she threw up what appeared to be a considerable number of whoopie pies into the lap of the boy sitting next to her. Unfazed, the boy continued stuffing his pie hole. Anne laughed at the scene, her mood lifting – life was good. Things would all work out. After all, she and Doug were in love.

People moved away from the puker and Anne noticed Doug standing next to the table, deep in conversation with a woman who had her back to Anne. As the woman turned and stalked away from Doug, Anne saw that she was crying, and that it was Beth, Doug's ex-wife. Even crying, Beth was a quite attractive woman, and had picked up an impressive tan and lost a few pounds since Anne had last seen her over a year ago. Anne's breath caught in her throat – "Just what I need right now," she muttered to herself as she left her shadowy refuge in the entrance tent and made her way over to Doug.

Doug saw her coming, and closing the distance between them, pulled her into a tight embrace. Pulling away, Anne scanned his face with concern.

"Are you OK Doug? What was all that?"

"A bad dream Anne. That's what that was," Doug replied, leading her across the parking lot to a bench in the shade. "She sure caught me by surprise. Just back in town. She walked right up and started right in on how fucked up her life is. It turns out that her relocation out to New Mexico was a disaster, and now she's back where she belongs, as she puts it. Did you know that Santa Fe is in the high desert, and it gets really hot in the summer? There aren't any trees, all the plants have thorns, and there are obnoxious Texans playing cowboy all over the place. Everybody lives in mud houses. And her lover man tired of her, apparently, and left her high and dry."

Anne looked away, hiding a smile. She should feel sorry for Beth, but didn't. The woman had made Doug's life miserable and now was back, looking for a shoulder to cry on. Suddenly wondering if Doug might feel obligated to try to help Beth, Anne stopped smiling.

"Sooo, what now Doug?" she asked, with some concern.

"What do you mean?" Doug replied, looking puzzled.

"You know, Beth being back and all."

Doug continued looking puzzled, and then realized what Anne was getting at and smiled.

"I have to admit, Beth is still a good-looking woman, and a master manipulator, I would say. And it does sound like she has had a rough time and could use some support and empathy. But she's not my problem any more Anne. All the time she was spilling her problems and seeking sympathy, I was thinking about how good our life is together, and how different it is from my marriage to Beth."

Doug paused, suddenly gave Anne his best come-hither look, which invariably made her snicker, and continued.

"But now that I think about it, since my ex-wife is back in town and looking fantastic, and clearly wants to rekindle our relationship, it would probably be a good idea if we headed back to my place so you would have the opportunity to remind me of how amazing we are together, and what a great life we have going here in the middle of Maine."

Anne would have liked nothing better than to spend the rest of the afternoon in bed with Doug, reaffirming their strong physical attraction to each other. She was about to suggest an early exit from the Whoopie Pie Festival when a ruckus broke out over by the stage. Inanna, an all-female drummer band from a small town halfway between Bangor and Portland, had paused their performance to watch the drama unfolding in front of the stage. Nigel Underwood was slumped up against the front of the stage with his crutches lying akimbo and his bright green fiberglass leg cast sticking out in front of him. Nigel appeared to have been punched in the face, given the swelling around his left eye and his bloody nose. His two bodyguards, incongruous in their suits and ties, stood in front of Nigel, blocking several local men from trying to kick the downed man.

"You fuckin prick," one of the men screamed at Nigel. "You try bringin one of them souped-up patio boats into Buck's Cove again and you'll end up with more than a broken leg. You'll be needin a wheelchair on a permanent basis, not those crutches."

Anne and Doug hurried over and pulled the three attackers away from Nigel and his bodyguards. Doug knew all three men, could smell the beer on their breath, and figured they were just letting off a little steam. If it had just been a spat between locals, Doug could probably have resolved things amicably with apologies and a stern talking to. But he wasn't sure how Nigel would react. It soon became clear that with the patio boat race only a week off, Nigel would not want to make even the smallest waves in the community. When Doug turned around to get Nigel's side of the story, he and his two bodyguards had disappeared.

The rest of the afternoon passed uneventfully, with Dover-Foxcroft racking up another record attendance at the Whoopie Pie Festival. There were no further fights, no more puking at the pie eating contest, and with the exception of a few fender benders out at the fairgrounds where out-of-towners parked, no more disruptions to an otherwise beautiful summer day.

20.

Sunday morning. The day after the Whoopie Pie Festival, and only five days away from the Friday time trials for next weekend's patio boat race. It was shaping up to be a beautiful sunny day, although the weather for race weekend was looking more and more iffy. Anne had headed out for an early morning paddle and Doug was sitting on the dock, watching her kayak disappear behind Pine Island and sipping from his third cup of coffee. Their dog Jack was snuffling around in the underbrush by the lakeshore, trying to ignore the red squirrel scolding him from an overhead branch.

After running into his ex-wife at the festival the day before, Doug was pretty confident that he had managed to convince Anne last night that the only real reaction he had to Beth's emotional meltdown at the festival was one of relief that he no longer had a role to play in her ongoing drama. He was also quite relieved to have Lou Binford in custody and charged with the killing of Don Robertson, along with two additional charges of attempted murder - for running over Ximena Lapointe with a powerboat and the shooting of Jack Walker. A search of Binford's house in Bangor had turned up canvas tarp scraps in a basement trash can that perfectly matched the piece recovered from the Sebec River that had been used to cover the cabin chimney where Robertson died. And Walker had identified her as the person who shot him at close range. Given the compelling evidence recovered in two of the crimes – the tarp fragments and the footprint on the boat used to run down Ximena, as well as the first-person account from Walker, Binford was facing multiple convictions and a likely life sentence.

Binford's arrest and the resolution of those three cases left just the John Eastman murder on Doug's plate, and he and Anne would be focusing on it this week – circling back to interview the widow

Eastman and her sister again, and also tracking down and talking to Ted Height and other Water Rat alumni who might be behind the more serious incidents, including the Eastman boat house fire and maybe even his killing. Things were definitely looking up.

Finishing his coffee, Doug remembered he needed to check the solar powered battery charger that kept the battery on his seventy-year-old wooden boat charged. The boat still leaked a bit, and without the charger the bilge pump cycling on and off would eventually drain the battery. The charger was working well, but as was often the case, Doug found several other things that needed his attention. He was on his back, scrunched up under the dashboard of his Chris-Craft, trying to figure out why the oil pressure gauge refused to work, when he heard a loud noise coming closer. Assuming it must be a low-flying float plane, probably Babs from down by Turtle Cove, he kept tracing wires and softly swearing to himself until his boat started rocking violently and he could hear waves washing up on the shoreline.

Pivoting out from under the dashboard, Doug looked up just in time to see a patio boat disappear around Otter Point. Solid black, with three large outboards on the back, the boat was traveling at a high rate of speed and passed within fifty feet or so of Doug's dock. At first Doug couldn't quite believe what he had seen. It wasn't so much the size of the boat, or its three huge outboard motors, or even the high speed – it was the total and apparently deliberate disregard for a basic shared tenet of lake communities everywhere –boats should slow down close to shore. It was common sense and common courtesy.

The black patio boat continued west at a fast clip and encountered Anne returning home in her kayak a few minutes later. Anne watched the boat approach, expecting it to slow down and steer away from her, but it did neither, passing close enough that even though she turned and paddled directly into the boat's wake, her kayak was almost swamped. Two middle-aged men wearing the bright red T-shirts handed out to patio boat racers waved at her as the boat passed. Anne flipped them the bird and turned her kayak to watch the patio boat fade into the distance. She hoped they might not see the warning buoys west of Pine Island and end up in the rocky shallows that had claimed many boats over the years. The boat's windshield had carried a red placard with its assigned race number, which Anne hoped would help the Water Rats target it for attention.

Both Anne and Doug were disturbed enough by the behemoth patio boat that they decided to track it down. Anne's phone chirped as they pulled away from the dock in the Otter, Doug's Chris-Craft.

"Anne, it's Jim Torben. Not sure what you and Doug are up to on this beautiful Sunday, but I'm hoping since you're close you could check out the boat ramp at Newell Cove. Apparently there's some sort of disagreement that's escalating. I know it's weird for a Sunday morning, but we received several irate calls already this morning."

"OK Jim," Anne replied. "We're in the boat – looking to track down a crazed patio boat that flew by Doug's place a little while ago. We'll go right by Newell Cove. I'll call and let you know what the situation is after we sort it out."

Soon after they rounded Ram Island and skirted around the rocky shallows at the edge of Newell Cove, the boat ramp came into view. A patio boat, still on its trailer, which in turn was still attached to a large RV, had somehow flipped sideways off the boat ramp and was now firmly wedged in among rocks on the lake bottom. Several men were struggling to try to disentangle the RV, the trailer, and the boat from each other- without much luck. Behind them a small crowd had gathered and was not in a friendly mood. Personal insults and vulgar language were beginning to enter the ongoing conversations around the ramp as Doug pulled his boat up on a small patch of sandy beach and he and Anne approached the angry boaters. Doug heard a familiar voice call to him from the crowd and recognized Dave Williams, whose lakefront lot was adjacent to the boat ramp.

"Hey Doug. Hey Bateman," Dave called out, waving his hands in the air. "Tell these people they can't just leave their trailers anywhere they want. They can't be trashing up my property and parking on my land."

Dave's complaint was immediately joined by a chorus of other cries from the crowd as soon as they realized that Doug and Anne might have some authority to address their anger. A large man sporting a red race-entrant T-shirt boomed out his complaint over the other competing voices.

"Get this piece of shit out of the way. I've been stuck in line for over an hour. There're at least a dozen race boats in front of me waiting to launch, and I don't know how long the line stretches behind me, but this is fucked up. I can't turn around, and this fool has blocked the ramp."

Doug raised his hands to quiet the crowd and offered a solution that seemed pretty obvious to him.

"OK, here's what we'll do." Pointing to the big man, he continued. "Would you walk back up the road until you reach the last person in line. Tell him the same thing you tell everyone else as you work back up the line toward the boat ramp. Turn around, last in line first, then continuing up the line. Drive back down Bowerbank Road the way you came, turn right at the intersection in Sebec Village, and then right again at the boat ramp sign just before the dam. The ramp there is wider than the one here and launching should be no problem. And there is more room for trailers to park there too."

While Doug was calming the crowd, Anne pulled Dave Williams aside and assured him that she would get some sheriff's deputies out that morning to remove the parked trailers from his property. Anne and Doug continued west in the Otter, stopping to check the Merrill's Marina boat ramp at Greeley's Landing, which was active but not backed up. Nigel Underwood was sitting at one of the picnic tables holding forth with a group of men in red T-shirts, his green leg cast stretched out in front of him. Doug went over to ask him how preparations for the race were progressing, and Anne headed for the roller rink to look for Becky Hull and see if she was still involved with the drone coverage of the race.

"Detective Bateman. Just the man I was looking for." Underwood boomed out as Doug approached the table. Turning to his red-shirted audience, Nigel continued.

"This is the man I was telling you about. Douglas Bateman here is the person in charge of making sure nothing and nobody interferes with the race this weekend or with our practice runs the rest of this week. No more pranks. Right detective?"

Doug paused before answering, and stepping closer to the picnic table, took a long look at Nigel, who seemed to have aged considerably since his accident. His face was drawn, his hair dull gray, and his hands shook slightly. Nigel's pupils looked dilated and his gaze shifted nervously back and forth between Doug and the group crowded around the table.

"Sorry to disappoint you Mr. Underwood, but I don't have any responsibility or authority to ensure that things go smoothly this week. I can certainly be called on if any state laws or regulations are violated, and that includes, I should emphasize, boating safety and speed limit laws. Which leads me to ask if any of you know the whereabouts of a large black patio boat that was doing a high speed run this morning. It should have come by here in the last hour or so."

Several of the men crowded around smiled knowingly to each other, but no one responded to Doug's question, which didn't surprise him. Probably the status of the patio boat in question, and its captain, had just increased among the red shirts. Once they realized that Doug was not very supportive of their concerns the men clustered around the table all decided they had other things to do and drifted away, leaving Doug and Nigel alone at the table.

"Is everything OK Nigel?" Doug asked. "Is all going smoothly with the race preparations?"

"As if you give a shit," Nigel replied angrily, dropping the friendly veneer he had presented in front of his small audience.

"Arresting my drone director, ignoring the eco-terrorist attacks on law-abiding boaters, not catching the people who tried to kill me. What are you doing, Bateman, to make sure Sebec gets the patio boat race that will transform it into a first-class vacation destination?"

Doug was a little puzzled by Nigel's comment about Sebec being transformed into a vacation destination by the patio boat race but decided to get right to the questions he wanted to ask.

"We still need to talk to you Mr. Underwood about your relationship with John Eastman. Were you two in business together?"

Underwood reached for his crutches, struggled to stand, and motioned to his two bodyguards who were standing over by the boat ramp, dividing their attention between Nigel and the patio boats lined up on trailers waiting to be launched. They started walking over.

"Not this week," Nigel replied. "Contact my lawyers and set something up for next week. Can't you see I'm pretty fucking busy here."

On full alert now, Doug realized that underneath Underhill's hostility and arrogance, the man was on edge. He could almost smell the man's fear. He wasn't going to get anything from Nigel. But the man might open up if he became frightened enough.

"I'm going to leave you alone Nigel, for now. But keep in mind that I'm here to help if you need it. I'm guessing you're in way over your head and will need to find some way out of your predicament pretty soon – sometime this week I figure. Give me a call."

Underwood was walking away now, flanked by his goons. He turned his head slightly and called a goodbye to Doug.

"Fuck you Bateman."

Anne walked in the front door of the roller rink and found Becky Hull ensconced in front of a cluster of three video screens, guiding a drone on the central screen over what Anne could recognize as the Bear Point Marina, down toward the east end of the lake. Becky turned and saw Anne. A few taps on the controls and she turned to smile up at Anne.

"I put it into hover mode so we can talk. Great to see you Anne. And kudos on your fencing gig."

Anne smiled at the compliment and replied.

"How are you doing Becky? Are you still going to be part of the race drone team?"

"Part of the team, Anne? I'm running the team. I contacted my professor at U. of Maine and she's sending over another two students to work with me. They arrive tomorrow. I'm a fucking star Anne, and I pilot these drones like I was born to it. It's a blast."

"That's brilliant Becky. Sounds like you might have a future in drones. Nigel's not giving you a hard time?"

"No. He barely asked if I was doing OK and hasn't really looked over my shoulder at all. I've been back and forth with ESPN folks a lot though, since you sidelined Binford, and we are pretty much set now on how we will be covering the race. They seem happy with my performance so far, so I guess that's good enough for Nigel."

"And how's Nigel doing Becky? Anything worth our interest?"

"He's been acting really weird since he got back from the hospital, Anne. He talks on the phone a lot, some overseas calls I think, sometimes the conversations get pretty hot – I can't hear what they're saying, but there's screaming involved, and I can pick out foul language now and then. And he's in constant motion, thumping around on his crutches and muttering to himself. It's getting pretty tense."

Anne asked a few more questions, trying to elicit more specifics about Underwood's behavior from Becky, but didn't get anything additional - just that he was tense and skittish. Anne and Doug climbed back in the Otter and continued west through the narrows to the big lake. They cruised around South Cove, Tim's Cove, and the rest of the west end of the lake but saw no sign of the black behemoth. They did, however, discover another race related kerfuffle, this time at the entrance to Bucks Cove. Half a dozen patio boats, all boasting the red signs with race numbers identifying them as entries in the upcoming competition, were crowded around a small ancient patio boat that was anchored directly in front of the narrow channel that provided the only access to the cove.

The race boat occupants, many wearing signature red shirts, were taking turns insulting the single occupant of the patio boat that blocked their way.

"They all want to try their luck at threading the needle where Nigel crashed," Anne commented to Doug. "That coverage on ESPN of his spectacular flip probably did more to publicize the race than anything else they did."

"That's George Olsen," Doug replied, pointing toward the ancient patio boat. "He's gotta be in his middle eighties at least and has lived on Buck's Cove his whole life."

Doug slowly edged up next to the vintage patio boat. Smiling now, the old man lounging in the boat got up, stepped over, and dropping several bumpers, took the line offered by Anne and moored the Otter to his craft. Reaching out to take his hand, Doug stepped onto the patio boat and then helped Anne aboard. The surrounding patio boats all erupted in a new round of insults hurled toward the occupants of the boat blocking their way, prompting Anne and then Doug to hold up their badges, which silenced the insults and lifted the spirits of the assembled daredevils. They mistakenly assumed Doug and Anne would soon be clearing the way for them. But neither Anne nor Doug knew exactly what the jurisdictional complexity of the situation required. Technically, Doug thought, the waters of the inland freshwater lakes of Maine were the responsibility of the Warden Service, which was part of the Maine Department of Inland Fisheries and Wildlife. But while the warden service could enforce fishing laws and general boat safety regulations, Doug wasn't sure they had the authority to make anyone move the location of their boat. And he wasn't aware of any state or local regulations that gave either he or Anne any powers to enforce a "must move your boat" statute, if it even existed.

"Mornin Doug," the old man said. "And I assume this is Anne - the fencer I have heard so much about."

He was courteous enough to not to cover his throat with his hands.

"Morning George," Doug replied. "This is indeed Anne Lapointe – the woman you have no doubt watched on YouTube. I see you have a couple of lines in the water. I would have thought you'd be in your usual spot over closer to Wilson Stream at Willimantic – nobody fishes here."

"Well," the old man replied. "I know that. I got lines in the water but there's no bait. I'm just taking my turn blocking the cove entrance. We got some legal advice that indicated that it's a gray area of the law. See, I'm not actually blocking the entrance. They can squeeze around me here if they go really slow and are careful. But they don't have the room to try any high-speed attempts to run the entrance. We got together, those of us who live in Buck's Cove, and set up a filibuster schedule. I drew today, but all week long and through the weekend there'll be somebody right here with some lines in the water. They might not be really fishing, but if the wardens come around we will have all the required safety equipment, fishing licenses, and boat registrations they have jurisdiction over. And just in case, we checked with Bowerbank – we're just within the Bowerbank boundary line. They confirmed that they wouldn't think of trying to tell anyone where they can or can't go fishing. Not gonna happen."

Doug turned to the crowd of irate race entrants.

"OK, listen up. George and his boat can stay right where they are for as long as he wants. Over there, by that cottage, there's a Sebec Lake website CCTV camera, which is recording us right now and will record any attempts to push George off his fishing spot. Lots of criminal charges could result from any such effort. And the Maine Warden Service is on its way to make sure everyone here, including George, have all the proper registrations, licenses, and safety equipment – fire extinguishers, personal flotation devices, whistles, distress flags, operational navigation lights, tow ropes, all that stuff. And also of course, to check for alcoholic beverages. Lakes are public places, I don't have to remind any of you, and drinking in public is illegal in Maine."

Doug paused long enough to make sure the red shirted crowd had gotten the message, then he and Anne climbed back in the Otter and they continued their search for the Black Behemoth. They passed several other hard-charging race boats on their way home, and when they passed Newell Cove it was crowded with a large group of patio boats full of red shirts celebrating the weekend with happy laughter and loud music.

Thinking of the Water Rats, Anne leaned over and commented to Doug.

"Looks kinda like fish in a barrel."

Anne's augury would prove to be all too accurate in the coming days.

21.

By sundown on Sunday it was clear that a considerable number of race entrants had decided to arrive the weekend before the race and enjoy a week-long holiday with time for practice runs, informal racing, and general merrymaking. A total of about fifty race boats had arrived by sunset. Parties continued till almost one in the morning, with fireworks, loud music, racing outboard engines, and garishly lit patio boats disturbing the night's silence. By three in the morning the last partier had turned in for the night and with the exception of a few loons and owls, silence returned to Sebec Lake.

Ted Height lived on the south shore, a few miles east of Greeley's Landing, and it took him less than a half hour by kayak to reach Merrill's Marina. There was no moon, which made it a little difficult for him to avoid rocky outcrops near the shore, but was perfect for what he was planning. Ted hid his kayak under some bushes near the marina, grabbed the pair of long handled branch cutters and the pole with a hook on the end he had brought along, pulled on his diving mask and flippers, and slipped into the dark waters of the lake. He swam cautiously, flippers moving silently under the surface, hook and snippers held firmly, to the first of a long line of race boats anchored in the marina. Slipping between the massive twin outboards on the stern of the boat, Ted reached up with the pole hook and pulled the fuel line for one of the engines down toward him. Once it was within reach he switched to the snippers and removed a two-foot length of the fuel line, slipping it into a mesh bag tied to his waist. Turning to the second engine, he cut its fuel line in the same manner before moving on to the next boat. Ted worked his way down the row of more than a dozen patio boats, continuing his outboard vasectomies in a deliberate, methodical manner. When he had completed snipping the entire row of boats, he spent another half hour searching out and incapacitating the other race boats scattered throughout the marina, easily identified by their distinctive red number placards.

Ted was looking forward with growing anticipation to the following morning, when he planned on getting an early front row seat to watch the patio boats power up and head out for practice runs, only to be stranded in the middle of the lake when the small amount of fuel in the engine's internal fuel storage tank ran out and there was nothing coming in from the external tanks. Ted had come up with the pole hook and snipper strategy on his own and was pretty pleased with it. The fuel lines could be replaced easily and inexpensively, but it would take a while to obtain new hoses, and the effort and time needed definitely qualified as a considerable inconvenience. No real damage was done to the boats or the engines, and only a day or two would be lost before they were back up and running. Just what Mother Moth had called for.

Alex and Owen Diehl, two teenage brothers who lived quite close to the Newell Cove boat ramp, took a different approach to disabling the two dozen or so race boats anchored in the cove. Rather than snipping fuel lines, they swam from boat to boat, each teen armed with a pair of pliers, a crescent wrench, a clamp-shaped tool called a prop puller, and a bag to collect their trophies. Owen and Alex had both been practicing for a few days, and they now could, by feel alone, in total darkness, use pliers and wrench to first remove cotter pins and lock nuts, and then employ the prop puller to pop the prop off the drive shaft. They got quite good at it after a while, and both could remove a propeller in under a minute. On the boats with more than one engine they would sometimes remove the propellers from all the engines, and on others they would leave one intact. While Ted was looking forward to watching race boats at the marina run out of gas the following day, Alex and Owen would be sitting on their dock and taking videos with their phones of boats moving much slower than usual, or not moving at all.

A few race boats, moored down by Sebec village, suffered a more serious fate. Here, without any direct instructions, a Water Rat alum had settled a few scores at the same time he was targeting race boats. Using a compressed air powered bolt gun like the one portrayed in the movie 'No Country for Old Men,' he punched holes in the pontoons of several race boats as well as his neighbor's patio boat, sending them to the bottom. In other scattered locations around the lake, younger Water Rats had simply untied boats and set them adrift.

Reactions to the events of Sunday night were quite varied. Water Rats of all ages, not surprisingly, were quietly upbeat that it had gone so well. Nobody had been caught or injured and sections of black hose which might or might not be from fuel hose snipping started showing up around town as informal neck wear. The owners of the disabled patio boats, who were understandably angry about the Sunday night attacks, none-the-less rallied in an impressive manner to the challenge. An anonymous phone call early Monday morning to race organizers alerted them to the return of the props the next day. As promised, all of the liberated props, lock screws, and cotter pins collected by Owen and Alex were found in a plastic bin left on the porch of the roller rink on Tuesday morning. By mid-afternoon most of the props had been reunited with their engines and the boats were back in action. Replacement fuel hoses for all the impacted boats were also tracked down by race organizers in various boat dealers across Maine, and by Wednesday morning many of them were also fully operational.

Reactions to Sunday night were not restricted to just the perpetrators and the victims. The story of the coordinated attacks on the race boats spread quickly on social media and by mid-week it had been picked up by national news outlets. ESPN thought it was excellent advertising for the race, while many people in the Sebec community seemed to support the Water Rats, particularly those who had witnessed high-speed practice runs by race participants.

By noon on the Monday of race week, as the full scale of Water Rat pranks of the night before came into focus, Sheriff Torben had taken the lead in coordinating with Nigel and the Kiwanis Club race committee, the Sebec Lake Association, the Town of Dover-Foxcroft, and the Maine State Warden Service to address the dramatic wave of attacks and protect the race participants from further vandalism. Torben also called Anne on Monday morning to ask her and Doug to focus on the Eastman killing and to not get tangled up in the pranking investigation. The sheriff had few expectations of actually discovering who planned the Sunday night attacks or who carried them out, as they looked to be the work of a very few individuals working independently of each other. No one had seen them, or at least no one was willing to come forward, and they had left no evidence behind. With the exception of the bolt gun sinkings, all of the pranks were also clearly misdemeanors, and juveniles were also likely involved. Not exactly a high priority for law enforcement.

After discussions between all of the stakeholders on Monday afternoon it was agreed that the easiest and most effective way to avoid additional pranking before the Friday time trials would be for race entrants to pull their boats from the lake before dark each night and park their trailers in well-lit locations. This recommendation was implemented, and many of the trailers carrying race boats ended up parked in the large lots at Greeley's Landing and at the Peaks-Kenny State Park in the South Cove. This caused long waits at the boat ramps each morning and afternoon but did serve to protect the boats from nocturnal pranking.

The Water Rats had expected just such a mass exodus of race boats to the safety of dry land, and hadn't scheduled any follow-up nocturnal forays after Sunday night. They did, however, have a mid-week second act planned. The parking lots at Greeley's Landing and Peaks-Kenny, where the patio boats were gathered for protection from the eco-terrorists, lacked lighting, but race organizers had established overnight monitoring by volunteer Kiwanis Club guards. Race organizers didn't anticipate any problems, and on Monday and Tuesday nights all was quiet. On Wednesday night, after guards had become a little less alert, it was pretty easy for Water Rats to evade detection in both locations. A half dozen of them flitted silently among the trailered race boats, disabling them using a simple tool.

Instead of targeting the boats, however, they focused on the trailers – specifically the trailer tires. Instead of puncturing the tires or simply letting the air out, they deployed tire valve core removal tools – small, inexpensive and easily discarded. Muffling the noise of escaping air with towels, the Water Rats removed the tire valve cores from all of the trailer tires. New valve cores would have to be installed before the tires could be inflated again. Valve cores could be obtained easily from auto parts stores in Dover-Foxcroft or adjacent communities. Most of the race boat owners opted to wait for new valve cores before trying to move their trailers. Moving the trailers even the short distance to the boat ramp on flat tires could cause damage that might not appear until they were on their way home after the races. As a result, very few race boats made it back on the lake for practice runs until Thursday afternoon.

Following Sheriff Torben's instructions, Anne and Doug called to try to set up a time to talk again with the widow Eastman. After several of their calls went to voicemail, Anne tried the widow's sister, Mary Payne. She indicated that her sister would be out of town until Friday but didn't offer any explanation. She did, however, offer to meet with Doug and Anne and answer any questions they might have. They agreed to meet at two at the Spruce Mill Farm and Kitchen, just across from the hospital in Dover-Foxcroft.

Mary was sitting at a table by the window and waved them over as they walked in the front door at Spruce Mill. She was sipping a cup of coffee and had started in on a muffin. Anne sat with Mary while Doug went to the counter, soon returning with coffee and donuts for the two of them.

"Pretty exciting about last night's pranking," Mary commented with a wide smile as Doug sat down. "Those Water Rats did themselves proud."

"So, you're in support of the attacks on the patio boat race?" Anne asked.

Mary looked surprised.

"Of course I am. My sister and I were born and raised on Sebec. It's a special place. We both love it. We don't want anyone trashing it all up with cheesy shit like patio boat races. What's next – a Sebec Six Flags theme park?"

Looking puzzled, Anne followed up with another question.

"But wasn't your sister's late husband John a big supporter of the race?"

"Sure, John had a boat entered and was involved in the planning. Once again, he got sucked in by Nigel. Their whole lives Nigel has been able to talk John into joining his schemes. John was always a hard-ass negotiator when it came to business, but somehow Nigel has drawn him into a number of fiascos over the years – always big plans and then eventually another failure. I always thought John must be indebted to Nigel for something Nigel did for him when they were kids."

"Nigel Underwood and John Eastman were boyhood friends?" Doug asked with unconcealed surprise.

"Oh sure – they grew up a few blocks from each other in a small town in central New Jersey – I forget the name of it. John and Nigel were best friends all through high school and continued to keep in touch after. But their lives went in very different directions – John became more and more successful as a developer and Nigel slipped further and further into sketchy schemes."

"Is the patio boat race another one of Nigel's sketchy schemes?" Doug asked.

Totally at ease, clearly enjoying herself, Mary answered.

"Oh, I guess so. Actually it could be a lot of fun if it was organized properly. But the abomination they have put together is an affront to everyone who values the tranquility of the lake. All these yahoos roaring around close to shore, cutting off boats that have the right of way, scaring the wildlife. Unacceptable."

"Did your sister Elizabeth share your views, or did she agree with her husband?" Anne asked.

"She strongly agreed with me but would never dare speak up too strongly to John. She loved the man, which I could never understand. You probably know already or will find out soon enough – the hospital here in town certainly has chapter and verse for you if you can get into their records. John was an abuser, almost from the start of their marriage. I could never understand why she didn't leave him, but she didn't. Mostly it was just slapping and an occasional body punch. He stayed away from her face, but he did break her foot a few years ago. He 'accidentally' dropped an outboard motor on it. Her foot never healed up properly. That's the reason she uses that clunky beaver-chewed stick as a cane now."

Doug smiled at that. Each year he would collect dozens of the sticks Mary had referred to along the shoreline of his place by Otter Point. Varying in size from sizable branches, like the one Elizabeth Eastman had used for her cane, to small twigs, such beaver-chewed sticks were easily identified by the distinctive teeth marks at one end, and the ubiquitous nibble marks where the bark had been stripped along its full length.

"She never reported the abuse?" Doug asked.

"No, she never did. I told her many times that she should leave him, but she wouldn't think of it. He was her husband and she loved him."

Glancing back and forth between Doug and Anne, Mary continued.

"I know what you're thinking. My sister had a pretty good motive for getting rid of her husband. But she didn't. I'm one hundred percent sure of that."

"Why so sure?" Anne asked.

"Because I know her. She isn't capable of such a thing. And for some reason, in spite of the abuse, she loved the man."

"When did you learn about John Eastman's death?" Doug asked.

"Liz called me right after she discovered his body. Our phone records should document when she called."

"How did she seem? What did she say?" Anne asked.

"Liz was hysterical – she just kept screaming 'he's dead. He's dead.' Over and over."

"You were at home when she called?" Doug asked, abruptly shifting the focus of the questions.

"Yes. The phone records will show that as well." Mary replied, sitting straighter in her chair.

Doug and Anne both noticed Mary's reaction to the question, and Anne quickly followed up.

"What was your relationship with John Eastman like? Did you get along with him? Did you two ever have words about him beating up on your sister?"

Mary leaned back in her chair and gazed past them out the window at the passing traffic. She took her time before answering.

"I despised the man. He was a puffed-up little fool, no matter what Liz tells you. I avoided him as much as I could and tried hard to fake it when we got together. But I much preferred it when he wasn't around. He was absent a lot before he retired, and things weren't as bad for Liz. But after they moved up here, and he had more time on his hands, Liz became more of a target."

Setting down her coffee cup and picking up her purse from the seat next to her, Mary indicated that the friendly chat had ended. Anne thanked her for talking to them and they both shook hands with Mary as she got up from her chair. As Mary walked to the door, she reached back to free her long hair from her purse strap, briefly exposing the back of her neck. Anne noticed a design of two small fern-like filaments peeking up above Mary's collar. The design looked vaguely familiar, but Anne couldn't immediately place it.

Doug's phone rang as they were pulling out of the parking lot. It was Tom Richard.

"Hey Tom," Doug answered. "Are you and the beautiful Rosemary engaged yet?"

"I'm going to ignore that Doug. But I will say that so far our relationship is developing nicely. And that's part of why I'm calling. I've got some good news and some bad news. Here's the bad news – Louise Binford was taken back to the hospital from jail last night and kept overnight for surgery on her larynx early this morning. But she disappeared from the hospital overnight. Made a clean getaway. The guard outside her room apparently went down to the cafeteria for coffee just after midnight and when he checked on her when he returned, she was gone. Her handcuff was still attached to the bed, but Lou wasn't on the other end. No leads yet on where the hell she went."

Doug muttered 'fuck' a few times in response before asking "What's the good news?"

"Oh, the good news. You can thank Rosemary for this little nugget. We're definitely coming up to Sebec for the races this weekend. But next week we are going in search of the elusive Arctic Char. Apparently it is still extant in some lakes up around Baxter. I know, it's weird, but anyway... Oh yeah – so we pulled out our dog-eared copy of The Maine Atlas and Gazetteer to plan our trip, and Rose wanted to see what Sebec Lake looked like on the map. We found it on page thirty-two, in the upper left-hand corner. The lake extended over several of page thirty-two's map squares, but the north side of the big lake, up by Buck's Cove, was in the corner square – 1A."

Doug waited for Tom to continue, and then realized that he had just told him the good news – page thirty-two, square 1A in the gazetteer, or 321A, was the code used to identify the file on Don Robertson's computer printer that included all the overseas bank account information. In some fashion, the millions of dollars that had vanished from Don Robertson's secret accounts was linked to the north shore of the western basin of Sebec Lake.

22.

The weather was clear on Friday morning, with no wind to speak of. But a line of dark clouds could be seen massing on the western horizon. The time trials for the race were scheduled to begin at eight. The final prank by the Water Rats, however, delayed the start time for almost ninety minutes. They targeted the weather balloon with a suspended camera that had been moored on Pine Island. It was to provide continual coverage of the race boats as they started near Merrill's Marina, powered east and rounded Pine Island, and then returned to the start/finish line.

Jim Lucas, who lived on the north shore of the lake, not too far away, had swum over to the island early that morning. He was an avid open water swimmer who liked to swim in the early morning, before boat traffic picked up. Lucas easily avoided detection by the family renting the island's cabin, and after snipping its mooring cable he watched the liberated balloon and its suspended camera rapidly drift east, never to be seen again. He imagined it continuing its lonely journey east over the Gulf of Maine and being lost at sea. Several people saw Jim swimming in the vicinity of Pine Island right· after the balloon release, and assumed it was just Jim out for his morning swim. The loss of the balloon mounted camera over Pine Island caused a brief panic at the roller rink command center, but Becky Hull, the newly crowned queen of the drones, was quite confident that the loss of the balloon camera was not that serious and that her team could make a few adjustments, bring a few more cameras into play, and actually provide better coverage of the time trials.

Becky might have gotten more pushback on her position, which turned out to be spot on, if Nigel had been present at the command center. But he was, of course, first in line for the time trials in his replacement boat. He was well aware of the line of storms moving in from the west, and the accompanying probability of high winds and substantial waves. Nigel wanted to post his time before things got dicey. The boat wasn't his of course, it was a short-term rental. Nor would he be piloting the boat. Trailered in from Indiana, the boat came with its own skipper, and Nigel was just along for the ride. With three 300HP engines, his was by far the most powerful patio boat on the lake. Doug recognized Nigel's boat as soon as he saw it later that morning. It was the black behemoth that he and Anne had tried to track down earlier in the week. Nigel rode proudly in the bow, with his green cast propped up on the bow rail, waving to the crowd of onlookers scattered in boats along the racecourse. Many of the people watching the time trials waved back, but a fair number also flipped him the bird. The previous week of patio boat escapades on the lake – racing, partying, and just basic rudeness, along with some free-floating hostility by race entrants – fueled no doubt by their frustration with Water Rat pranking, had in turn resulted in many more locals siding with the water rats in opposition to the race.

For the most part the time trials went smoothly. The threatening storms never materialized. Starting at one-minute intervals, one hundred and seventy two pontoon boats completed the out and back course around Pine Island on Friday, with the last boat crossing the finish line a little before one in the afternoon. Nigel's black behemoth was one of only a dozen boats entered in the unlimited class, with another fifty or so in the over twenty-two feet class. The remaining hundred entries were in the under twenty-two feet class, and most of those were from Maine. Becky Hull's drone, stationary, and boat mounted cameras worked well, capturing highlight reel footage which ESPN would be broadcasting that afternoon as promotion for the next day's match races. Although the time trials were completed without any complications, there were two interesting developments.

First, the sixteen entries in the twenty-two feet and under length 'powder-puff' class all objected to the offensive label. Rejecting the attempt to diminish and ghettoize them, they demanded the right to compete with the men. Their demand was easily accommodated by simply adding their time trial times in with the men's times. This combining of classes to create a unisex category of patio boat competition resulted in a compelling story line for the upcoming match races. Alice Delany, of the Delany family, whose women had been perennial skillet throw champions at the Piscataquis Valley Fair, posted the second fastest time in the now combined twenty-two feet and under class, setting up a next day battle of the sexes showdown on live TV.

The second development involved Wesley Fuller's entry in the race. Wes, the ex-boyfriend of Ximena Lapointe and an early suspect in the death of Don Robertson, ran into trouble for below the water modifications of his patio boat. He had driven his boat up from his camp near Sebec Village that morning and had tried to evade the inspection station at the boat ramp before joining the long string of boats lining up single file for their time trial run. Kiwanis Club volunteers watching for just such shenanigans checked his race number, saw that his boat had not yet been cleared, and pulled him out of line. An underwater inspection, watched with interest by the other competitors lined up for the time trials, quickly uncovered multiple modifications, any one of which was enough to disqualify his entry. Despite angry objections by Fuller, he was informed he could not rejoin the line of competitors and would have to talk to Bob Lutz about what was and wasn't allowed below the waterline.

Wes Fuller found Bob Lutz in the roller rink command center about an hour later, talking to Ximena Lapointe and Mary Payne. The time trials were almost finished by then, and Bob, Ximena, and Mary had joined the crowd that had begun to congregate in anticipation of the scheduled announcement of the qualifiers for the Saturday match races.

"What kind of bullshit are you pulling," Fuller blurted out as he rushed up to Lutz. "You can't keep me from racing – I paid my money. I want back in line."

Lutz was taken aback but stood his ground.

"We can't allow you to participate Wes. Sorry, but the rules don't allow modifications, like the ones you made, below the water line. It wouldn't be fair to the other competitors."

"Fair," Fuller replied, "I'll show you fair."

Before Lutz could react, Fuller rushed forward and punched him in the chest. Lutz staggered backwards before regaining his balance. Fuller goaded him.

"Come on little man, show me what you got."

Glancing briefly at Mary and Ximena, Lutz reacted to Fuller calling him out in what initially seemed a rather peculiar manner. Bob used the toe of his left foot to push down on the heel of his right shoe, slipping it off. Lutz then bounced on his toes a few times, eliciting a disdainful laugh from Fuller. The laugh was cut short as Lutz executed a traditional Mawashi Geri – a roundhouse karate kick that caught Fuller on the side of the head and dropped him to the ground. Ximena laughed out loud and others nearby looked on in surprise. Fuller rolled away from Lutz and scrambled to his feet. Holding a hand to the side of his head, he looked at Lutz, thought a moment, then turned to walk away, calling back over his shoulder.

"Next time, Lutz, your sissy kicks won't help you."

Anne and Doug had arranged to interview Elizabeth Eastman at the marina before the announcement of the qualifiers for the next day's match races, and they arrived just in time to witness Bob Lutz's karate lesson for Wesley Fuller. Anne whistled softly, impressed by Bob's seemingly effortless decking of Fuller.

"I didn't expect martial arts skills from Bob. I thought he was the introvert nerdy type."

"He is. But winters here are long. People find lots of things to do that you wouldn't necessarily expect, like souping up pontoon boats, or taking karate at the dojo down in Bangor. I think he started karate in high school, so he's been at it a while. Bob's a gentle guy, but nobody to mess with. And his kick there was pretty gentle. He could have broken Fuller's jaw with a serious kick."

Mary Payne noticed Anne and Doug and walked over to them.

"Hi Anne. Hi Doug. Liz is over at the picnic tables. I'll take you over."

They followed Mary through the crowd that had gathered at the marina, finding Elizabeth sitting at one of the tables, her loon cane leaning against the table next to her. Across from Liz a young man in a business suit pulled together a pile of papers and shaking Liz's hand, walked away just before Anne and Doug reached them. Mary Payne intercepted the man as he walked back toward the roller rink, and they stopped near one of the food stands and talked briefly before he took out car keys and headed for the parking lot.

"I hope we didn't interrupt anything," Doug said after they had greeted the widow and took seats across from her.

"Oh no, That's fine. Just a few loose ends from the estate. Brought that nice young man all the way up from Augusta on the weekend. And I might have to go back down there tomorrow."

"Thanks for talking with us again Mrs. Eastman. It shouldn't take long," Anne said.

"Sure thing," Liz replied. "Fire away."

Doug started the questions.

"Have you thought any more about who may have been responsible for your husband's death?"

"I've thought a lot about it and I can't think of who might have had it in for him,"

Liz replied. "Maybe somebody from the past – he made a lot of enemies in business, and real estate development can be particularly cutthroat. But John didn't mention any difficulties in the last few years. And he didn't have any ongoing litigation as far as I know."

"How about local disputes? Any problems with neighbors, acquaintances, or any business dealings locally?"

Liz paused before responding.

"Well, there was a disagreement with our contractor – John was always seeing where he could save some money. It was like a game with him. It amused him. But I have settled that debt, and I don't expect anything else to surface."

"Can you tell us again about discovering your husband's body the night he was killed? About what time did you find him in the garage?" Anne asked.

"It was maybe two or two thirty in the morning. He often stays up late, and I had already gone to bed. I woke up about two, and he wasn't next to me in bed. So I went looking for him."

"Had you heard anything before you went out?" Anne continued.

"No, not really. I never hear noise from the garage when he's working out there."

"Any unusual happenings in the week or so before that night?" Anne asked.

"No, like I mentioned when we talked before – nothing out of the ordinary."

Switching topics, Doug asked about Nigel Underwood.

"What can you tell us about your husband's relationship with Nigel Underwood?"

"Oh, John and Nigel were very close. Had been since growing up together in New Jersey. He and Nigel talked almost every week. Nigel's a nice man, always coming up with new ideas, new ways to make money. Most of the time John just laughed at Nigel's crazy schemes, but every now and then he would invest in one of them, mostly for the amusement value."

"How about recently, Liz?" Doug asked. "Were they cooking anything up that you knew about?"

"Well…." Liz paused, choosing her words with care. "Yes – they were scheming about something, I'm pretty sure. Nigel and that nice young man who died last winter – Don Robertson, came for dinner at least once a week here for a while there. Ximena was also at their dinners here occasionally. I never heard any of their plans at dinner, but the three men would often go out and sit on the dock after dinner and man talk for an hour or so while I did the dishes and cleaned up. When she came, Ximena would help with the dishes. She's very nice."

"So, you had no idea what their plans were?" Doug asked.

"No, not really."

"How about now? Has anything turned up since John's death that might suggest what they were planning?" Doug asked.

"No. I'm sure there would have been some sort of files in John's office above the boat house, but it was all burned in the fire we had."

"Do you think Ximena was involved in their plans?" Doug asked.

"I wouldn't have thought so. But I can't be sure." Liz replied.

Doug glanced at Anne, who picked up the questioning.

"Did you ever contemplate getting a divorce because of your husband's physical abuse?"

Liz was silent for a while, clearly not pleased with the question. Finally, she replied.

"Early on I thought about it. But John was a good man, and it wasn't that frequent. Marriage isn't always easy. He had a temper and I learned to live with it."

Anne had more questions, but the PA system suddenly came to life, and a voice indicated that the time trial results and the pairing for the match races tomorrow was about to be announced. Nigel Underwood stepped up on the front porch of the roller rink and took the microphone from Bob Lutz.

"Welcome. Welcome. I hope everyone enjoyed the time trials today, which I am sure you will all agree were a huge success. You must all be hungry after the races, and we have lots of different food choices for you to pick from in the food stalls set up around you, all run by Kiwanis Club volunteers, so please get something to eat. I have the results of today's races here, as well as the pairings for tomorrow. So let's get to it."

Nigel read through the time trial results, and Anne recognized the name of the competitor who would be going up against Alice Delany in the twenty-two feet and under category first thing tomorrow morning – it was Dave Oliver, the guy who had fashioned an airfoil and outriggers for his patio boat and done a few unallowed modifications to his motor. Anne smiled as she realized that Oliver had avoided detection so far. Nigel's boat made the cut, of course, and there were a few boos from the crowd when the unlimited category match race pairings were announced. Rich people from away were never that popular.

Doug expected Nigel to conclude his remarks after announcing the pairings for tomorrow and the changes in the racecourse necessitated by the Buck's Cove blockade. But Nigel continued holding the microphone, and nervously cleared his throat before continuing.

"I also wanted to share with you today some very exciting news about a new development project that promises to transform Sebec Lake into something spectacular, which I am sure will thrill all of you as much as it does me."

Nigel paused here for dramatic effect as he gazed out across the crowd.

"There are still a few details to work out, but in the next few weeks we will be formally announcing the creation of a new community on the north shore of Sebec Lake. It's called Club Borestone and will extend along about two miles of shoreline east of Buck's Cove. Right now the land is undeveloped, neglected, and woefully underutilized. We've been in discussions for some time with the timber conglomerate Weyerhaeuser, which owns all that unused shoreline and thousands of acres back into the forest, and will be finalizing the acquisition of the land for Club Borestone within a week or two. We were hoping to be able to announce the completion of the deal today, but these complex negotiations take time."

Nigel did not seem to notice the shocked expressions on many in the audience, and continued with his announcement.

"Club Borestone will be like other so-called mega-resorts such as the Yellowstone Club in Montana and Club Intrawest in Tremblant, Quebec. Right now there are less than a dozen such resorts across the country, and we believe that Club Borestone will outshine them all."

Nigel paused to allow the outpouring of excitement he expected would erupt at his news about the planned development, but the crowd seemed stunned into silence. Nigel hurried on.

"And here's the good news. It's not going to impact the lake or the people who live around it very much at all because it's going to be completely private and pretty much self-contained. It will have its own airport, which will be an expansion of the small Two Falls airstrip that exists nearby now. There will be a marina developed on Bear Pond, with a channel cut through to Buck's Cove for access out into the lake, along with a community center and fitness facility. We're not sure yet how many vacation homes will be built, but the construction boom will bring hundreds of jobs to the area. There will be a golf course, miles of nordic ski trails and snowmobile trails, and we are hoping to develop a small downhill ski area. All in all, it will transform Sebec Lake forever. Property values are bound to go up, Bowerbank gets a huge increase in real estate tax revenue, and it will put Sebec on the vacation destination map."

Nigel paused again to consult his notes and was about to continue with more on the wonderful mega-resort for the ultra-rich that would be coming to Piscataquis County, but was interrupted when a chilidog thrown from the crowd hit him square in the face. As Nigel retreated back into the safety of the roller rink, the crowd broke up into small groups of angry conversation as people tried to come to grips with what Nigel was laying out as the future of the Sebec Lake community.

Doug's jaw dropped and Anne covered her face with her hands at the news. Doug glanced across the table at Liz Eastman, who returned his gaze, smiled sadly, and confirmed what he had suspected, but was afraid to acknowledge.

"Now you know what Nigel and my late husband were planning."

23.

By the next morning Doug and Anne had finally absorbed the reality of the planned Borestone Club and how it would forever alter the lake and its community. But they still had trouble accepting that they had somehow failed to see what was right in front of them. It appeared that they had been lied to by more than a few people.

"Did you see who joined the widow Eastman after we talked to her at the marina?" Doug asked, "Her sister Mary, and Bob Lutz, and Ximena – all causally sitting at the picnic table and chatting like Club Borestone was no big surprise. They must have been in on it from the get-go, and all the time keeping it quiet."

"It sure looks like it," Anne replied. "And how did we miss it? All the pieces of the plan were there. I don't know who came up with the idea of a resort development, but we knew John Eastman had a long career developing high end real estate. Nigel likely came up with the idea of the patio boat race as a way of advertising for the new ultra-rich private club. Don Robertson handled the money laundering- no doubt he was the conduit for oligarch investments. Bob Lutz was the inside man who handled the Kiwanis Club and organizing the race, and Ximena could have been instrumental in bringing the property acquisition possibility to their attention. She's been doing real estate up here for years. And I think meek Elizabeth and her sister Mary enjoyed being along for the ride, or maybe they were just afraid to say anything."

"And Eastman and the rest likely got inspiration for their Club Borestone scheme from the attempt by Plum Creek to build a huge vacation resort on Lily Bay up at Moosehead Lake," Doug continued. "Those plans died due to the recession of 2008, but this time it looks like it's going to happen. I looked up those two places Nigel mentioned. Both are private enclaves for the ultra-rich –

condos at that Club Yellowstone in Montana cost maybe nine million dollars, and the homes start at twenty million or so. Nigel was certainly right that Sebec will be transformed forever, but not in a good way."

The mood was somber at Merrill's Marina when they arrived for the Saturday match races. Many of the race entrants who had failed to make the cut had departed the day before, no doubt because of the dramatic shift in mood after Nigel's announcement about the Borestone Club. What had been a jolly, boisterous crowd, busy eating the brats and burgers sold at the Kiwanis Club food booths and enjoying the beautiful summer day, had abruptly turned quiet and taciturn, and increasingly less friendly to race entrants that weren't locals – those 'from away.' People were angry. Their dog Jack, however, was having a wonderful time going from food booth to food booth, hustling for handouts.

The morning's first race was the battle of the sexes match between Alice Delany and Dave Oliver. It turned out to be the most exciting contest of the day. The course started near the marina, and Alice and Dave were neck in neck as they roared through the narrows and then slalomed through a winding course of buoys west almost to Tim's Cove. The wind had come up out of the northwest just before they started, and the two patio boats were plowing into two-foot-high waves with whitecaps. Dave's airfoil seemed to give him an edge in the rough water. He was a good four or five boat lengths ahead when they finally reached the final buoy in the slalom portion of the course and turned south toward South Cove. He continued to maintain his lead around a final buoy near the beach at Peaks-Kenny State Park, but Alice slowly ate into his lead during the return leg of the race. She had almost caught up with him by the time they reached the narrows again, where all of Dave's dreams of victory suddenly vanished. He had deployed his port outrigger when he rounded the buoy at Peeks-Kenny, and he couldn't get it fully retracted after the turn. As Dave and Alice raced back toward the narrows his port outrigger remained stubbornly only a foot or so above the waves. It didn't look like the stuck outrigger was going to cause any problems, only occasionally slapping the tops of waves, until the boats reached the midpoint of the narrows. The water here was quite choppy, and the damaged outrigger that Dave had been watching nervously suddenly drilled into a wave, pitching his patio boat into a chaotic cartwheel before it landed upside down in the shallows. Alice motored slowly up to Dave's boat and hauled him out of the water. He was unhurt, except for his pride, and no doubt he was already thinking about next year.

The other races were not as close, or as exciting, and went off uneventfully until the last match race of the day, which pitted Nigel Underwood against another entry from Indiana – another triple hull Manitou designed for high speed and costing north of a hundred grand. Nigel's professional driver surged off the starting line and had opened up a two-boat lead before they even reached the narrows. By the time the two boats had traversed most of the course and reappeared back through the narrows his lead had grown to more than six boat lengths. Nigel appeared to be cruising to an easy victory. He began waving to the crowd in triumph. His driver put the hammer down, wanting to wow the crowd with the boat's acceleration, and Doug heard gasps of awe from people close to him. Doug also heard someone near him quietly chanting a strange mantra in a sing-song manner – "Wait for it. Wait for it. Wait for it."

Seemingly in response to the mantra, Nigel's boat suddenly lost power and slowly drifted to a stop. The other Manitou quickly caught up and passed Nigel and roared across the finish line, only fifty yards or so from where Nigel's boat sat dead in the water. Doug looked around for the source of the magical mantra he had heard and noticed Bob Lutz and Mary Payne standing behind him, smiling at each other and sharing a high-five. Doug thought he saw Bob slip what looked to be a garage door opener into his pocket. Bob saw Doug looking at him and pulled the remote out of his pocket again. Holding it up so Doug could get a good look at it, Bob explained.

"You can turn lots of things on, or off, with one of these, Doug. I got this one off of Amazon. Adding the cutoff control device to Nigel's boat was a bit of a challenge, but the Water Rats got it done."

The assembled crowd jeered as two Water Rats in their small outboards towed Nigel's disabled patio boat to the boat ramp. They apparently had been standing by in anticipation of Nigel's engine problem. Grabbing his crutches and clearly enraged, Nigel was helped off the boat. He started swinging his green leg cast and hobbling toward the roller rink and the microphone that waited for him. He had almost reached the steps to the roller rink when one of his bodyguards stopped him and whispered in his ear. All the color drained from Nigel's face, and he sagged on his crutches. His bodyguard put his arm around Nigel, supporting him and leading him quickly away from the roller rink and toward the parking lot. Nigel and his bodyguard got into a black SUV, which quickly left the lot and headed east back toward town.

Watching the SUV depart, Anne wondered if Nigel would end up like the weather balloon that had floated above Pine Island – cut loose and drifting off east, never to be seen again. Nigel did in fact resurface, however, late that year. His body was found floating in a sewage lagoon in New Jersey. The corpse was badly decomposed but still showed signs of torture, including missing digits and teeth. Someone apparently was not swayed by any explanation Nigel had offered for how the plans for Club Borestone collapsed that beautiful Saturday afternoon in central Maine.

Puzzled by Nigel's abrupt departure, Doug turned to ask what Anne thought was going on. As he did so he was further surprised to catch sight of Mary Payne standing over by the roller rink talking to Bob Lutz and Ximena. There was no sign of Liz Eastman. She must have had to head back down to Augusta to sort out estate stuff, he thought. Mary was wearing a one-piece purple bathing suit and had her back to him. A tattoo of a pale green Luna moth covered most of her upper back, it's twin antenna extending up the nape of her neck. Stunned, he leaned over and whispered in Anne's ear as he pointed to Mary.

"Mother Moth is revealed."

This third surprise of the morning, following Nigel's defeat and abrupt departure and Mary's moth tattoo, came a few minutes later during the award ceremony. Bob Lutz was congratulating Alice

Delany and handing her the twenty-two feet and under winner's trophy when Rebecca Hull came tearing out of the roller rink where she had been orchestrating the drone coverage of the races. She yelled excitedly to the crowd.

"Ya gotta see this. Ya gotta see this."

Waving her arms and dancing a little dance, she disappeared back into the roller rink.

Lutz stepped aside as people pushed past him and followed Rebecca back into the patio boat race command center. Becca and her interns were sitting on the floor, glued to the large flat screen monitor used for drone videos, which was now showing the feed from one of the local TV stations out of Bangor. As Anne came up behind her, Betsy looked back at her.

"We were watching the Red Sox game, Anne, but the broadcast was interrupted for this.

It wasn't immediately clear what was being shown on the screen. Doug recognized the Maine State Capitol building in the background and a lectern carrying the state seal was centered in the foreground. As if on cue, the governor of the state of Maine stepped up to the podium, arranged a few papers in front of her, and began to address the assembled crowd and the TV audience. She was clearly in a good mood.

"Good afternoon. First let me apologize for the lack of advance warning about today's event. This all came together just over the last few days and I didn't want to delay the remarkable good news even another day. Particularly given the recent unfounded rumors that have been swirling around."

Pausing briefly, gathering her thoughts, she continued.

"Today I am pleased to announce a landmark three-way agreement between the Weyerhaeuser company, the Eastman Foundation, and the state of Maine. A few days ago, Weyerhaeuser transferred over twenty thousand acres along the north shore of Sebec Lake to the Eastman Foundation."

Pausing to allow the news to sink in, the governor continued.

"The Eastman Foundation yesterday in turn donated the entire parcel of land they acquired from Weyerhaeuser to the state of

Maine, to be added to our public reserved lands as a nature preserve. This donation of land by the Eastman foundation continues a very hopeful trend in central Maine, exemplified by Roxanne Quimby of Burt's Bees fame, of setting aside privately-owned lands for the public good."

Pausing again, the governor turned to look at several people standing behind her before continuing. The small group crowded around the screen in the roller rink took the opportunity to exchange excited glances and high fives.

"At this time, I would like to introduce Elizabeth Eastman, President of the Eastman Foundation, who has asked to say a few words."

Elizabeth moved to the lectern and joined the governor, her loon cane thumping with each step. She looked nervous as she started to speak.

"I just wanted to thank the governor and her team for all of their efforts to make sure that our negotiations with Weyerhaeuser reached a successful conclusion. And I also wanted to say a few words about my late husband John Eastman, who was the inspiration and the driving force behind this initiative. I wish John was alive today to share this moment with us. John was a lovely man and he cared very much for Maine's environment and its beautiful inland lakes. In particular, John fell in love with Sebec Lake and its people, and I am very pleased that the newly established nature preserve will carry his name. Without John, none of this would have happened. I know he would be thrilled with what we are celebrating today."

Liz turned the microphone back over to the governor, and the broadcast concluded a few minutes later.

Mary Payne had moved up beside Doug as Elizabeth was speaking on the TV and now spoke to him in a low voice.

"Now that's one of Liz's better whoppers. And she has had some good ones. John couldn't wait to rip up that forest, build huge homes for the ultra-rich, and make lots of money for himself. Liz has done just the opposite of what he was working toward. If John was here today, he would no doubt have a stroke. Liz tried for months to get him to drop the Club Borestone development scheme that Nigel and Don Robertson pitched to him. But he wouldn't budge. John got what he deserved."

Doug's reply was succinct as he stared at Mary.

"Looks like lots of people around here have been telling whoppers, Mary."

Bob Lutz managed to hand out the rest of the race awards against a rising background noise of celebration over the dramatic turn of events. A keg of beer mysteriously appeared adjacent to one of the Kiwanis food booths, and for the rest of the afternoon no one made any effort to enforce, or even acknowledge, the state law against drinking in public. Only a few people got fall down drunk. Dan Grant, the biology teacher at Foxcroft Academy who ran the summer program for high school students monitoring Sebec Lake for invasive aquatic plants, was one of them. Late in the afternoon he staggered over to where Doug and Anne were sitting at a picnic table learning more from Mary Payne, Bob Lutz, and Ximena Lapointe about the plan to scuttle the Club Borestone scheme.

"I must be dreamin," Dan Grant managed to blurt out, sloshing beer from his plastic cup on their table. Realizing who was sitting at the table, Grant made a supreme effort to appear sober, and did a pretty good job as he continued.

"We just got a huge chunk of money from that Eastman Foundation to expand our study of Sebec Lake. We'll be establishing new labs, new ecology courses, and new grant programs to attract university researchers to come to Sebec Lake, bring their students, and involve our youth in their work."

Another well lubricated teacher from Foxcroft Academy materialized next to Dan and started pulling him away. Grinning now, sloppy drunk, Dan yelled back at the table as he disappeared into the crowd.

"We're gonna call it the Luna Labs."

Doug was relieved when Dan staggered off. He and Anne had been trying to pry information out of Ximena, Bob, and Mary for several hours and were just starting to get to the good stuff. After the third beer Bob started loosening up, and Mary and Ximena soon were adding their own comments, amid much laughter and high spirits. Doug and Anne had been nursing their own beers and quietly topping off their companion's glasses, and as the afternoon wore on, and the beer kept flowing, they managed to get most of the story.

Nigel had been up spending a weekend with the Eastmans a few summers ago, Bob explained, and one afternoon he and John had taken out one of John's vintage boats for a ride around the lake. Nigel's eyes lit up when he and John cruised past the undeveloped north shore just east of Buck's Cove, and he floated the idea of a mega resort. John Eastman, bored without a project, immediately signed on, and Nigel suggested they approach Don Robertson. Nigel had used Don in previous schemes and knew that he had connections that could provide overseas investment cash for real estate acquisition. The overseas investment, of course, was dark money in need of laundering through real estate ventures like theirs, which didn't bother the three plotters.

Ximena picked up the story from there. The three plotters – Eastman, Robertson, and Underwood, were careful to keep their plans quiet, but Nigel in his enthusiasm would get careless during the long and alcohol-fueled dinners that John Eastman hosted that summer. Both Elizabeth Eastman and Ximena soon suspected what they were up to. Both women were appalled, and after exchanging shocked glances across the dinner table on several occasions, they shared their concerns with each other. Ximena and Elizabeth then hatched a plan of their own, hoping they could talk some sense into their partners. Ximena thought she had been making some progress with Don when Louise Binford complicated things by inadvertently killing him in her effort to do away with Ximena.

"Unfortunately," Ximena continued, "John Eastman was able to access the dark funds from the overseas accounts Don had set up, and he successfully transferred them to his own accounts. Club Borestone was back on track once Eastman had the needed funds in his own accounts. But with his death, his estate, and his accounts, passed to his window, Elizabeth."

Mary took up the story then. She knew someone who could put Liz and the foundation in touch with the right people at Weyerhaeuser, and when they immediately warmed to the three-way deal, state officials quickly signed on. It was a three -way win, all parties agreed.

When Mary finished the story Anne and Doug asked a few questions to resolve some minor loose ends, and then Doug looked around the table and raised the final loose end, which was a big one.

"So, the only unanswered question then, is who killed John Eastman?"

No one spoke until Ximena broke the silence.

"One of the Water Rats told me she thought he was killed by a loon. That's pretty silly."

"Maybe not," Anne said, looking around the table.

She was about to say more, but Doug placed his hand on top of Anne's on the table and interrupted.

"Probably not such a good idea to talk about a still open homicide investigation in public. I should not have brought it up."

Smiling broadly now, Doug started to get up from the table and Anne followed, quickly coming up with an excuse for their sudden departure.

"You're right Doug. And we need to get home and feed our dog."

24.

Anne had realized her mistake as soon as Doug interrupted her. They still didn't know who was involved in John Eastman's killing, and it could have included one or more of the people who were sitting with her at the picnic table. She started to apologize as soon as they had rounded up their dog and climbed into her truck, but Doug interrupted her again.

"OK Sherlock, lay it out for me."

Relieved, and eager to see what Doug thought, Anne outlined her still half-formed suspicions as she drove back toward town.

"Elizabeth Eastman is no meek little housewife who tolerated her husband's abuse and womanizing. I think she had planned this from way back. Her sister Mary is also involved, I would bet, and Mary's partner Bob Lutz. When Liz's loving husband dropped that outboard motor on her foot, ensuring she would need a cane for the rest of her life, I think Liz decided to have a cane custom made – a clunky thick cane that one day she could use to cave his head in. And the cane, with its loon-head handle and beaver-stick shaft, also served as a symbolic instrument of revenge for the hideous transformation that Eastman, Underwood, and Robertson were planning for Sebec Lake."

Anne slowed to let a logging truck pull out from a side road and then continued.

"Liz must have somehow found out that her husband had managed to transfer the dark money from Robertson's Deutsche Bank accounts into his own account, and that she and her sister's dream of saving the north shore from development was now within reach. With her husband gone, the money would be Elizabeth's to manage. So she followed him when he walked out to work on his boat that night and buried the loon-head handled cane in the back of his skull."

"How did she get him into the garage?" Doug asked. "There were no footprints or marks on the floor."

"Mary likely helped her carry him, or maybe Lutz." Anne responded. "Once they had him positioned under the patio boat, they propped it up with the sturdy loon cane. Then they removed the original stand supporting the boat, and when they kicked the cane out, the pontoon dropped on his head. If we measure it, I bet the cane is in the thirty-seven to forty-inch length range that Peter Martell estimated."

Anne paused briefly before continuing.

"And I bet that Mary and Liz learned that we knew Eastman had been murdered within hours of us figuring it out. While we were driving over to Monson to interview them, someone, my money is on Ted Height, had already been contacted and was on his way to burn Eastman's boathouse and destroy any evidence that might implicate them."

"But they would have had to set up the Eastman Foundation almost overnight in order to head off the Borestone Club plans." Doug responded.

"Not necessarily. I bet if we check we will find that the foundation was set up years ago. Probably at Elizabeth's urging. Liz and Mary could have been hoping to change Eastman's mind at some point and talk him around to donating the land to the state rather than developing it."

"You have motive and opportunity, Anne, now all you need is proof. Where's your evidence? We didn't find anything at the crime scene, and Eastman's skull was turned into a pancake by that patio boat – we won't find a nice loon shaped hole in the back of his head. I doubt the cane would have any remaining blood or bits of brain remaining on it, and if it's in the length range you mentioned, so what? Unless some of the others who may have been involved decide to spill their guts to us, or Elizabeth decides to confess, we have nothing to work with."

Anne frowned in agreement.

"Yeah, I know. We got nothin."

"How about this." Doug replied. "I'll meet with my boss, Stan Shetler, along with someone from the criminal division of the attorney general's office. I'll run all this by them. Let's see what they think."

"We both know what they'll say Doug. If we tell them we think the director of a major foundation here in Maine, who has just spent tens of millions of dollars of her foundation's money in donating a huge chunk of prime real estate to the public trust, has also committed a murder, they're gonna want to see some pretty convincing hard evidence to back up our suspicions."

"Which we don't have." Replied Doug. "We might be able to make a case if we push hard on the investigation, but I don't think we'll get far. And any ongoing investigation could definitely throw a monkey wrench into the deal between the Eastman Foundation and the state. And if course there's also the town to keep in mind. Elizabeth Eastman is close to beatification status now – she saved Sebec Lake from the forces of evil. If we go after her, the community will support her and turn against us in an instant."

"That's for sure." Anne replied. "And what about the environmental groups and the politicians. I doubt the attorney general's office would be keen on pressing the case, even if we did come up with strong evidence."

They drove in silence for quite a while until Doug summed things up.

"I'll set up an appointment with Shetler for tomorrow and talk to him face to face. No phone calls, no emails or texts on this – strictly face to face. My prediction – he's going to shit his pants and tell me to immediately and forever cease any unfounded rumors about one of our most outstanding citizens being a murderer. Period. End of discussion."

Doug met with his boss Stan Shetler and a representative from the attorney general's office later in the week, and his prediction was borne out. Doug was given clear instructions to waste no more time or effort on actively pursuing the Eastman murder. There were other more pressing matters. If new evidence fell into his lap, or if

Elizabeth Eastman or an accomplice confessed, then he could move forward. Otherwise, leave it alone.

. . .

Things pretty much got back to normal on Sebec Lake after the patio boat racers departed. In late July Bob Lutz announced that the Sebec Lake Association and the Kiwanis Club had reached agreement with ESPN on holding the fourth annual Sebec Patio Boat Challenge the following summer. Several open meetings had been held to solicit public comment, and the final plans involved moving the race entirely to the big lake – west of the narrows. The boat traffic and number of lakeshore cabins was much lower on the big lake, and by keeping the racecourse restricted to the center of the west basin there would be much less impact on the local community.

Next year the staging area for the race would be shifted from Merrill's Marina at Greeley's Landing over to Peaks-Kenny State Park. The fifty- six camp sites at the park would be reserved for race participants on race weekend. That wouldn't accommodate all of the patio boat racers of course, and camp sites would be allotted on a first come, first served basis. Two hundred entries would be allowed again, with the overflow RVs and campers going to the Piscataquis Valley Fair Grounds. There would be only two classes of boat entries –those over twenty-two feet in length, and those twenty-two feet or less. Horsepower limits would stay the same. There would be no unlimited category of entries, no fat cat racers from away. There would be no powder puff class, and Alice Delaney was looking forward to defending her title in the unisex under twenty-two-feet class.

The race would also have a new logo – a Luna moth, which would appear on all the announcements and advertisements, and underscored the expectation of an absence of Water Rat pranks targeting race entrants. As for the Water Rats – through the summer the nature and number of their pranks returned to what they had been pre-race, with a single notable exception.

At about two in the morning on a Saturday night in mid-August, at the peak of vacation season, Doug and Anne woke when their dog Jack started barking from the foot of the bed. He had been disturbed by a light coming in the lakeside windows of Doug's place on the north shore. When they looked out their bedroom window a bright light in the middle of the lake, a fire, was oddly moving slowly past their dock, illuminating Doug's vintage Chris Craft as it past. Doug ran down to the dock and tried to start his boat, with no success. The next day he would find the distributor cap for his boat sitting on the dashboard of his jeep, where he would be sure to find it.

Looking out at the passing blaze, Doug realized it was a burning boat, like a Viking funeral ship, being slowly pulled on a long line by a second small boat. The tow boat was almost silent and was only visible as a slightly darker shape leading the pyre boat off into the darkness. Doug couldn't tell whose boat had been set on fire and was being towed for the late-night entertainment and edification of the lakeshore audience. It wouldn't be until the next day that the burned hull of Wesley Fuller's go-fast boat, widely reviled on the lake, would be found on the bottom near the narrows. The person who towed Fuller's go-fast boat on its last late-night run was never identified. But when Anne ran into the fledgling at Will's Shop 'n Save a few weeks later, the teen proudly showed off her Luna moth tattoo.

ABOUT THE AUTHOR

B.D. Smith is the award-winning author of a number of fiction and non-fiction books, including the highly-praised *Doug Bateman Mystery* series. He and his wife live outside of Santa Fe New Mexico in the winter, and in Bowerbank Maine in the summer.

Note from the Author

Word-of-mouth is crucial for any author to succeed. If you enjoyed *Dead to the World*, please leave a review online—anywhere you are able. Even if it's just a sentence or two. It would make all the difference and would be very much appreciated.

Thanks!
B.D. Smith

Thank you so much for reading one of our **Crime Fiction** novels.
If you enjoyed the experience, please check out our recommended
title for your next great read!

Caught in a Web by Joseph Lewis

"This important, nail-biting crime thriller about MS-13 sets the
bar very high. One of the year's best thrillers."

−BEST THRILLERS

Made in the USA
Monee, IL
06 December 2024

72617410R00125